BIRDS OF
A FEATHER

BY

ASHLEY ANTOINETTE

BIRDS OF A FEATHER Copyright @ Ashley Antoinette

All rights reserved. No part of this book may be reproduced in any form or by any means without prior consent of the Publisher, except brief quotes used in reviews.

ISBN: 9798306626864

Trade Paperback Printing June 2024
Printed in the United States of America

This is a work of fiction. Any references or similarities to actual events, real people, living, or dead, or to real locales are intended to give the novel a sense of realism. Any similarity in other names, characters, places, and incidents, is entirely coincidental.

Distributed by Ashley Antoinette Inc.
Submit wholesale orders to:
Mgmt@asharmy.com

CHAPTER 1

The emptiness. It was overwhelming. Even as Charlie sat in the living room, with a growing life filling her belly, she still felt the barrenness that accompanied winter. No life grew in this bitter season. Nothing survived, apparently not even children. It was wicked the way life tricked us into believing we had all the time in the world. Charlie was always taught to hunker down and ride out the frigid months until life bloomed again in the spring. One life wouldn't return when the earth thawed. Not this time. In fact, the coldness would last longer. This house was filled with everything she could ever dream of. Every little luxury that she hadn't even known she needed existed between these walls, but on this night, this home that Demi had made for her was void. This home didn't matter; she didn't matter. It was almost like she didn't even exist. Only she did. She could feel her existence with every painful breath she took. Every single one…two…three…because she was counting them to calm her anxiety and stop herself from panicking. With every knock of her aching heart, and every stab from the dread quickening her pulse, she was reminded that she had chosen this. DJ, her fiancé's son, was dead, and she couldn't quite process her emotions. Demi had sent her home from the hospital, and she didn't know what to do. What was expected of her? Should she cook? People always cooked when someone died. Surely, Demi would be starving by the time he made it home. Or was he not coming home? Demi's son was lying on a hard slab in the morgue of the hospital. She knew leaving that building would be a challenge for Demi. He had walked in as a concerned father. When he exited, he would be a grieving one. Should she check in? Should she pray? She had called out the name of God all night from the shock of the tragic news, but she hadn't prayed. She wasn't even sure if she had a right to pray for a child who had hated her. Lo wouldn't want her prayers. *Should I call him?* Charlie desperately wanted to hear his voice. She yearned to be at his side, to hold his hand, because she knew he was out of his mind, but she was afraid to pick up her phone. She was petrified to misstep because as much as she loved Demitrius Sky, she knew this wasn't her place.

The nervous energy in her belly made her feel like she had to throw up. She felt guilty for carrying Demi's unborn child while he was grieving the loss of his firstborn. How could she ever look Lauren in the eyes after this? How could Demi ever fully love their new child without feeling guilty? The burden was already so heavy. A puzzle of human dynamics.

The house felt bigger than it ever had. Suddenly, it was lonely, impersonal, and cold.

"I don't know how to fix this," she whispered. She felt like crying, but also felt like she had no right. Her last interaction with DJ hadn't been a positive one. She had yelled at him. She had been angry with him. She never thought there would be no time to fix the misunderstanding. Would Demi remember her last moments with his son and bear resentment? Would Lauren hold them against her? Charlie couldn't help but feel culpable for DJ's death.

When Demi left, DJ's world fell apart. I'm the reason he lost his daddy, Charlie thought. The shame of that had always been present. For them to love one another, DJ's world had been forced to change. Charlie didn't know what to do with this. The emotions were almost unbearable. A picture of DJ and Demi sat on the end table beside the sofa she sat on. From the smiles on both their faces, it had been a happy day. Charlie knew that Lauren was the one who had taken it. Even something as small as a father-and-son photo reminded Charlie that she was out of place. Charlie couldn't sit still, so she stood, and the inevitable pacing of the living room floor commenced as she fought back tears.

She pulled out her phone, hoping that Demi's name would appear on her screen. She desperately needed to hear his voice, but she wasn't surprised when the time was the only thing staring back at her. She knew him. His grief would turn to anger, and anger would turn to vengeance, but who could he seek revenge against when the two of them held the most blame? Their affair had cost Demi his son's life. She dialed Stassi. The pounding of her aching heart echoed in her ear as she waited for her sister to answer the phone.

"Charlie, my goodness, I heard! Are you okay? How's Demi?" Stassi fired off questions as soon as she picked up the line. Charlie didn't have answers.

"He died, Stass. He's been cutting himself, and nobody knew. How the hell didn't we know?" Charlie asked. "He was a normal kid. Did I do this to him?"

"What? Nooo," Stassi answered. It was loud in the background, and Charlie could barely hear her sister. "This isn't on you, Charlie. Don't even start that shit. You hear me?"

"Stassi, we need you to come troubleshoot. There's something going on with the audio system, and people are showing up saying they're VIPs who aren't on the list."

Charlie knew her sister couldn't talk right now, and even if she could, there wasn't anything Stassi could say that could make this okay.

"Go ahead, Stass. I know you're busy," Charlie dismissed sadly.

"I'm not busy," Stassi countered. "One sec!" Stassi shouted to someone in the background. "Well…yeah, I'm busy, but not too busy for you. Day left this event in my lap when he got the phone call about DJ, so I'm just trying to hold things together, but I'm here. I'm listening."

"It's okay, Stass. Handling that for him is more helpful than sitting on the phone babysitting my feelings. I'll call you later."

"I'm really, really sorry, Charlie. Please tell Demi, too. This is terrible," Stassi said.

"I will."

With that, Charlie ended the call.

It was close to midnight. She had left the hospital hours ago and had heard nothing since. She knew there would be questions to answer, from the social workers, from the police, and from the doctors. There would be so much to handle. She told herself she shouldn't expect to hear from Demi for a while. It was completely reasonable that he hadn't called, but it didn't stop her from checking her phone every few minutes. The silence was eating her alive. She knew it was selfish to look to him for comfort when his heart had been obliterated, but he was the only one who could reassure her right now. Being dismissed from the hospital had filled her with an insecurity that was growing by the second. Charlie was trying her hardest not to overthink. She and Lauren had just found common ground. They were finally communicating; and while they weren't friends, they had at least been able to accept one another. Now, they felt like enemies. Charlie felt like she was on a deserted island while Demi and Lauren watched from a bypassing ship. She wasn't even sure if they noticed her.

Was he just going to leave her there? A part of her felt expendable. Like Demi could just clock in and out of his life with her because she wasn't truly a necessity to him. Lauren felt like the necessity, meanwhile, Charlie was the hobby. She felt like he picked her up and put her down whenever he felt like indulging in her. This had to be the hardest moment of his life, and he didn't seek her for comfort. He didn't even fight for her presence. He had just gone along with Lauren's desire to make her disappear—almost like he wanted her gone, too. There was no way Charlie would be able to get through something like this without him at her side. Yet here she was exiled.

Charlie did the only thing she could do. She removed her clothes and showered. She wished she could rinse the trauma of the day away, but it clung to her. She couldn't even get lifted to lighten the anxiety or have a glass of wine because she was housing another human. She washed her body, checked her phone, tried to eat but couldn't, and then checked her phone again. The checking of calls was the intermission between all her actions. It would be until she heard his voice. She was driving herself crazy, but in a world where little boys were alive and well one moment, and then dead and gone the next, crazy was the only way to be.

She had half a mind to drive her ass back to the hospital to check on her man, but in this grief-filled moment, he wasn't her man at all. He was a mourning father, and Charlie was the last thing on his mind. She had to find comfort in that space, in this unknown, in this hurting, because it was a space that would exist for a while. Perhaps forever, because unlike losing any other person in a lifetime, the aching behind losing a child would prolong eternally. It was something she couldn't relate to yet. The baby in her belly was still a thought. She wasn't even out of her first trimester yet. There was no face attached to the flutters in her stomach, no notions of unconditional love, no attachment to an upbringing she had worked hard to provide, no memories of sleepless nights, no nothing. Just a man who had planted a seed that she hadn't even wrapped her mind around yet. Just nausea. Just fear.

Nah, Charlie couldn't fathom motherhood at all. She hadn't walked that walk, but it was coming, and her child's father was going through a darkness that left no room for the light she was growing inside her. How could he balance the two? Was it even possible? Balance requires a distribution of equal weight. An equilibrium between life and death, between Lauren and Charlie. She was outmatched. She would lose. There was that island again. The loneliness and impending abandonment she faced felt inevitable, but still, she walked into the bedroom she shared with Demitrius Sky and crawled under the covers, hoping sleep would find her. It didn't. Grief located her instead.

    Lauren Sky didn't understand. It was like they were speaking a foreign language around her. She was concentrating as hard as she could, trying to follow the conversation. They wanted to move him to the morgue. Her son. Her precious little baby was headed for the morgue. He was just at football practice. How does one go from football practice to the morgue? She was almost numb. The only thing that told her she still had feeling in her body was the pressure from Demi squeezing her hand. He was squeezing it so hard that it hurt, that the blood had stopped flowing. He was squeezing her in disbelief. He was squeezing her desperately like he was screaming for help without uttering a word. They were united in solidarity for the first time in years—over death. She didn't know if he was holding her up or if she was keeping him on his feet, but together they absorbed this devastating blow.

There was something being said about grief counseling. An Autopsy. An investigation of the home.

"For what?" Demi asked, interrupting the social worker. His tone was aggravated and short. "What the fuck is there to investigate?"

"We need to know the circumstances and the state of the home to ensure that the cause of death was indeed self-inflicted. We need to see where it happened."

"It wasn't self-inflicted. DJ might have held the blade, but everything that led to him feeling like he had to do this, none of that shit was his to carry," he said. "My boy." Demi could barely choke out the words. The blood flow returned to Lo's hand when he released it and walked away to conceal his emotions.

"Can I be with him?" Lauren asked.

"There are things we must do to the body," the doctor said.

"DJ. He's not a body. He's my son. He's my baby. Please don't talk about him like he's not a person anymore. I just need to see him."

Lauren was fully prepared to press these doctors. She would bend this man's fingers back until he called mercy if that's what it took. If they thought they were going to keep her from her child, she would have her attorneys on the line so fast that their heads would spin. They wanted to keep her in her grieving mother bag because if she got in her boss bitch bag, there would be hell to pay. She saw the doctor debating in his mind. To follow protocol or to tap into humanity and allow this mother another moment with her child. Lauren was grateful when the man said, "You can sit with him until the morgue comes for him. After that, we legally must process things on our end."

Lauren nodded. She didn't even attempt to find Demi. She wanted these moments alone with the child she had birthed. She had brought him into this world, and now she had the heavy burden of returning him to the earth. It was the most unnatural thing she had ever felt. She hadn't been given enough time. He was supposed to bury her, not the other way around. The fact that she hadn't seen this coming made it impossible to process. Oh, how she wished she could rewind the clock. All she needed was a few hours. If she hadn't invited Nyair over, she would have been more alert, more aware of DJ, and more attentive to his needs. They probably would have been watching a movie together or catching up on his favorite show, *The Walking Dead*. If only she had been tuned in. God, one moment of selfishness, of feeding her irresponsible urges, of wanting to be carefree and throw caution to the wind and call a man to the crib, had resulted in this. Catastrophe. One moment where her motherhood had slipped had come with a consequence she couldn't roll back. How? Why? She had seen Demi put himself first so many times over the years to no detriment. The world just continued to spin. DJ lived to see another day and Lauren picked up the slack whenever she could. Who was there to pick up her slack? She had one night where she had given away her focus just a little, and now her son was dead. How was this fair? How was she supposed to reconcile this without rage? How could she go on day to day without wanting to die right behind her son?

    She followed the doctor to the back. Her feet were heavy, her stomach churned, and her eyes blurred as the energy that was death pulled her near. It was sickening. Her motherly instincts had always triggered her body whenever she was near her son. Often, she could feel his spirit when she was miles away. When she would be at work, and he would be at school, she could feel if something went wrong in his day. If she was away on vacation, her gut would churn with worry, and she would call home only to discover some illness or issue that had suddenly plagued him. A mother was just connected to her child, but as she walked down these halls, she felt disconnected. Their connection had dissipated into the air when he had breathed his last breath. There was no feeling that could compare to this. Not her divorce. Not the loss of her grandmother years ago. Not the miscarriages she had suffered in the past. This was irreparable. Lauren would never bounce back from this. Her world was forever changed, and the light within her eternally dimmed.

    As soon as she saw the white sheet that covered his body, she stifled a cry. Dewy emotion clung to her lashes as she took her place by his side, rolling down the sheet to expose his face. He had already lost his color. His ashen, lifeless face tore her right in two.

    She couldn't speak. The apologies and I love you's that she wanted to scream were overpowered by a hopelessness that she couldn't beat. All she could do was lay over her child and weep.

CHAPTER 2

Nyair sat shirtless on the couch. He leaned over, elbows meeting knees as he held a cup of joe in his hand. Shannon Sharpe's voice boomed through his television. It was a program that Nyair rarely missed, but today, he couldn't focus. Today, his mind was stuck on a woman who had become a fixation out of thin air. He had left the hospital with no resistance. Lauren and Demi had a right to privacy in their time of distress. He couldn't imagine their loss. He had witnessed it before. He had prayed for others during their time of need, but he had never experienced the loss of a child. If he was honest, no parent he had ever counseled had bounced back the same. Tremendous sorrow filled him, and his empathy wasn't reserved only for Lauren. He felt for both parents. So, when he was asked to leave, he complied without taking offense because it was their right to lean on one another. Only the two of them knew what this tragedy was like. He didn't belong there, and he knew it. It was too sacred of a space for someone casual to linger in, and that's all he and Lauren were, friendly fucks to each other.

Nyair wasn't looking for a relationship. He wasn't interested in love. He was trying to stay focused, trying to repent for so many years of selfishness and bullshit. Lauren, however, was a lovely distraction. For a man like Nyair, a woman like that, with her vulnerability, with her pain, with her neediness, with her effortless sex appeal, and unassuming expectations was dangerous. She spoke a need to him without ever moving her lips, and he couldn't control his primal instinct when she was around. Years of self-control had gone out the window. He didn't know how to feel about it. He couldn't even focus on feeling anything because his craving for her was too strong to feel anything else. Nyair required Lauren in a way that was unreasonable. Every part of him wanted to be enveloped in her. Inside her body. Inside her mind. Inside her heart. Her thoughts. Her legs. That mouth. My oh my, the work she did with that throat. Lauren had swallowed him in ways that women were normally too shy to partake in. It was like her body had been dormant, and his sex had awakened her because she fucked like she was making up for lost time. He was so unfocused because even now, his dick reacted just thinking about it. But at this moment, he wanted to be more for no other reason than she needed more. He wanted to take root inside her spirit because he could feel that it was drained. Her faith was gone. He knew at this moment, the devil was whispering in her ear because nobody blamed God more than a mother who had lost a child. If Lauren gave in, she would never recover. DJ's death would lead to her destruction. He had seen it time and time again. Addiction, alcoholism, promiscuity, all symptoms of a woman with a broken heart, and not just any type of injury caused that type of despair. A maternal travesty. God didn't design the realm of humanity for mothers to bury their children, but time and time again, the natural order of things was disrupted. To pick up the phone and call would be too aggressive, but Nyair was an aggressive man. In all ways, on all days, he was assertive. Grieving left no room for him. He would be lucky if he ever heard Lauren's voice again.

"Get your head right, G," Nyair whispered to himself. He took a sip from his mug and then lifted the diamond cross he wore around his neck. He lifted the chain to his lips and kissed it. "Prince of Peace, do your job. Don't leave that woman's cries unanswered," he prayed aloud. He shook his head, his chest aching, a symptom of caring too much. He wasn't supposed to know Lauren enough to care at all. He was her son's football coach. He had crossed a line. Plenty of his players had beautiful moms who had shot their shots at him over the years. He had only given in once. How complicated this thing had become. He had helped to create confusion, and he couldn't be sure that his involvement didn't push DJ to hurt himself. The weight of the possibility that he was to blame was taxing. Nyair set down his coffee mug and reached for the Bible that sat on his table. He opened it to the book of Psalms. Instantly, his eyes fell upon the highlighted verses. Nyair was a student of this book. He studied it, deciphering the Word of God because it was written by men so long ago that it was hard to bring things current. He contextualized every word from cover to cover daily so that he never forgot. Life was hard. It was impossible at times, and he didn't know how a man could even attempt to face it without a playbook. That's the type of man he had always been. He had needed coaching and guidance ever since he was a boy. It was how he had become a star athlete. He memorized the playbook. When his career had come to an end, the Bible had become his playbook and God his coach. He needed to brush up defensively for this loss. He didn't know how to move life forward after this.

"So much life left in that kid," he mumbled, sniffing away an unexpected bout of overwhelm as he gritted his teeth in protest. He hated to hear about the loss of anybody, but a child, especially one that he had coached and engaged with closely, hit so much harder. He couldn't help but wonder if his interactions with Lauren had been that straw that broke the camel's back. He tried to run memories back in his mind to see if he had missed anything. Had there been a sign of distress that Nyair had ignored? He was a football coach. He could normally pinpoint the kids who were troubled. He usually fed the ones who came to him hungry. He counseled the ones who came to him angry, teaching them how to control their emotions and minds. He had bought shoes and clothes and taught hygiene to some who showed up to his practice without knowledge of self-care. He had sent home care baskets, wiped tears, all that. How the hell had he not noticed the crater of self-harm and self-hate growing within DJ? It didn't make sense. Little boys committing suicide? How had DJ become so unhappy that self-mutilation was mistaken for relief? Where did he even learn it from? He clamped the Bible shut, suddenly angry at…at…hell, even he didn't know, but he had resentment in his heart, and DJ didn't even belong to him. He kept replaying the sound of Lauren's screams. The octave was so agonizing that it hurt to hear. It was the kind of cry that evoked tears from the eyes of men. Misunderstanding lived in him. He had done this with his friend Alani. He had watched her be eaten alive after losing her daughter. He didn't know if he could do it again with Lauren. He cared too much, and it fucked him up because he couldn't even pinpoint how he had begun to care at all. To witness another strong woman unravel before his very eyes would make him begin to ask questions about life, death, and divinity. He was good at calming the heartbreak of others, but how many times could he witness it without tainting his own faith? Nothing hurt worse than seeing a woman hurt. He had seen a lot of that in his lifetime. He had caused a lot of it, too. A big part of his life had been spent making up for the damage he had caused to a woman he had loved once. All this death around him triggered memories that he didn't welcome, which meant it was time to distance himself from Lauren. It would be best for them both to establish boundaries now before they were too far gone. He needed to cut her off before either of them became too attached, or before her trauma became his mission to heal. He opened his phone and went to her name in his contacts. His thumb lingered over the screen for a while before he deleted it. He didn't know her number by heart, so he wouldn't be able to give in to temptation and call her. She would have to reach out to him, and he knew that under the circumstances, he would be the last thing on her mind. He doubted he would ever hear from her at all because he knew that she also thought their rendezvous was the inciting incident that had caused DJ to hurt himself. A mother wouldn't soon let go of that blame. Neither would Nyair. So, this was it. He was out, and they had to be done. It was for the best.

"Where the hell is Kiara Da'vi?" Stassi asked as she spoke into the headset while maneuvering her way through the thick crowd. "According to the call sheet, she was supposed to be here an hour ago."

Stassi was trying her hardest to remain focused. She hardly knew DJ, and she wasn't too fond of Lauren and Demi, but she would never wish this type of tragedy on anyone. She couldn't imagine what they were going through. The fact that Day had up and left this multi-million-dollar event in her hands without thinking twice meant that he trusted her wholeheartedly. *He trusts me too damn much,* Stassi thought as she tried not to panic.

Kiara Da'vi was the biggest act of tonight's show. She was the headliner and Dynasty Records' most viral artist. TikTok had blown the bubbling rapper and mumble singer out of the water lately, but with the rise in popularity came an inflation in ego. The star was late, and if Stassi didn't get her on that stage soon, the entire night would be a bust. She didn't want to have to call Day to fix this.

"Helloooo? Am I talking to myself? Where's my goddamn headliner?" Stassi shouted into the headset.

"Her manager says they're en route. ETA is 15 minutes, but she isn't stage ready." It was the worst thing that the production assistant could have told her. Glam would take the singer another two hours. There was no way the audience would wait that long. Stassi beelined for the dressing rooms where the house glam team was set up. She knocked on the door out of courtesy but didn't wait for permission before entering.

"Hey, ladies, I'm Stassi. I'm producing the show tonight. Which one of you is on hair and has lace wigs on hand?"

"I have wigs, but I was about to get out of here. The label only paid me for one look tonight. Why, what do you need?"

Stassi sighed in relief. "What's your name?"

"Everybody calls me MiMi," the girl replied.

"Well, MiMi, I need you to stay and prep one wig on the mannequin for Kiara Da'vi. She normally rocks blonde. You got any colored units?"

"If you got green, I got color," MiMi replied, rubbing her fingers together. "Cuz this is feeling like overtime."

"I'll double your rate, sis. I'ma make sure the label takes good care of you. Come see me at the end of the night. Can you get a blonde wig wand curled in half an hour?" Stassi asked. She opened her Instagram and went to Kiara Da'vi's page, then showed MiMi. "This is how she normally wears her hair. Can you emulate that?"

"I got you," MiMi answered.

"Thank you. I'll send her back when she arrives." With one problem resolved, she felt her chest lighten some, but sure enough, the small win was short-lived.

"Stassi, do we have a permit on hand? Fire department is trying to shut us down." When the voice came through her headset, she groaned. Stassi wanted to snatch that bitch off her head. Good news never came through. It was always someone paging her to tell her something catastrophic.

She felt like she was being pulled in a million different directions. Every time she put out one fire, another sprouted out of thin air. She was juggling a million balls, and if she dropped even one, she would fail.

"No, they are not! Do not let them in! I'm on my way to the front!" Stassi shouted as she hightailed it through the venue. Her toes screamed in excruciating pain from the high heels she was wearing. If she had known she would end up working, she would have worn sneakers.

"Wait! Wait!" she shouted as she neared the door.

"I'm sorry, sir, can you step over here for a moment so we can discuss this?" she asked as she moved out of the doorway. I'm Anastassia. I'm the producer of this show. I can assure you we have a permit for this event. Why exactly are you threatening to shut us down, and what can I do to stop that from happening?"

"What's the point of applying for the permit if you aren't going to follow the law? You're over capacity. If the parking lot is any indication, I'd say by about 30%. Cars are spilling out into the street, and you've got people parking in the fire lane," the fireman said. He was pleased. His tone was impatient, and she needed all the patience she could get tonight.

"Okay; what if we start towing the cars that are in the street and in the fire lane? That'll clear some of the crowd out." Stassi hated to ruin somebody's night like that, but it was either sacrifice a few or the whole damn crowd was going home. "I just need another two hours to close out this show. Please. I'm desperate here, and I'm at your mercy."

The fireman removed his helmet, and Stassi was instantly taken aback. The man underneath this suit was so handsome that she was instantly distracted. He was the type of Black man that hadn't been seen since the 90s. Brown-skinned, tall, with dark eyes that were made to stare into. He was fine, and his fine ass was about to shut her down.

"I…umm…" Stassi shook her head, refocusing as she grasped at straws. "Please. The owners of this event had to leave. His son died tonight. I was left in charge. If I fuck this up…" Stassi sighed in frustration. "I just can't fuck this up."

The fireman was brooding as he stood over her. The dip in his brow expressed his irritation.

"If the fire lane and the overflow aren't cleared out in half an hour, I'm shutting you down and writing you a citation," he warned.

"That's all I need! You have no idea how you just saved my life. Thank you so much for not being an asshole!" she said, smile returning as she backpedaled away from him in a hurry.

"Yeah, you're welcome," the man said, unenthused. "I'ma swing back around personally to make sure it's done."

Stassi held up praying hands and shook them in his direction. "I swear, it'll be taken care of. Thank you!"

A voice was in her ear again, beckoning her. Stassi was a puppet on a string tonight. "What now?" she shouted into the headset. She gave the firefighter one final glance. "I'm sorry, I got to go, but thank you!"

She turned around and rushed back toward the dressing rooms. Kiara Da'vi had arrived. She heard the commotion of the up-and-coming R&B sensation before she even made it to the door. She was known for her diva-like expectations. It would take all of Stassi's patience to put up with it.

"I'm sorry, I don't know who you are, sweetheart, but I don't let randoms style my hair. This blonde wig doesn't even fit my aesthetic."

Stassi rolled her eyes as she paused outside the door. She didn't knock this time. Instead, she took a deep breath before barging inside.

"Hi, Kiara, I'm Stassi. I'm running the show tonight. We need you in and out of hair and makeup in 30 minutes," Stassi said.

"Running the show?" Kiara asked with a laugh. "I mean, considering that my brother is a partner in this business, I'd say you don't really run shit, sis. More like this my show, and you didn't even know it. All this shit in here is done wrong. Where's my catering? My hair stylist? My Fiji? Matter of fact, where's Day? He knows what's on my rider," the singer shot back.

"Day isn't here. I'm here, and rider or no rider, brother or no brother, you're late. You have a packed house out there, and they've been waiting. I had the house team pre-style a wig for you and…"

"Girl, get me the boss. If Day isn't here, where's Demi? I'm not using no new stylist that I've never worked with before. No offense," Kiara said, looking at MiMi before crossing stubborn arms over her chest.

"None taken. I'm paid regardless," MiMi answered.

"Listen, I don't know what Day and Demi tolerate when you work with them, but tonight I'm in charge. You can either sit in that chair and let MiMi get you together, or you can risk letting your hair stylist start from scratch. Your choice! But if you're not on stage in 30 minutes, you won't be hitting the stage at all, and you can explain to your fans why in an apology post on IG. It won't be me getting cleared online for flaking, so it's on you."

"Who the hell do you think you are?" Kiara asked. "Let me call Day. The nigga around here, giving out fake power when he knows I call all my own shots around here. Was just in this nigga bed, I'll be damned if I take orders from his assistant. Ain't you the same bitch he called the help?" The girl snickered, and Stassi saw red.

That hit a nerve. Not only had Kiara Da'vi staked claim over Day, but she was throwing shade. Kiara was marking the man and the territory, and Stassi felt her temper rage. Day had just professed his affection for her in front of thousands of people, and now here another woman was throwing her weight around the room because she was clearly fucking him.

"Are you done?" Stassi asked. "You just wasted five minutes. Now, you got 25 minutes to be on stage or I'm shutting this down." Stassi stood her ground and kept her poker face strong. She was rattled, but nobody in the room could tell. She wouldn't give them the satisfaction, but in the back of her mind, questions about Day's relationship with this woman were nagging, and a rehash of the humiliation she had felt when he had belittled her on the radio flashed through her mind.

Stassi walked out of the room and prayed that Kiara Da'vi would comply.

Difficult-ass bitch, Stassi thought. The sooner this night was over, the better. Manning this job was a huge responsibility. She just wanted to make it through the evening without messing anything up. Demi and Day had enough to deal with without worrying about losing money tonight.

CHAPTER 3

The silence that filled the car was one that only visited when death called. It was the kind of silence that came from not knowing what to say. It was the kind that was summoned when something hurt too badly to be explained. There was no consoling it. There was no ignoring it, no dulling it or treating it. It just remained, and it was immeasurable.

Demi's eyes burned. He was filled with an unyielding anguish. It was like someone was holding a branding iron to his chest, marking him with a burn that would never heal. It was the invisible mark of a grieving parent. Demi hadn't even known that a feeling like this could exist. To think, his world was ordinary just a few hours ago. It felt like another lifetime ago. Happiness. Wholeness. Lying next to the woman he loved. Yeah, that shit was an alternate universe. It may as well have been a dream because, in this reality, he could never see himself feeling anything except brokenness.

He felt himself driving, but he had no idea how he hadn't wrecked his car. His mind was void of logic. His eyes were on the road ahead of him, but he didn't see anything. Images of DJ flashed in his mind the entire way. Lauren sat in the passenger seat. If he didn't smell her signature perfume, he wouldn't even know she was there. Her silence matched his. They were both vanishing before each other's eyes.

Day followed in Lauren's car all the way home. Demi was afraid of this house. Suddenly, it was intimidating to be inside the space where his son had taken his life. He turned off the car and neither he nor Lauren moved. He could hear DJ's laughter ringing in his ears. He could hear their playful banter. He could hear his son being braggadocios through his headset as he played video games. Those were the sounds that used to exist inside this house. It was unbelievable that he would never get to hear those sounds again. If he had known the last time was going to be the last time, he would have cherished the noise. Memories were all he had now. He didn't even have Lauren to share this emptiness with. He had given her up before realizing what they would have to face. The boy in him needed the woman he had hurt now more than ever, and he was too proud to tell her. As he glanced over at her, he was sure she was too destroyed to care.

He opened the door, and his feet left trails through fresh snow as he rounded the car to open Lauren's door. Day pulled in behind them and exited as well.

No words, just actions, just zombies as he held out his hand for her. She stared at it, almost like she was afraid to take hold of him.

"It's cold, Lo. Let's get you in the house," Demi said.

"Is it? I don't feel anything," she replied. Death was a cruel encounter, and its grip was firm around her neck. It had narrowed its glaring stare on her family, and its kiss was poisonous. That venom was spreading through her body, decaying everything. Her heart…her lungs…the pit of her stomach, all rotting from the inside out. If she touched Demi, would he start to rot too? How long could two decaying hearts continue to beat?

"When we…go in this house…and he's…not there, Demi." Her words tripped out of her throat as each sob interrupted her. "Demi, fix it, please. Please! I'll never ask you for anything again just go get my baby!"

There hadn't been a lot that Lauren had asked him for that he hadn't delivered, and it made him feel powerless that he couldn't deliver this miracle for her. If only he could. If the attempt was even halfway possible, he would give it his all, but life didn't work that way. Regrets remained because time didn't tick in reverse. If he could redo it all, he would. He would treat Lauren better and be more appreciative of the moments they had on those simple days when they were all under one roof—and their son, their creation, their sum was breathing.

"I can't, Lo."

"You can't ever do the shit you're supposed to do!" Lauren screamed, her wails carrying through the pitch-black sky as the freezing wind howled in harmony. "Where were you?!"

Her question awakened Demi's guilt because, in the back of his mind, he knew that DJ had veered into the danger zone the moment he had moved out.

"He needed you! You're so fucking selfish!" Lauren wailed. She rushed Demi, emotion fueling her. Her despair motivated balled fists to fly his way as she punched and pushed Demi. He was so solid she barely moved him, and Demi grabbed her hands to stop her from knocking his head off his shoulders. Her resentment and aggression were so great, and rightfully so.

"I'm sorry," he whispered as he tried to subdue her.

"Let me go! This is your fault!" Demi's eyes stormed as his vision blurred. Was she right? Was he to blame? It sure felt that way, but hearing the accusation stung. It filled him with embarrassment because what kind of father couldn't protect his own son? Lauren fought against him until Day intervened.

"Come on, sis, not out here," Day said, pulling her away from Demi.

"I hope you're happy. My son is dead because of you," Lauren accused, sobbing before giving into Day and sobbing on his shoulder. Day stared at Demi as he held Lauren tightly, and he could see his best friend's misery. Day knew Demi. They had been friends for a long time. Demi needed the type of support he would never request, but silently, Demi was tasking Day to come to Lauren's aid. She was in shock. Her world had been turned upside down, as had his, but Lauren was looking to place blame. She had to, to make sense of it. Someone had to be the cause, and in the crevices of her broken heart, the cause was Demi.

"Take her inside," Demi instructed.

Day hesitated. The look in Demi's eyes was haunting. Day had never seen hopelessness like that before. Demi had never felt it, and if he was honest, he didn't know what to do with the grief. He didn't have the privacy he needed to give into the loss. He couldn't cry. He couldn't scream. He ached to hurt someone, to punish something. Instead, he stood there, lost and confused.

"I just need a minute," Demi reassured.

Day nodded and escorted Lauren into the house. Demi walked back to the driver's side of his car and climbed inside, turning up his heat to knock the chill from his bones. He sat in that car in silence for two hours as he waited for the light to go out in Lauren's bedroom. The blunt he sparked was company enough as he stared at that amber glow in the window. He knew Lauren down to a science. She would go inside, shower, pull out her journal, write down her thoughts, read a passage from her Bible, pray, and then sleep. Although tonight, he doubted if sleep would come. Not for him, not for her, but he waited anyway for the bedroom light to go out. Only then could he go inside when he knew it was safe. He would wait outside forever to avoid her wrath. He didn't need Lauren to assign the blame, he already felt it. Her judgment would only push him over the edge of a steep cliff, and he knew he wouldn't survive the descent.

He thought about calling Charlie, but he was afraid of the probing he knew would come with dialing her number. He went to her Instagram and clicked on one of her posts. She sat in front of a camera, with no makeup, locs pulled into a messy bun on top of her head, and guitar in her hands. Demi closed his eyes as she sang to him. Pain leaked from his eyes, and he stubbornly wiped it away, trying to remove all evidence of this breakdown. Charlie sang, and Demi cried in the shadows of this dark, snowy night. In this solitude, he wished he had never met her. If he hadn't walked into that club that night, he would have never laid eyes on her, and he would have never had a desire to love her. He would have been satisfied with his wife, and he would be inside this very home on this night, with his woman and their child. It hadn't been a bad life. Demi had just taken it for granted. As he felt his heart cracking in two, he realized, that every small moment spent under this roof with Lauren and his son had been the biggest moments of his life. Now, they were memories. Now, those times were impossible to recapture, and suddenly, the sound of Charlie's voice made his stomach flip.

A knocking on his window caused Demi to shape up. A click of a button turned his screen black, and he cleared his wet face with one swipe of his hand.

He opened the door and stepped out to face Day.

"She needs you in there," Day said.

Demi nodded and bit into his bottom lip as his chin shook against his will.

"I fucked this up," Demi hissed.

"We all fucked this up. DJ is a part of all our lives, bruh. We all could have done more…"

"I'm his father," Demi countered.

"And you were a good one. A damn better one than either of us had," Day said. "Don't doubt that. Nobody did this. We just missed it, that's all," Day said somberly.

"How, tho'?" Demi asked. "How the fuck did I miss this?"

"I don't know what's needed here, but I'm right here with you. I'm gonna reach out to the funeral home. We'll send him to the sky in style, spare no expense. I got this part. You and Lo don't have to worry about shit. Just take care of each other," Day promised.

"You talking about my little boy's funeral, Day. You talking about putting my li'l man in the dirt. How this happen, bruh?" Demi asked, genuinely confused. The tears were back, sliding down the bridge of his nose. No matter how much he wanted to appear strong, they both knew he had never been more vulnerable. This was one of the most unnatural things he had ever felt.

"I don't know, man," Day replied. Demi turned and placed his hands on the roof of his car, balancing his weight as he lowered his head in defeat. He sobbed. He felt a hand on his shoulder, and then a squeeze of support, and Demi knew he had to pull it together. He stood, clearing his throat in embarrassment, and Day said, "No tough guy shit this time. No gangster shit. No pretending like we aren't fucked up. We just two brothers who about to go in this house and have a drink while we figure out how to put one foot in front of the other. I'm here, my nigga. You hear me?"

Demi nodded. He couldn't speak, but he complied and followed Day into the house.

The scent of the home was so familiar that it somehow soothed Demi. His new place still smelled like plaster and paint. It had been built from the ground up for Charlie, and it was still too new for her scent to settle into the walls. Lauren's house had scents and sounds that had burrowed into his psyche for years. Along with the familiarity came comfort. He didn't know how he had missed this appreciation for this space before. The way he had sighed in relief as he crossed the threshold symbolized safety. Demi knew this place. His son's energy was alive between these walls. It was the only place he could see himself being tonight.

Day headed for the bar, but Demi kept walking down the hallway toward DJ's room. The sight of the blood took his breath away. He could smell the iron in the air, and it was so overwhelming it turned his stomach. He couldn't fathom his son's last moments. He walked into the adjoining bathroom. More blood. So much more blood. When Demi's eyes landed on the razor on the floor, he folded. He had to sit. He sat on the edge of the toilet as he reached for the razor. It belonged to him. It was an old-school straight razor that he had left behind. The tool his son had used to hurt himself…to kill himself.

Demi sat there stunned. Day entered the room, standing in the doorway to the bathroom.

"Get out of here, man. Let me get this cleaned up. I know how you is," Day said.

Demi shook his head. "I'll do it." It was a big task for a man who hated filth, but it was his responsibility. This blood was his blood, and no one else could do this part. Lauren definitely shouldn't have to, so he stood and opened the closet.

Mop.

Bucket.

Cleaning solution.

He retrieved it all, filled the bucket with hot water, and went to work. Day opened the closet, grabbed more supplies, and joined him. They had spilled a lot of blood over the years; never did they think they would be here. There was a screaming silence in this room. Demi emerged from the bathroom and rested the mop against the wall. He grabbed the bottle of Louis that Day had placed on the dresser and then grabbed the two glasses. Pour up. Drink. Pour up. He passed a glass to Day and then took a seat on his son's bed.

He leaned over, resting elbows to knees, as he swirled the brown liquor around in the glass.

"Say, man," Demi said. "This shit gon' kill me."

"I ain't gon' let it, my nigga. I can't stop the feeling, though. You got to find a way through the hurt."

"He's a piece of me. He's mine. Made of me. And now he's dead." Demi swallowed the drink in one giant gulp. He invited the burn, hoping it would wash the devastation away.

"I don't know what to say to this shit. Niggas just talk to talk when shit like this happens. So I'ma shut the fuck up and just listen, bruh. I'ma just be here with you and sis. Whatever y'all need."

Day took a seat next to Demi and held out his glass. Demi tapped it with his own, and then the two men sat in silence as they refilled, settling into their brokenness. The fabrics of their lives had been dismantled. An invisible hand had plucked a loose thread, and the entire garment upon which they existed had come apart. It just wasn't right. The death of a child would never make sense.

CHAPTER 4

"Great job tonight, Stassi. This is honestly the smoothest show I've been a part of. I hope they keep you around. Have a good night!"

"Thanks. I hope so, too," she replied. She gave the final crew member a wave as she watched him walk out the back door.

Only once everyone else was gone for the night did she give herself permission to breathe. She sighed and wandered out onto the deserted stage. The emptiness of the building made her realize how massive it really was. Day and Demi had built an empire for themselves. To be able to pack a place like this wasn't easy. It was the biggest event Stassi had ever successfully run. It made her want to shift her focus completely and focus on the music industry. If there was room for her, she wanted a seat at the table. The sound of the doors opening at the rear of the auditorium startled her, and she placed a hand over her eyes to try to see past the beaming stage lights shining down on her.

"The buildings closed!" she shouted.

"Just coming to make sure you're a woman of your word."

The firefighter came into view. He entered, wearing navy blue cargo pants, heavy boots, and a fitted navy-blue t-shirt. He was stripped of the uniform he had worn earlier, but she could tell he was still on duty from the badge that adorned his shirt. She traveled down the stairs to greet him.

"As you can see, I am," she said. "I really appreciate you giving me a break earlier. You have no idea the type of night it's been."

"Are you all set here? It's late. I can walk you to your car if you're headed out," he said.

"I caught an Uber," she said.

"Well, if you don't mind riding in a fire truck, I don't mind dropping you where you need to go," he offered.

Stassi looked at him curiously. "I'm Grayson, by the way," he said, holding out his hand.

She reluctantly placed her dainty hand in his. His palm swallowed hers as he curled his fingers around hers for a shake. He was a mountain of masculinity. Tall and built, like he worked out every day of his life.

"What kind of name is Grayson?" she asked.

"A trustworthy one," he shot back. It was the certainty in which he said it that caught her attention.

"Grayson the firefighter," she said. "Hmm."

When he smiled, his face lit up. His goatee was lined to precision. His hair was cut low in a fresh fade that waved. She was trying to size him up, but he was difficult to read. He wore a simple watch on his wrist, but other than that, no jewelry, a work hazard she assumed, and he smelled like burning wood. Oddly, it was intriguing.

"I feel like a million assumptions are going through your mind about me right now." He chuckled and folded his arms across his chest. "I'm just being a gentleman, no need to overthink it."

"You're right," Stassi agreed. "I'd appreciate a ride."

He stepped aside and motioned for her to lead the way. "After you."

The red fire truck that sat outside filled her with excitement for some reason. He glanced down at her as they walked side by side. He chuckled.

"What?" she asked, smiling.

"Everybody has that reaction when they ride in one for the first time. It's something about it that makes you feel like a big kid," Grayson said, already knowing what the look on her face revealed.

"I mean, it's kind of cool," she admitted. He walked her to the passenger side and opened the door.

"Watch your step," he said. She hopped up, and he closed the door before joining her on the driver's side. He reached across her, secured her seatbelt, and then started the engine. She felt the truck come alive beneath her, and she giggled.

"Correction, this is very cool." She couldn't stop smiling.

"Glad you approve," he said.

She put her address in the GPS and turned up the volume so he could hear the instructions as he pulled out of the parking lot.

"How long have you been a firefighter?" she asked.

"Long time. About 15 years now," he said. "Did four years in the navy, came home, and this was destined for me."

"So, you got a hero complex." She covered her mouth as soon as she said it because she hadn't meant to say it aloud. "I'm sorry. That was rude as hell."

"I'm a lot of things. A hero isn't one of them," he said. His message was cryptic, and his tone a bit sad. "I do love what I do, though."

"You aren't afraid you'll get hurt one day? You walk into burning buildings to save complete strangers." She knew it took a level of selflessness to even consider the profession. She was much too selfish to ever sign up for the task.

"Somebody has to make the sacrifice. Why not me?" he asked.

"I'm sure somebody who loves you is asking why it has to be you," she offered.

"There's nobody asking that question."

The answer was so somber that it put a pit in Stassi's stomach. How could there not be someone waiting for him out in the world? A wife? A child? A parent? Hell, a sibling? She wanted to probe but decided not to.

The awkward silence that followed was uncomfortable. The conversation had gotten too deep, too quickly. They were strangers making small talk, and lack of love was the biggest topic of them all.

"Tell me about you. You're a promoter?" Grayson asked.

"Not at all," she replied. "I was just filling in for a friend. I'm an event planner. I typically do much smaller events."

"Well, maybe it's time to level up. I mean, if tonight was

any indication, I'd say you can handle it," he said.

He was only speaking what she was feeling, but it felt amazing to have someone acknowledge it aloud.

"Yeah, I think so," she smiled because she was proud of how she had commanded the night. "My exit's right up here." She pointed to direct him off the freeway. He eased out of traffic and onto the ramp that led to her street.

He pulled curbside, and Stassi turned to him.

"Thank you for the ride home."

"You're welcome, Anastassia," he replied.

"Stassi," she corrected. "It's easier," she shrugged.

"It's okay for some things to be hard," he answered. "You have yourself a good night."

"You too, Grayson."

She looked at the sticker on the windshield. "Better get back to Station 10 before they find out you're using their fire truck to pick up girls," she teased.

He laughed and nodded. "I think they would give me a pass." Stassi waved goodbye before turning to walk into her building.

She heard the loud horn of the truck just as she stepped inside. She made her way to her door, and when she placed her key in the lock, she froze. The lock was already turned. She pulled her hand back like the door was hot to the touch.

It was like all her senses came alive at once, and the hair on the back of her neck stood up. She pushed the door in slowly and eased into her home. There was a small glow coming from the hallway.

I know I didn't leave that light on. Did I? She made her

way to the knife block on her kitchen counter before easing down the hallway.

She took a deep breath before pushing forcefully into the guest room.

"Charlie?! Shit!"

Charlie practically jumped out of her skin.

"What are you doing here?" Stassi yelled as she placed the knife down on the dresser. "You almost gave me a heart attack!"

"I called you! I left you a message!" Charlie shouted, holding a hand to her chest and heaving in distress as she tried to calm down. "Bitch, what your butcher knife was gon' do?"

"Stab a mu'fucka up if I needed to," Stassi said, laughing as her anxiety subsided. Charlie fell into laughter, too, as she shook her head.

"That shit don't work against no real robber, ho. You need a gun, living here by yourself," Charlie said.

"Well, thank God I don't have one tonight cuz your ass would be grass," Stassi snickered. "What's going on? Why aren't you with Demi?"

"Demi didn't come home, and I'm pretty sure he doesn't plan to," Charlie said. "I really don't know what to do. He lost his son, Stass. What am I supposed to do?"

"Not be here, Charlie," Stassi said empathetically. Stassi sighed and sat on the end of the bed as Charlie sat up against the headboard. "You have to just be there for him."

"How can I do that? He asked me to leave the hospital. He hasn't even called me to update me. It's going on four in the morning, and he's not home."

"Did you call him?" Stassi asked.

"I can't call him. I don't want him to think I'm down his back. I want to give him space, but it feels so…" Charlie paused. "I don't know. It feels like…" Charlie swiped away a tear as she lifted full eyes to Stassi. Stassi could almost hear Charlie's heart crushing under the weight of her fears. "Like he's never coming back."

"Charlie, he lost his son," Stassi whispered. "I don't have a kid, but I can imagine that he wants to die right now. He may not be home right now, but when he finally does walk through that door, he's going to need you."

Charlie nodded. "What if I can't comfort him?" Charlie asked. "What if I'm to blame? He's going to hate me. I love him so much, and I'm going to lose him to this. I can feel it. It's already happening. When he put me in that car and sent me home, I felt the disconnect."

"You felt grief. He probably can't get to the love he feels for you through the clouds that are over his head right now, Charlie. Don't overthink this. He loved you before this happened. It's a tragedy. He won't be the same for a while, but he'll love you after. Go home, girl. The last thing you need is for him to make it there and you're gone. I don't even like Demi's ass, but I know he needs your support through this."

"You're right, and I know you're right. So why does it feel wrong for me to be there with him through this?" Charlie asked.

Stassi sighed and rubbed the back of her neck. "Okay, look, Charlie. I'ma keep it all the way real with you because I love you. It's gon' sound real bitchy and judgmental because I been working all day and I'm tired, but I promise I hold no judgment. The time for you to feel like this was wrong was when you were riding that married man's dick. He's yours now. He's divorced. He left his family for you. You don't need anybody's permission to be present for your man in his time of need. You asked for this, so put your big girl panties on and ride this shit out."

"It kind of sounds judgey, bitch. Like you done said this shit to somebody else before," Charlie joked.

Stassi smiled. "Well, I warned you it was gon' sound bad, shit. Now, go home! I'm exhausted, and I ain't got the energy to talk to you all night about your insecurities that don't even make sense. Catch me in the morning, and I'll do the whole sister circle thing with you."

Charlie crawled across the bed and wrapped Stassi in a hug.

"Call me if you need me," Stassi said. "For real."

She walked Charlie to the door. "Text me when you make it," Stassi said.

"I will. Love you," Charlie replied.

"I love you more," Stassi answered.

Stassi locked the door and retired to her room. She didn't envy Charlie at all. Demi was a dominant man. He was big, mean, and intimidating. She could only imagine what he was like when dealing with a pain he couldn't control. She prayed Charlie could handle it.

"Couldn't be me."

CHAPTER 5

Sleep was a stranger. Demi laid on top of his son's bed. His head throbbed. It felt like an earthquake was splitting his skull in half. Orange specks of light were breaking through the dark sky. The world was awakening. It was the first day of his new life without his son. He had forgotten how to live without DJ. He wasn't sure he could. Every part of his body felt different. His feet didn't know how to hold his weight. His shoulders rounded down as depression tried to force him to fold. His eyes burned constantly, begging him for a little relief. All they wanted to do was shed tears, but he held back. He pulled himself from bed and found his way to his old bedroom. The sounds coming from behind that door made him bow his head and close his eyes. Wetness threatened his lids, and he sniffed his feelings away. He cleared his throat and knocked on the door.

"Lo," he managed to call out.

Retching followed. Uncontrollable gagging—it sounded painful. Demi pushed into the room and found her in the bathroom, on the floor. Her knees kissed the tile as she gripped the toilet seat. She had cried all night, for so long that she had made herself sick. She flushed the toilet and rested her head on the seat.

Demi didn't think twice about picking her up from the floor. He was a man who hated filth. He hated everything that felt unclean, but he ignored the smell of vomit as he turned on the shower.

"I...don't want...your help," she whispered. She couldn't even talk without her words fumbling out, competing with the sobs that were trying to reach him first.

"I know," he said, pulling her shirt above her head anyway. He bent down on one knee and unbuttoned her pants, rolling them down and pulling them away from her body. When he exposed her stretch marks, he froze. He remembered when those marks had first appeared on her belly. She had been seven months pregnant when burgundy dots had started at her hips and spread further day by day. Lauren had been so insecure about those marks. She had hated them and had tried to rid herself of them every day since. They were proof that life had grown there. They were DJ's signature etched in permanent ink on her skin. He placed a hand on her stomach and then let his forehead rest there. His jaw shook violently, and he locked his teeth, gritting, grinding. Lauren placed a hand on top of his head, and Demi quickly stood to his feet. The feeling of her hands consoling him would break him. He couldn't break. He wouldn't know how to put himself back together if he allowed it, so he plugged the hole up quickly, stopping any evidence of emotion from draining from him slowly.

"I'ma leave a towel here on the sink and give you a minute to shower. I'll fix you something to eat," he said.

"I'm not hungry," she mumbled.

"Hey," he said, jarring her attention and forcing her to look at him. "Our son needs you. You're his mama. You're the soft one. He needs you to lay him to rest, Lo, and he needs me to tell him not to be scared. We aren't done being his parents. We're not done."

She blinked, and heavy tears fell from her eyes, but she nodded in agreement.

Demi walked out, giving her privacy, but he kept the door cracked because, for some reason, he didn't trust her behind a closed door. He had seen her through a lot. There had been deaths of loved ones before. She had suffered miscarriages. Even his infidelity. None of those things had brought about this type of agony. He hadn't seen her suffer like this before. He wasn't sure if she still had hope. Hell, he wasn't sure if he did either.

Demi pulled out his phone and saw that he had two missed calls. The spark that flickered inside his chest told him he wasn't hopeless. His nature wanted to get in his car and drive an hour to her side. He was bleeding out, and he knew that her presence would be a temporary bandage that stopped him from losing it. Charlie was peace in human form, and his body called to her, but his duty was here. This was one vow he couldn't break; this was one responsibility he couldn't abandon. He couldn't leave Lauren in these trenches by herself. He didn't know what to do or how to handle this death. He didn't know if he was right or wrong for the decisions he was making. Being by Lauren's side just felt necessary. He didn't know if he was saving himself or her, but there was the possibility of survival in their togetherness. Nobody could hurt over this in the way he was, no one except her. They shared this sorrow. Half on a baby. Half on the death of one. The shit hurt so bad it had the power to end him. He hadn't thought anything could make him this vulnerable. He had never experienced an injury this severe. He wasn't sure if he would have had children at all if he knew that this was even possible. It didn't feel earthly; it didn't feel like it was supposed to be a part of the human experience.

Demi went through the motions of preparing breakfast. He didn't know why. If he was hungry, he couldn't feel it, and he knew Lauren would refuse him, but he needed to keep moving. By the time she emerged from the bedroom, he had a plate set out for her. Her short hair was wet and slicked back. Her face lacked color. She almost appeared green; she was so sickened. Her eyes were bloodshot red, and it matched the tip of her nose.

"I can't eat," she said. "I can't sleep. I can't live, Demi. There isn't even a point in trying. I'm going to blow my brains out as soon as you leave this house. So, just get out. Just get out, Demi."

The hole in his heart deepened because he believed her.

"I'm not leaving, Lo," he said. "And you can't make me bury my son and my…"

"I'm nothing to you. There's no burden here. You aren't responsible for me. You can go."

"You're my wife, Lo," he stated. He stated it like they hadn't signed divorce papers. He stated it like he hadn't walked out on her. "You'll always be my wife. Life looks different for us, but I do love you, Lauren. You're my family. Dried ink and disagreements don't change that."

"It doesn't matter, Demitrius! None of it matters anymore!" Lauren couldn't control herself. She braced a hand against the wall and clutched her stomach with the other as she sobbed. "What did I do to deserve this?"

All Demi could do was embrace her. "How did this happen to my babyyyyy?" The wails of a grieving mother were torture. This was incurable. It was abhorrent, and nothing could stop it.

"We're gon' get through this," Demi whispered in her ear as he tightened his hold on her. "I don't know how, but that's my word. I'ma see you through."

He didn't know how to disconnect from one life to check into the one he shared with Charlie, but he knew the instability under this roof was too detrimental to desert. If he had recognized that before, his son would still be alive.

"We need to go to the funeral home. They're taking DJ there. Do you want me to handle that part?" Demi asked.

Lauren was an event planner. She had built her career on being the best at meticulous execution. She should be the one to do this, but no way could she do it. What a task to ask a mother. Who would be so cruel to put that expectation on her plate? She couldn't sit at a table and choose between the finishes of caskets for her child. She couldn't organize a program to say goodbye. She shook her head.

"I can't."

Demi nodded, fighting down his own torment to keep hers in check. "I can't leave you alone here, Lo," he said. He didn't trust her not to harm herself. The shock was too new, the wound too deep. The emotion hadn't diluted even a bit. The intoxication of heartbreak would force Lauren to make bad decisions. "I'm going to have to start making some calls. Let the family know, your mama. Get some people in here around us. We can't do this by ourselves."

The thought of dealing with relatives—her mother, especially, was a burdensome task. The relationship was strained, hostile even, but he knew Lauren needed her around. DJ was her grandchild. There was no excluding the woman from this goodbye. A funeral would be the thing that brought a family back together. It was a bad habit of Black families, to let time pass only to be forced to reunite over death. Why couldn't the good things bring distant relatives around?

Lauren couldn't even speak to agree. Demi felt like he was expecting too much from her. Lauren was only good to exist right now. Asking anything else would be setting her up for failure.

"You want to ride with me for a minute? Hmm?" he asked, lifting her chin with one finger. She shook her head, declining him, but he had to move around. Things needed to be done, and they couldn't wait. He feared that if he left, when he returned, he would find her body, and that, he couldn't risk. "Ride shotgun with a nigga like you used to. We ain't did that in a long time, Lo. I want to be here for you, but I'm fucked up too. My mind sending me to places that make me want to kill somebody. I need you to keep me leveled, too, Lo. You ain't got to do nothing but sit and ride. We ain't even got to talk. Okay?"

Just the blink of her eyes sent tears sliding down her cheeks. She nodded, and he retrieved everything she would need. Her purse, her coat, her shoes, a hat, and her phone. He grabbed his coat next and retrieved his shoes by the door. He paused because a pair of DJ's boots sat next to his own. It was the simplest trigger, but it was all it took to hollow his soul. He sucked in a desperate breath and then ushered Lauren out the door.

Demi's eyes never left the road, and Lauren stared out her window as they made their way to the funeral home. They were two parents, two people, navigating through the fog that existed in the lapse between the living and the un-living. Forever broken. Forever bonded.

Charlie didn't know what to feel. Throughout her relationship with Demi, she hadn't really connected with DJ. She had wanted to, but the tension that existed when they were in the same room made it hard for her to break through to him. She hated that she hadn't been given more time to earn his affection. She hated that she hadn't redeemed his trust. Now, it was too late, and the memory of him made her sick to her stomach because in what reality was this normal? She ached for Demi, and she wished she could just wrap her arms around Lo. She wished they had space for her support, but she knew there was none and that ostracization felt like the loneliest place on earth.

To love someone and be excluded from their grieving was hurtful. Charlie was trying her hardest to be understanding.

Night had transformed to morning, and the stars yielded to the sun, yet no news had come. She reluctantly dialed Demi's number.

"The person you have dialed has not set up this voicemail…"

He wasn't taking any calls. Not even hers.

She opened a new text thread.

Charlie
I just want to make sure you're okay. Please call me.

A few seconds passed before she saw activity on her screen. The bubbles dancing on her phone matched the flutters in her stomach.

Demi
I'm okay.

That was it. Two words. No added information. No update on what was happening. No instructions for her. No reveal of where he was. Just two fucking words. Charlie didn't know if that was helpful or if it was worse than not hearing from him at all.

Charlie
I just want you to know that I'm here.

Charlie waited and waited. Demi went to type a response, but when no message came through and the bubbles stopped, tears filled her eyes. This was catastrophic. The amount of relief she felt when her phone vibrated in her hand wasn't normal. It wasn't healthy. She shouldn't be dependent on a phone call to breathe.

Demi
I know, Bird. I'ma be home as soon as I can. Honestly, don't know how long I'ma be. Walking into this funeral home.

Charlie dropped a tear at what she knew was about to unfold when he saw his son.

Charlie
I love you.

Demi
And I you, baby. Real bad.

He was a walking, talking, red flag, and Charlie had run to this man like he was an amusement park ride. She couldn't stop chasing the thrill if she tried. Even now, at the bottom of the hill, she wanted to beg him to take her back to the top. Charlie chose her next words carefully. Typing, then erasing. Then typing, only to erase again, because she needed him but couldn't demand his presence—not right now, not after this.

Charlie
When can I wrap my arms around you, Demi?

Demi
Soon, I hope. You don't even know what I'm facing, Bird. I'm losing it.

Charlie
When you lose it, come find me.

Demi
I'm not worthy, Bird. On God, I'm not.

"How fucking dare you?!"

Day looked up from his desk as Kiara Da'vi stormed into his office.

He stood and rounded his desk, bypassing her to close the door before he turned and put a firm grip around her neck.

"Bring your volume down," he warned.

She pushed him off, and her eyes watered as she hissed. "You bring some bitch into my show acting like she's running shit! Are you fucking her?"

"I have," Day said honestly. Why lie? Niggas lied when they weren't the boss. He was, so it was his rules. Kiara Da'vi was a participant in his life in the capacity he allowed.

"When my brother helped you and Demi start this label, you promised him you would take care of me!" Kiara shouted. "I know how this fucking company started. I know the 50 bricks that built this bitch. It's the same dope that sent him to jail. He died in there for you and Demi! Don't try to have me playing second fiddle to no bitch. Not Demi's nappy-headed mistress turned wifey, and for damn sure not no uppity-ass bitch like the one you let play in my face at the showcase!"

Day regretted the day he had crossed the line with this one. Their old partner and friend, Duke, had been a part of the initial investment of the record company. It was a three-way split, but when Day and Demi went legit, Duke refused to pull out of the streets. Day and Demi dabbled here and there to make sure their soldiers stayed strong, but they stopped throwing rocks at the penitentiary and focused on building reputable wealth. Duke didn't follow suit, and he got caught up. Day and Demi had promised to look out for his little sister, Kiara, and they had over the years. Day had even put the girl on his arm, blowing her up overnight and setting her up for a hell of a career. Every single she had dropped had taken the culture by storm, and every time they were linked together, her streams soared. The popularity made her ego soar, too, however. She was becoming a diva, and she was becoming possessive. Anytime she saw him out with someone other than her, she felt like her opportunity to shine was being taken away.

"We aren't in a relationship, Da'vi, remember who you talking to," Day reminded.

"The dick, the trips, and the cash say differently, but whatever you say, Day. Just check your hoes when it comes to me. My brother helped start this label. I deserve to be Queen B around here. When you know how it's built, you know how to burn it to the ground, too," she threatened.

"Need I remind you who you're talking to?" Day asked. The calm before the storm. He was known for it. He had taught plenty of lessons over the years when niggas had mistaken his calm demeanor for weakness.

She piped down, huffing and puffing, but she knew she had no wins in a fight with a man that wasn't hers to claim. She rolled her eyes. "Who is she anyway?"

"Nobody that concerns you," Day answered. "You're focused on the wrong things. I need you in the studio more, making music; leave these clubs alone, hop less flights, and let's get focused. You do more shaking ass on IG with the baby mama gang than you do anything else." He was referring to her frequent trips to Miami to hang out with the rappers' baby mamas. "We got a lot of paper invested in your project, and that shit moving at a snail's pace."

"I got you, Day," Kiara said, toning down the attitude.

"Then have me then," he shot back. "It's a hard time around here for everybody. Shit is about to get dark. Don't need no extra static."

"I heard about Demi's son. I'm really sorry to hear about that," Kiara stated sincerely. "He was a cute kid."

Day went back to his seat and rifled through the papers on his desk.

"Yeah, it's unfortunate," he said casually without looking up at her. She waited for him to say more, and when he didn't, she scoffed.

"You know the cameras will be out for the funeral…"

Day lifted his head and deadpanned on her. His stare was so cold that she stopped speaking mid-sentence. He knew where this was going. Kiara Da'vi lived for the cameras. Professional, cell phone, and otherwise, it didn't matter. She documented every aspect of her life for the social media stage.

"Tell me you not about to try to use my nephew's funeral as a press opp," Day stated. He shook his head. He didn't even wait for a response. "See yourself out, Da'vi. I got somewhere to be. I got a funeral to plan."

Day stood inside Williams Funeral Home. He had been in this position many times. Only this time, it wasn't some fallen rapper or an old friend from the block that he was there to pay respect to. This time, he was there to make arrangements for his nephew, and it made him want to vomit. He had been there the day DJ was born. He remembered it like it was yesterday. They had popped champagne right in the waiting room to celebrate. It had been a joyous occasion. It was the day that Demi had forced him to make a pact to take their business legit. He hadn't wanted to be a father who brought dirt into his home from the streets. He didn't want his wife to worry about him not coming home one day. They transitioned into a full-blown corporation and pulled out of the drug game the day after DJ's birth. The boy had basically saved their lives because shortly after that, their old partner, Duke, had gotten sent upstate for drug trafficking. They would have been right beside him if they hadn't made the decision to fly straight. They still had a firm hold on their old territory and collected taxes from the local hustlers for allowing them to occupy those blocks, but on paper, they were clean. They went from block huggers to CEOs. Day was positive that he wouldn't be alive today if DJ hadn't been born. A baby being in the picture had forced them to accept their responsibilities as grown men. DJ was a gift, and they had failed him. It never should have ended like this. Day had been around death his entire life, and never did it shake him to this extent. DJ's body was hard to stomach.

"They can't see him like this, man. This ain't my nephew," Day stated as he turned away from DJ's body. It was so hard to see this child lifeless in front of him.

"It's just a natural process that happens after death. Gas starts building up almost immediately. It's just bloating," the funeral director said. "There isn't much that we can do to stop it. That's why we urge families to hold quick services. Within the week is best. Do you have any idea when the parents will want to hold the funeral?"

"Soon," Day said as he checked his phone. "They're pulling up now. I want this as uncomplicated as possible. The insurance isn't necessary. They can keep all that. I want every bill to come to me, and don't hit me with no inflated prices. Just give my nephew the very best on his way out." Day went into his back pocket and pulled out a platinum card. "Put it all on there and be sensitive. Whatever they want, you hear me?"

"Understood, sir," the man replied.

Lauren walked into the building and her body reacted. Her stomach twisted as pangs of panic caused her throat to constrict. She was so lightheaded that she had to reach for Demi's forearm to steady her.

"Mr. and Mrs. Sky, I'm Michael. My deepest sorrows. On behalf of Williams Funeral Home, I'd like you to know we will make this process as uncomplicated as possible for you."

"My son died. How can you uncomplicate that?" Lauren asked. No sarcasm lived in her. She was truly inquisitive, desperate, in fact, for the solution to this conundrum. "It's the most difficult thing I've ever had to live through. It's taxing. To breathe. To walk. To talk. It hurts. Please help me uncomplicate this," she whispered, tears returning. She spoke with so much despair that the man's eyes misted.

He took one of her hands and clasped it. "God be with you, Mrs. Sky." He gave Demi a glance and a concerned look. "God be with you both. May I show you some options for you to lay your boy to rest in? We can't control when they go, but we can control *how* they go. I want your boy to go in something handpicked by his mother."

Lauren wanted to resist this entire process. She kept waiting for this nightmare to end. She had dreamed of things like this before. Usually, the moment before doom arrived, she would pop up in a cold sweat and thank God that it hadn't been real. That had to be what this was. It was a bad dream, the worst dream. She could tell by the look in everyone's eyes that it wasn't. She wouldn't wake up this time.

"Come on, sis," Day encouraged gently. "We got you."

Demi's hand on the small of her back reminded her legs to work, and she followed the man through double doors into a conference room. Kleenex rested on the table in anticipation of her tears.

Michael sat at the head of the table while Demi and Lauren sat beside one another. Day stood near the door, arms folded in front of his body.

"We have many options for you guys to choose from, but I think the most important will be deciding how you want to prepare the body," Michael stated.

"There's more than one way?" Demi asked.

"Well, we could embalm him and prepare him for burial, or we could cremate him and send him home with the two of you."

"You want to burn my son's body?" Demi asked, offended.

"Typically, parents of young children prefer it," Michael informed.

"We're not doing that," Demi protested. His answer was astute. He didn't even need time to consider it. His son would be laid to rest peacefully, not burned into nothing.

Lauren was silent. She reached for a tissue and then soaked up the tears racing down her face. "If we cremate him, we'll still have him with us. He'll still be here. I don't know if I can just stick him in a hole and walk away."

Demi looked at her in shock. Of the many conversations they had indulged in over the years, dealing with death had not been one of them. Her answer surprised him.

"We're not walking away, Lo. We're giving him back. The earth is a living thing. The dirt. The grass. It all grows. It's peaceful. My son went through hell these last few months, and you want to burn him? He got to know peace now. It's my job to lay him down peacefully."

"He's not just your son! You don't get to come in here and play dutiful father after how you abandoned us. You get a say, but I pushed him from my body. The final say will be mine."

Demi saw red. He leaned into Lauren and took her face into the U of his hand as he gritted his teeth. He was stuck somewhere between sadness and rage. He could feel sorrow burrowing in. The sting behind her accusation was enough to hollow his stomach, and he was a grown man. Life was undressing him, exposing him. The man presenting the information to them tensed, and Day stepped forward to intervene, but Demi conceded, releasing her as he shook his head.

"That's the bullshit he heard you say time and time again? How many times did you tell him that shit after I left?" He couldn't imagine how many bitter moments Lauren had put negative thoughts in DJ's head about their divorce. Demi hadn't abandoned DJ. He had left Lauren, but the way she had presented the split damaged DJ's perception of things. Demi knew he had been wrong for cheating; he wasn't innocent, but he had a right to move on. He had never wanted to leave DJ behind, however. Lo had made things difficult for him following the divorce. She had played games. She hadn't respected the custody agreement all the time, and he didn't press it because he knew she was hurting. He wished he had. He wished he had insisted on having DJ in his presence more than he conceded to her wishes to keep him home. He pushed his rolling chair back from the table. "You still think them cuts on his arms came out of nowhere?"

Demi opened the conference room door with so much force he cracked the glass pane. He doubled back and placed a stern finger in her face. "Marriages end, Lo."

"Marriages don't end, Demi! They aren't designed to end! You deserted ours! The truth fucking hurts, don't it?"

"I don't think we should focus on the negative in this…"

The funeral director tried to interrupt the chaos, but Demi was on Lo's ass like white on rice.

"We could have made that shit easier for him. You could have helped me make the transition easier! He was my boy, my blood, Lo. That shit is forever! You ain't tell him about the weekends you said I couldn't pull up. You ain't tell him about the times you blocked me from calling his phone. You ain't want him around Charlie, so you kept him from me."

"Say that bitch name again and watch me go the fuck off," Lauren threatened.

"Yo, Dem," Day stated, scratching his temple and wincing as he watched the start of World War III commence.

"Mind your business, Day," Lauren warned. "I don't need rescuing."

Day lifted his hands in offense as the funeral director looked at him in dismay.

"That's your fucking problem. You put your hurt feelings in front of my son's well-being. Tryna punish me made my son think I didn't want him."

Lauren was astonished. Tears flowed everywhere. Snot too. "How is this my fault? You cheated, Demi!"

"I cheated! I lied! I left. YOUUUUU! I did all that shit to you! I ain't never not wanted him. You played tug of war, and I let you because I knew you needed him more than me for a little while. I wasn't looking to pick no fights with you, so I let you have some shit. I never abandoned my fucking son. Now I got to live knowing he thought that shit. If you were anybody else, you'd be under my trigger for that shit."

"Just fucking leave, Demi. That's what you do best," Lauren spat.

So much animosity in one room. One parent versus the other, both spewing pain and looking for someone to blame.

"Make sure she gets back to the house for me, bro."

"I got her," Day replied.

Charlie lay on the couch, curled under a blanket, stomach in knots, remote control in hand. She changed the channels out of habit, not interest, as her thoughts ran rampant. The nausea was exceptionally bad today, and she didn't know if it was because of the baby or if it was because of the circumstances. The sound of the house alarm deactivating drew her attention to the door. She stood and nervously waited for Demi to come into view. His presence was so gigantic. The enormity of his energy was exciting but also intimidating. Demi was just the type of nigga that made people pay attention. Women wanted to fuck him. Men wanted to be in his position. He was a dominant-ass man, even now, in his weakest state. As soon as he spotted her, his feet sped up until he was wrapping his arms around her, pulling her entire body into his. His hand fisted a handful of her golden locs as his cold nose defrosted in the crook of her neck.

"Oh, baby," she whispered.

"I'm not going to be the same after this, Bird," he said.

Charlie pulled back to look him in the eyes. She placed her hands on the sides of his face. She was so full of caring and affection. So potent with love that it poured from her touch. "You don't have to be. Nobody expects that."

"She said I abandoned him. I loved my son, Bird. On me, I did," he said, breathing in a heavy breath and then holding it as his eyes swelled with anguish.

"I know you did, Demi. Lauren knows you did. She doesn't mean that," Charlie whispered. Demi turned away from her and slammed his fists on the kitchen island.

"Fuck!" he shouted as he swept the dish rack off the counter. Glass shattered as it hit the floor. Charlie was shaken, and she jumped, yelping in shock. He leaned into the counter, fists still balled, head bowed. He doubled over as agony tore through his body.

Her hand on his back was like magic. She felt the tension in his muscles ease. He turned to her. "I don't deserve shit like this."

"Like what?" she asked, confused.

"Like you."

His words struck a sour chord with Charlie. The world saw the harshness in this Black man, but Charlie saw the protector, the lover, the friend. She saw the father he had been. The one who lit up with pride when describing a story that involved his son and the one who ached for his son's presence during the aftermath of a tumultuous divorce. She noticed how he tried to overcompensate with DJ whenever he was around, just to make up for the fact that he was no longer in their home. Demi carried guilt about that while DJ was living, so she knew he held even more now. He wasn't the unforgiving CEO at home. He wasn't the unyielding boss or the iron-fisted reformed gangster. He softened with those he loved. He would do anything for them, for her. Reciprocity was easy with Demi because he cared for her with 100% effort. Her wants were supplied before she could even ask, and her needs, they didn't even speak of because that was second nature to him.

"Oh, but you do, Demi. You really do, baby," she said.

"I'ma need to go back to the house for a while, Bird. Lauren ain't in a good way at all. She can't be by herself," he stated.

Charlie felt an instant conflict in her spirit. Her knee-jerk reaction was to catch an attitude because why the fuck did her fiancé need to go be with another woman? She understood their loss, but why did her man have to be the shoulder Lo cried on? She held back, however, and softened her approach because she already knew that Demi was on edge. She grabbed the broom from the cleaning closet and began to sweep the mess off the floor.

"What about her family? Her mom? They can't stay with her?" Charlie asked.

"If I thought she would let them, I would make sure it happened, but she won't. This is something I need to do," he responded. "I owe her this. I owe my son this. It's my responsibility to be present while we bury DJ. I can't leave it on her shoulders. I can't pop in and out. The family, the arrangements, the breakdowns. If she hurts herself and I could have been there to stop it…"

"Hurts herself?" Charlie repeated. "You think she would do that?"

"I don't know what to think. I've never seen her like this before. I just know she's not okay," Demi responded. Charlie could see the weight on him. To be responsible for your own healing was one thing, but to be tethered to another and be accountable for theirs was a different type of pressure.

"And while you're holding her together, who's going to take care of you?" Charlie asked. "You're not okay either, and you're *my* responsibility."

She swept up the last of the glass and emptied it into the trash.

"I'm so worried about you, Demi. Like sick with worry," she admitted. Demi pushed out a forceful sigh and reached for her hand, pulling her into him.

"You are the guiltiest pleasure I've ever had, Bird," he said. "I'm doing the best I can with what's in front of me. Right now, Lo needs me. It doesn't really matter what I need. I just want to get through this funeral. I just need you to bear with me, baby. You have my heart, but she had my son, and this thing right here is only something me and Lo can do. You understand?"

Charlie didn't want to remind him of the child she was carrying, but in her mind, she was screaming, *what about me?* Perhaps it was because she wasn't showing yet that Demi didn't consider that she, too, had needs in the situation. Lauren was a woman he loved once. If Charlie was honest, she would admit that he still may love her. He hadn't loved her enough to save their marriage, but she wasn't naïve to the fact that fifteen years of a bond didn't disappear in an instant. They had built a life and a family. The nucleus of that family had perished. Charlie was sure Demi's old feelings were resurfacing and it terrified her. Lauren was the total package. She was beautiful and successful. From what Charlie could gather, she was kind and accommodating. And now she was vulnerable. The threat of Demi returning home to Lauren and realizing he had made a mistake was an insecurity that formed in Charlie's mind before she could stop it.

She nodded because the lump in her throat stopped her from speaking. She would come off insensitive if she protested, so she suffered silently as he placed a kiss on her chin and then her lips before he turned for the bedroom.

"I'ma grab a bag and head over there," he said. "I don't want you here by yourself. Maybe you should call your sister over here to stay with you for a few days."

So, my family can look after me, but nobody else but you will do for Lauren, Charlie thought. Was she not a priority? Did Lauren matter more than she did? How could she be engaged to a man and carrying the child of someone who didn't put her first? Charlie didn't know if her offense was selfish or justified, but she felt it all the same. She was too fucking embarrassed to even call Stassi and admit that Demi was going back home to Lauren, so she would not be extending an invitation for her sister to come to pity her. This felt like something she needed to hide, and it was only a reminder that when they started, she had been a secret, his mistress. It seemed that stain never went away. Ring or no ring, Lauren's title as wife trumped hers. Hell, even as the ex-wife, she was put first. Under the guise of support, Charlie allowed it. She didn't want to be the jealous girlfriend. She didn't want to bring about little problems and make the situation worse. She swallowed her pride and watched her man pack his bags, all the while feeling like she was on the verge of tears. She stood at the door to their bedroom, leaning against the frame with her arms folded over her chest.

"Will you be able to make it to our doctor's appointment?" she asked. "Should I just reschedule?"

Demi paused. Going to hear their baby's heartbeat for the first time had been on the calendar for weeks. He turned to her, and Charlie held her breath.

"Rescheduling might be better, Bird. I need a little time to wrap my mind around things. I don't know how to celebrate and mourn at the same time," he said truthfully. "We have time. The baby won't be here for months. I can't see past the next week."

She nodded and then walked out of the room before he saw the disappointment in her eyes. Charlie didn't want to rush his healing. She didn't even want him to completely abandon Lauren. She just wanted to be a part of the process. She wanted to matter enough for him to lean on her when he was weak. She could see him struggling. She could almost see the pain radiating off him like sun rays from a car on a blazing summer day. How could he not seek her for relief? Did she not provide that for him? Was she capable of being that for him? She wanted to be, but he didn't seem to expect that of her, and as his fiancé, it bothered her because that meant the position was open and Lauren was overly qualified.

She stayed in the living room as she heard him preparing to leave. He showered, packed, and then rounded the corner to face her. The duffel in his hand made her eyes burn with emotion.

Why does it feel like he's not coming back? Charlie thought.

"I'll call you," he said.

Those were his departing words. No kiss. No hug. Just a promise to reach out, like he was a nigga who had taken her on a date, and he was skating out with false promises because the vibe had been off.

Charlie wanted to call his name. She wanted to stop him, but she didn't feel like she should have to. He should know. He should feel her the way she felt him, and he should have known that every step he was taking felt like a sledgehammer to a glass heart.

When those taillights rolled down the driveway, a heat wave of anger started at her head and radiated through her entire body.

She felt so many things she didn't know if they were rational. She was jealous, and it was absurd. What kind of woman was envious of another woman who had just lost a child? She didn't know if it was the pregnancy hormones or if she was truly losing her mind, but the duty she was witnessing from Demi to Lauren bothered her. It felt intimate, and it felt reserved for a party of two. Another woman was doing a dance with her man, and Charlie didn't like it. She hadn't realized that even after divorcing, Demi and Lauren would have moments reserved for them. She had thought eventually they would form some kind of family and that life would include her, especially now that they were getting married and having a baby. Charlie's mistake was only planning for the happy times. She could have never predicted a time like this, and in this world, family didn't include her. Demi was being summoned by obligations she hadn't prepared for.

"Just get through this week. It's just until the funeral," she whispered, but there was a nagging in her gut that taunted her because this could be the thing that caused Demi to spin the block on Lauren and choose to leave her behind.

CHAPTER 6

Day
I'm sending a car for you in an hour.

Stassi frowned as the text came through to her phone. It had been two days since the showcase. She hadn't heard from him. She knew he had a lot going on, so she didn't necessarily expect to hear from him, but to burst into her head out of the blue so casually annoyed her soul.

Stassi
So, your mama didn't raise you with any manners, huh?
Hi, Day. I'm fine and you?

No sooner than she had pressed send, Day was calling. Stassi hadn't expected a phone call. He was clearly not in the mood for games. She answered on the third ring.

"My day is already hard enough, Anastassia. Why you got to make it harder?" he asked.

She felt an instant sympathy for giving him attitude because he sounded drained.

"Not trying to make your day hard, sir. Just making sure you know that rude shit you do with other women won't fly around here."

"Now, if I was texting you *good morning, beautiful*, you'd have a fit, call a nigga cliché," he said. She laughed. The one thing she loved about Day was this back-and-forth shit. The witty banter, the making her smile, even in the midst of a bad day like the one today where she was trying to get a new car, but the salesman was making it hard for her. She held up one finger to the older white man that she had walked away from to take this call. "One second, I'm on a very important call," she said, stalling him out.

"Don't spit that starter kit game on me. You got to try a little harder than that."

"How about this?" he proposed. "I'm fucked up over here over my nephew's death, and I really want to see you. Can't lie, though; I don't have the best intentions. I'm looking for a distraction."

Lauren knew the exact distraction he was talking about, and as tempted as she was, she wasn't going to be that for him.

"Then I think you need to call Kiara Da'vi or one of your other little girlfriends," she said. She hadn't forgotten the smart remarks the singer had dropped on her.

"Here you go," Day said. "I thought we were past this?"

"Past what?" Lauren asked.

"Past…playing…games," Day replied. His tone was indifferent, and he paused between each word like he was smoking or doing something in between time.

"No games. I just don't want to be a dumping ground for your trauma, Day. We started in a crazy way. Everything else we do, if we do anything at all, I'd just like it to be normal, you know? I don't want to fall down a rabbit hole of dysfunction with you again. Which means, no, I don't want to be your fuck buddy while you're grieving."

"My what?" He laughed. "I swear you overthink every mu'fucking thing. But cool. No dick for you."

Stassi chuckled against her will because she was trying her hardest to establish boundaries with this man.

"Ma'am, we have other customers. I don't think we're going to be able to get you approved. I need to see about this couple over here." The salesman was hasty as he interrupted her call.

"Yo, where you at?" Day asked, annoyed that their conversation was being interrupted.

"Wait! I need a car, and I need it today. It doesn't even have to be new. I know you have something I qualify for. My credit score isn't that bad."

"You have a recent repossession, ma'am. Now, there are customers here who can afford to be here, and then there's you. I don't want to waste any more of your time or mine. Have a good day," he said, walking away. The man was so damn nice and nasty at the same time that Stassi didn't even know how to respond. She was mortified. She felt small in this building like everyone's eyes were panning on her.

"Yo, where you at?" Day asked again. The annoyance in his voice embarrassed her even more. Although he knew she was down on her luck, she didn't need him to hear it. She had a quarter million sitting in her bank account from him, but she hadn't touched it. It just didn't feel right to spend.

"I'm at the dealership," she said. "I was trying to get a car. Can I just call you back? I was in the middle of something. They acting like I'm asking to drive off this lot in a Benz. I just need a little used Honda to get around. Damn."

"Which dealership?"

"Day, I don't…"

"Anastassia. You need a ride. I'm sending a driver for you. Which dealership?" he insisted.

"The Honda lot off 23 in Fenton." She surrendered the information, and he hung up the phone instantly. She knew his driver was on the way, but she was so embarrassed that she just wanted to get out of there. She walked outside and waited on the curb. She would rather be in the cold than spend another second inside.

Within 20 minutes, she saw Day's driver pull into the parking lot. She was freezing by that time and shuffling from foot to foot to generate heat. When the back door popped open and Day hopped out, she was stunned.

Okay, nigga, in your Chelsea boots, pea coat, and your Tom Ford sweater, she thought. He looked like money, and when he pulled her in for a hug, she discovered that he smelled like it, too. She didn't know where he was coming from, but he had cleaned up for the occasion.

"They made you wait outside?" he asked, brow dipped in aggression as he headed toward the entrance.

"No, I just needed some air, Day. Really, it's fine. Let's get out of here," she said.

"Nah, who was you working with?" he asked as he pulled open the door and marched inside. She followed behind him, wondering if he knew how much authority he exuded. It just infected the air whenever he was around. Dark-ass, fine-ass nigga. Stassi could feel the intrigue dancing up her spine.

"Day, please don't act like no nigga up in these people's establishment. I already did. I'm a walking stereotype with my Black ass and my fucked-up credit," she whispered. Day pinched her chin and tilted her head back slightly so that she was staring into his eyes.

"Which one?" he demanded.

Stassi sighed because she knew they weren't leaving without making a scene.

"That guy over there," she said, looking past his shoulder. Day turned around and saw the middle-aged white man in his Docker pants and cheap collar shirt shaking hands with a couple he was helping.

"Let them have him," he said. "Come on." He walked over to a man sitting in one of the side offices.

"Excuse me. Are you the manager?" Day asked.

"Yes, sir, I am. Dave Mitchell. What can I do for ya, big fella? I saw this pretty lady test-driving earlier. Did Jake take care of you? You ready to write up a contract?"

Another white man with faux authority. Stassi just wanted to get out of there.

"He didn't, in fact. He told my lady here she was wasting his time," Day explained.

"Well, there must be some kind of misunderstanding. I'm

sure he didn't mean to rub her the wrong way," the man said. "Hey, Jake. Come on over here."

Jake, the asshole, strolled over cockily.

"We're trying to get this young lady in a car. What seemed to be the problem?"

"Well…she didn't qualify. Can't get her financed," Jake answered. "If you don't mind, I need to pull some keys for that couple. They want to test drive."

"No, we don't mind," Day said. He turned to the manager. "I'd like to buy whatever she wants."

"I take it you're going to co-sign? We'll have to run your credit app," the manager said.

"You can put it on this," he said, pulling out a Black American Express card. "Matter of fact, I'll take three of 'em. Whatever she chooses, I need three. I trust that the commission won't go to someone who didn't earn it. Do we have a deal?"

"We've got a deal," the manager said.

Jake's face flushed red, and he stammered as he tried to find words to defend himself. "I didn't realize that she didn't need financing. I would have been happy to…"

"No worries, Jake. Too much of your time has already been wasted, my man. You missed this one. Might catch the next one. Better go fetch them keys," Day said.

Stassi folded her lips in to stop herself from gloating, but damn it, Day had saved her pride, and she just wanted to rub it in.

With your bitch ass, she thought.

"Let me come from behind this computer and put on my

salesman hat. You two look around, and we'll take something out for a spin," the manager said happily.

When he walked away, Day turned to Stassi. "You got a bank account full of money. Why you choosing struggle?"

"Your money," she said.

"Spend the money, Stassi. I can't take it with me. You tripping on it more than you need to." He tossed an arm around her shoulder, and she relaxed into his body as they walked around the showroom.

"You really buying three cars?" she asked. "What you gon' do with the other two?"

"Give them shits to my aunties or something," he said.

She shook her head in disbelief. "Not you dropping off whole vehicles like they're flowers," she said.

"I have more money than I can spend; more than I can invest even. It's not a big deal. People with money don't talk about money. Which is why we don't have to do all this overthinking about you spending whatever I give to you," he stressed.

He shrugged and opened the car door to one of the floor models. She climbed inside, and he watched her as she gripped the steering wheel. "Day, this is really not necessary," she asked.

"Nigga, quit playing coy. That game over. You want it?" he asked.

"I swear I'll pay you back," she promised.

He didn't respond, and she knew he was letting her ego win the moment.

"Thank you, Day," she said, smiling.

"Anytime," he replied. If he didn't value money, then how could she measure his affection for her? If gifting a car was no big deal, what gesture would signify a grand gesture? She decided to take his advice and not dwell on it. For now, this was a major resolution to a big problem, and she was appreciative.

An hour later, they were walking out, and Day had arranged for her car to be delivered to her place because he needed more of her time.

He escorted her to the back of the awaiting SUV. As they pulled away from the dealership, Day stared out the window.

"Thank you for covering for me the other night," he said.

"Of course. I'm really sorry about DJ," she said.

"Yeah, it's fucked up," he answered, voice drenched in a sudden sorrow that seemed to spread over the entire car. "I forgot about it for a minute when I saw you."

It was the strangest and most flattering compliment she had ever received.

"Have you eaten?" she asked.

"Damn, honestly, I don't even remember the last time I ate. I ain't even hungry for real. I just been on go, trying to make sure bro good."

"And is he?" she asked.

"Nah," Day responded vaguely. "Shit is all bad. Lauren can't even plan the funeral."

"How about we get you fed, then we start doing some of the things Demi and Lauren can't handle? I can take care of the planning part if they need help."

"You'd do that? I mean, I know y'all ain't got the best history with her firing you and all," he said.

Stassi scoffed. "I would hope that somebody would step up for me if I ever lost someone I loved so tragically. It's not about the past. I just want to help."

Day turned back to the cityscape as it passed by his window.

"This conversation didn't help me, Anastassia," he said.

"Why not?" she asked, confused.

Day leaned over and whispered in her ear so that his driver wouldn't overhear.

"Cuz a nigga really, really want to lay his head between your thighs now," he said.

The way Stassi felt her pussy jump, shit, she wanted to let him.

She blushed and shook her head. "Boy, go to your side of the car." She may have been dismissive aloud, but she lusted after him in her head. She hadn't forgotten the ways he had made her body sing. She hoped to get back to that place with him one day, where she felt comfortable enough to be the girl in his bed, but first, she had to be sure she was the girl who was in his heart. If she didn't occupy both spaces, she couldn't risk it. It would only lead to toxic attachment and disappointment. She had learned to lower her expectations with Day and to make her boundaries higher. Did she want him around? Yes. Did she need him around? No. So, if he was going to be around, it would be in a capacity that she knew she could handle. They were going to take this thing slow or not at all.

"Not that far," she said, closing the distance between them. She leaned her head on his shoulder, and he placed one hand on her thigh as they rode in silence.

"You're starting something, Day," she whispered.

"Seems like it," he replied.

CHAPTER 7

Nyair stood over DJ solemnly. He wished this outcome had never come to be.

"I'm sorry, man," he whispered as he bent down to kiss the child's forehead. He had come to bless the body and to check on the arrangements. He removed the small vial of holy oil he brought with him and touched his finger to the top. He left a dot of the oil on DJ's forehead, before bowing his head in silent prayer. This was a grave tragedy of epic proportions. He didn't suspect that Lauren would need financial assistance, but he still felt obligated to reach out to make sure things were handled. He hadn't even spoken to her, but this visit to see DJ was necessary. Since the body was being prepared by the funeral home Messiah owned, it was easy to gain access without disrupting Lauren.

"You got some investment here, or is this a church visit?" Messiah asked.

"I wish I knew," Nyair responded. The two men weren't particularly fond of each other, but they shared a common thread. "I appreciate you letting me in."

"Mmm hmm," Messiah responded. "The mortician needs to know what to do. Whether they're cremating or moving forward with a burial. If you can get word back soon, it'll be appreciated."

"I'll see what I can find out."

Nyair wasn't surprised that he hadn't heard from Lauren, and as much as he wanted to not be involved, his concern wouldn't allow it. He was certain that she was surrounded by support, but he was also certain that none of it helped her. To help a woman like Lauren, you first had to earn her trust, and after everything Lauren had been through, she trusted no one, not even God. He knew she needed guidance. This type of loss required prayer warriors far superior to him. Nyair was flawed, and the more Lauren crossed his mind, the farther down the rabbit hole he slipped. Nyair had lived life at the highest limit. His days in the NFL were filled with luxury and a world of people who never uttered the word no. The league was made up of overindulgence, and Nyair had become accustomed to living by a different set of rules. Everything was fair game. Drugs, alcohol, money. It was a normal day to bump a line of cocaine after a win and get fucked up until the wee hours of the morning. Nyair had witnessed it all. He had participated in it all, and it had almost killed him. The women, the drugs, the money. It was a lot of false idols in the land of the rich and famous. He had been worshipped, and his fall from grace had been a long one. Lauren felt like the precursor to relapse because he had worked hard to find discipline and restore his self-control, but the only thing that controlled him when he was around her was an overwhelming urge to be inside her. Lauren, with her difficult nature, challenged his, and he was a man who enjoyed a good hunt. He was trying his hardest to not complicate his life further, and after the death of DJ, Lauren was anything but simple. Hell, even before this had happened, he had some reservations, but now, they were both damaged. What else could they do besides destroy one another? Yet here he was, preoccupied with a heavy soul over her suffering. The mere thought of her grief bothered him. He wanted to call, but he had deleted the number. Checks and balances. He didn't want it to be easy to slip back into her life, but he hadn't anticipated how hard it would be to stay out of it.

He wasn't surprised by her disconnection. He hadn't expected to be someone she would call on during this time. Apparently, they were on the same page. They both were trying to scrub their connection out of their memory. What they had done had led to something unchangeable, something unforgivable, and facing one another after that meant being accountable for their irresponsibility. It meant admitting that it had been wrong, that they had hurt people, specifically Little DJ. He imagined it was harder for her to face that fact than for him, and it felt unfair that she was being judged solely, without him there to take half the blame.

"Mommy, this hurts so bad," Lauren whispered as she lay in DJ's bed, hugging his pillow. Lauren inhaled her son's scent on the duvet. She prayed the smell never faded.

"I know it does, baby," Lillian said as she stroked Lauren's hair. "We've got to get out of this bed, though. There are people here. There are many plans to make."

"Make them go away," Lauren protested. "I never knew how much of a show someone is expected to put on after they lose someone. Who's here?"

"Your cousins. Your aunt, your uncles. Nona and Papa are on their way," Lillian informed.

"I haven't spoken to any of them in years. What are they supposed to do for me now?" Lauren was unapologetic. "They just want to see me fall apart. I'm a train wreck, Ma."

"They want to love you. No matter how long it's been, they're your family," Lillian whispered. "And I know you want to give up, but we're not doing that, baby."

"I don't have anybody else! Other women get through this because they have other children to take care of. They have other little babies to live for, so they can't give up even if they lose one. He was my everything. It was only him. I have nothing. I am nothing anymore!" Lauren wailed, breaking down and squeezing her eyes tight as the ugliest sounds of woe filled the room.

"You got me."

Lauren and Lillian turned to the door to find Demi. His red eyes revealed he had found a moment to himself to cry, and for some reason, his sadness made hers feel appropriate.

"Demi, why don't you just get out of here? You've done enough!" Lillian stated. "She needs a minute!"

"Mommy, stop," Lauren intervened. She sat up on the bed, Indian style, and Demi walked over to her.

"I know, Lo," Demi said, and just from the tone of his voice, she knew that he knew exactly what she was going through. Lauren sobbed as Demi reached for her like she was a child, picking her up underneath her arms and hugging her snugly to his body.

"Shh. I'm sorry, Lo. We can do whatever you want to do. Whatever you need. You hear me? If you want to cremate him, that's what we'll do." Lillian stood to leave to give them privacy. The moment felt too fragile to witness, and Lauren was grateful for her exit.

Lauren nodded against his shoulder, finding so much comfort in his presence. Demi hadn't held her like this in years, maybe not ever. "I don't want to fight anymore." It was a truce. No matter how brief. They needed it to be able to trudge forward.

"Say, man," he muttered as he sighed in relief while squeezing her tighter. Fighting Lauren while fighting the devil was hell on earth. He was grateful for whatever had allowed her to extend him this grace.

"I'll be out front with your guests," Lillian said, her judgmental eyes full of disdain for her son-in-law. Demi put Lauren down. She shook her head as she took a seat on the bed.

"I'm so mad at you, Demi, but it's like ever since the doctors told me DJ was gone, I can't even feel it anymore. I can't feel how mad I am at you, so when I see you, I just forget that you aren't a safe space for me to run to. You're the most dangerous space."

"We did a lot of shit wrong, Lo. And really, that ain't even fair. I did a lot of shit wrong. The one thing you and I got right, though, was that little boy. You can always cash that check at the bank. I don't give a damn what life takes us through, how many times you scream fuck me, how many fights we have…because you gave me him, I will always be here if you need me. I know I fucked up, but that has never changed in my mind. You're important in my life, Lauren. I can't see a day when you won't be. Especially now."

Lauren leaned her head onto his shoulder, and he placed his large, tattooed hand on her knee.

"We can cremate him," Demi whispered. His voice hitched, and Lauren knew he was only agreeing to this for her. "I know you need him with you."

"Thank you, Demi."

"You ready to go out here?" he asked.

"No, but they're not going anywhere so…"

Lauren shrugged, and Demi stood, grabbing her hand and leading her out of the room.

As they entered the room, everyone's chatter dulled to silence. All eyes panned to them. She felt their pity. She gripped Demi's hand tighter. The way he held her back told her he needed her just as much. Demi wasn't a hand holder. He despised it, in fact. He was OCD in nature and would offer her a clothed elbow before he would ever touch his fingers to hers, but today, his grip was Vise tight. She looked at him in wonder as thoughts of how much distance had existed between them in their marriage made her eyes mist. Something this simple as the holding of hands was foreign to her. How damaged they had been. She couldn't help but think that damage had leaked onto their son. Perhaps DJ's pain had come along before the divorce ever happened. *Did he see love when he looked at us?* Lauren thought.

Day entered the home, and Lauren's entire body stiffened when she saw Stassi walk in behind him.

Day pulled Stassi through the crowded living room until the couples were face to face.

Demi released her hand to embrace Day. Lauren was glad Demi had a best friend like Day to keep him centered, to anchor him during this storm. Old Demi would have blown everything away by now, but this new version of him was steady, dependable, calm even. She had no idea that it was Charlie who was responsible for that transformation. It had nothing to do with friendship; true love had settled him.

"I'm so sorry to hear about your son. I umm," Stassi paused. It was uncomfortable for them both. They didn't like one another. They weren't even on the same team. Charlie was Stassi's sister.

"Why are you here, Stassi?" Lauren asked frankly. It wasn't even her nature to be that mean. Refined Lauren would have been polite. Professional Lauren would have tolerated the uninvited guest on behalf of Day. The Lauren who had fallen into a sudden nightmare was unapologetic.

"She's with me, Lo. You know I ain't with none of that bullshit. She's helping a nigga keep his peace right now, and I know you have your hands full. She's here to help."

Lauren scoffed. "Help with what?"

"Help with whatever you need. Both of y'all," Stassi said. "You don't have to work your son's funeral, Lauren. I can make things easier for you." Stassi paused and glanced at Day unsurely. She sighed and shrugged. "I don't know, Lauren, but if you need help...I know we aren't friends, but I'm available for you."

"We could have been friends," Lauren stated softly. "I thought we were, but I don't trust you, Stassi. This is the most important thing anyone can do for me. I can't trust just anyone with it."

"Trust me, sis," Day said. "Trust me to take this burden off you."

"I'm the best at what I do, Lauren. I promise to handle every detail with care. If you want me to. It just feels like everybody should be responsible for doing something. Everyone should be helping. He was just a kid. That feels bigger than any disagreement me and you have had."

Lauren's heart was so disturbed. She was shaken in a way that didn't lend room to find her way back to normalcy. She did need the help, and she was in no position to do this herself. She didn't trust her tacky-ass family members to do it the way she would want it done, but she also didn't want a stranger to plan this important goodbye.

"He's my baby," Lauren whispered.

Stassi reached out a hand and gripped Lauren's wrist. She looked her dead in the eyes. "I know," Stassi said. The sympathy and humanity coming from Stassi couldn't be missed. Lauren felt guilt in that moment. Stassi could have used this moment to gloat on how low Lauren had fallen. She could have rubbed the loss in. Lauren had fired her and blackballed her career. Stassi had every right to be vindictive at this moment. Instead, Lauren saw compassion in Stassi. Lauren was trekking across a bridge she had set on fire, and still, Stassi didn't inflict a burn.

"Thank you," Lauren said. Stassi hugged Lauren tightly.

"You're welcome," Stassi whispered softly. "I've got him. I promise. "

Day guided Stassi away from Lo and into the kitchen to greet the rest of the family.

Demi turned to Lauren. "You sure you good with that?" Demi asked. "I can shut it down. If it feels like she on some funny shit. You're my wife…I…" He caught himself, and he wasn't exactly quiet about it. Lauren's eyes widened in shock because sharing this space, this moment, this heartbreak together was like sharing one heart. It was convoluted and confusing, but they hadn't asked for this. Nobody would ask for this. She understood how he had forgotten. He had gone right back into their routine, retreating into the life they once shared because she, too, felt like she was staring at her husband right now. She wondered if that was what marriage did. It wasn't like a normal breakup where you could write the existence of a human being off forever. Marriage seemed to be forever. The imprint lasted even long after the ink dried on the divorce papers. Ownership still existed. They were like an abandoned building, still standing, but vacant inside. The sign was still on the door, though. Husband and wife. It didn't matter if the word ex was in front of it. The identity of that role still lingered. They depended on the routine of the institution they had built to get them through this.

"No, Demi. It's fine. She really is good at what she does," Lauren admitted. "She'll make sure it's beautiful."

Demi swiped both hands down his face, realizing that his head was fucked up. He addressed the elephant in the room. "I want to be here with you, Lo. I am going to be here with you. I'm not going nowhere. Every morning. Every night. Until this eases up, but I have to ask, and I'm sorry that I have to ask you this, but is Charlie welcome here? I know she wants to be here."

"Your mistress wants to be here for you?" Lauren asked, scoffing.

"And you, Lo. She wants to support us both," he said, ignoring the insult Lauren threw out.

Lauren's eyes turned to fire. "I want to be crystal clear with you, Demitrius. She's not welcome anywhere near me or my son—ever. She can't come here. She can't come to the service. If that's where you want to be…"

"I told you where I'm trying to be," Demi interrupted in frustration.

"Until when, Demi? What's my time limit? You said until this eases up? This will never ease up! I will always feel this! So, watch what you promise me. You know you're not good at keeping them."

"I need you to work with me here. Be reasonable. You know my situation. She's pregnant, Lo."

"And that's not my fucking problem," Lauren snapped. "I'm burying my son because of the damage caused by you and that bitch. I don't give a damn about anybody's child but the one I'm saying goodbye to. Did she give a single care in the world about my baby when she took you from this house? She didn't give a fuck about the family that ended so she could have you. Don't talk to me about her, and if you're that distracted and concerned about it, you can leave. Go be there with her!"

Lauren stormed off, and Demi reached for her, but she snatched her arm away before retreating to her mother's side. She wasn't sacrificing her comfort to make room for Charlie. Charlie was the worst thing that had ever happened to Lauren, and if she never saw her again, she would consider herself blessed. She was too angry to cross paths with Demi's little girlfriend. Before this tragedy, she had been able to be the bigger person, but to come face to face with her again, while she was growing life and Lauren was grieving it, nah, that would be like two trains colliding. Lauren didn't want anything to do with Charlie, and if Demi forced the issue, he would be cut off, too. She was no longer committed to peace because her storm would rage regardless. To draw a truce would only be for the sake of Demi and Charlie's happiness, and she would be damned if she accommodated that.

Demi walked into the kitchen where Stassi was pouring herself a drink. He stood next to her as they stared out over the growing family.

"You had a whole life with her," Stassi whispered. She passed him the Hennessy sidecar she had prepared, and he accepted it silently, taking a sip before clearing his throat. "It looks like you still have a life here with her."

"I can't erase history," Demi said. Stassi made him feel like he was doing something wrong. He felt the sudden urge to defend his presence. "She's my family."

"Your wife," Stassi said. "That's what you called her. That's what everyone in this house is calling her."

"Did Bird send you here?" Demi asked.

Stassi scoffed and shook her head. "To watch you? You think my sister smuggled me in here to keep tabs on you? Nigga, no. I'm here because Day asked me to help, and because I truly feel bad for you and Lauren." Stassi calmed some, remembering the pain that drew them all to this commonplace. "I know you're in a tough position, but do not hurt my sister while you're going through this. She doesn't deserve it, and she can't handle it. Be respectful to her while being present for the mother of your child."

"Your sister is a light in my world. I've never felt anything like what I feel for her. I know you don't like it. I know Lauren hates it. She distracted me from something important, though. I have to live with that. We all do. I need to figure out how to do that."

Stassi nodded. "You and Charlie love one another. I see that. Everyone sees it. You and Lauren belong to one another. Everyone also sees that. You tried to stay where you didn't belong, Demi, and people ended up hurt. Love isn't all it takes. I can see your loyalty to Lauren. I see your duty to her.

You're like a knight standing by her side in here. You're not letting anybody get close enough to break her. Meanwhile, my sister is in pieces in a home you're supposed to share. She's not here because you know it hurts your wife. You're choosing without saying a word. Between the two of them, you're protecting Lauren. So, as highly as you speak about Charlie, your actions don't match, and as her sister, I can't unsee that."

Demi couldn't deny what Stassi was witnessing. He only contested the interpretation of it. Women assigned too much meaning to things. They added narratives to things that didn't need an explanation.

"There's nothing to tell here, Stassi. I'm doing what I got to do. That's it. Lauren isn't a threat to my relationship. I know where the line is."

"I couldn't tell on you if I wanted to. She worships you, Demi!" Stassi exclaimed in a harsh whisper. "I'm asking you to be man enough to tell her yourself. If you want to be here and make things right with Lauren, nobody can blame you for that. We all know what you're both going through. Just don't string Charlie along. She's young. She doesn't have to have that baby. Spare her, Demi. If you love her like you say you do, you would."

"I'm really trying to be patient with you right now. Off the strength of your sister. But this whole conversation is out of bounds. This ain't your place," Demi stated. "I lost my son. Outside of that, nothing else is up for discussion. If you want to help Bird, make sure she's not alone. If you can't do that, just stay in your lane." Demi went to walk off, but one last thought occurred to him. "Do she even know you're here?" Stassi was charged, tried, and convicted within seconds. She was vocal about everything except that, and he recognized the flash of guilt in her eyes before she could form an answer.

"You're over here begging a nigga to send your sister packing. I ain't the one Charlie need to be side-eyeing."

With that, he walked away, making a mental note to keep a watchful eye over Stassi because even he couldn't tell where her loyalty lay.

Floating through this growing crowd that called themselves family felt inappropriate. They were Lauren's people. He hadn't bothered to call his side of the family. His parents were gone, and his brothers were distant. They had never even met DJ, so informing them felt fake, and Demi couldn't exist in any realm other than real. Lauren's mother had put the call out, and people he hadn't seen in years were walking through the door full of sympathetic salutations and aluminum pans full of food he wouldn't eat. He was sure he seemed cold as he stood in the kitchen. He was the overseer, sipping his drink silently, watching Lauren and no one else. He spoke, but there were no hugs being accepted. He didn't even need the handshakes they offered. Prayers were appreciated, but he was even weary of accepting those because the hearts of men were flawed. The wrong person sending prayers up on his behalf could easily be misconstrued as curses. Perhaps that's how this had occurred in the first place. Someone had cursed his son.

"She had that fake-ass pastor in this mu'fucka praying over my kid. Nigga everything but holy," Demi grumbled to himself. He was looking to assign blame in a situation that was hard to make sense of. He was careful where he placed it, however, because he knew Lauren couldn't hold any more weight. He suffered through the distant relatives and their fake sympathy for her sake. They seemed to make things better for Lauren. The lack of solitude forced her out of bed. It made her engage in the world. He hoped this kept her mind from venturing too far into the grave behind their son. He knew the type of devotion Lauren had as a mother, and she would undoubtedly follow DJ straight to heaven if he let her depression have full control. Her family was needed, no matter how intrusive it felt. The one person he wanted to walk through the door was unwelcome, so unlike Lauren, no matter how many people showed up, he would suffer regardless. His only reprieve was in Charliezonia, and he couldn't get there right now. It was the consequence he had to live with for starting his relationship with Charlie without honor. She was his love, but in certain spaces, she was also his biggest indiscretion. He was trying to lead with respect, and he couldn't lie and leave out the love he felt for Lauren through this loss, but Lauren's downright refusal to allow Charlie to be present made his pain intensify. Not many things could hurt Demitrius Sky, but this one hurt, unlike anything he had ever felt before. It was such an empty feeling. He couldn't explain it, and if he couldn't explain it, he was afraid that he would never be able to heal it. How could one heal what he didn't understand? It was an infection of a different kind, and it was spreading through his soul like a virus, ruining every part of him.

He grabbed the entire bottle of cognac and slipped down the hallway. Lauren hadn't changed his office. It was still as it had been when he lived there. It was almost like he had never left. He was grateful for the escape. He walked inside and closed the door, sighing heavily in relief as he sat in the executive chair. He poured himself another drink and then pulled out his phone. Even her name on his home screen stirred him. Since the day he had laid eyes on her, she was like a stimulant to his system. Charlie had texted him. The message, no matter how small, even before reading, was like paddles to his dead heart.

Bird
I can't reschedule the baby's appt. They don't have openings for another few months. I can go alone.

Demi frowned. He wasn't sure how he was going to balance two worlds at once. He wanted to be excited with Charlie. He had been elated upon finding out about her pregnancy, but now it felt wrong. It felt wrong to even hope for this new baby. It felt inappropriate to even mention life when his son no longer had his. It felt inconsiderate to even imagine the notion of celebration when he felt like the whole sky was falling.

Demi
When is it again?

Charlie
Tomorrow.

Demi
I'll be there. Send me the address and the time.

The information came next, and Demi set the reminder in his phone before swallowing a copious amount of brown liquor. It seemed to be the only thing to numb him, and so he poured up again, taking down another glass full.

The fact that it sounded like a growing party outside this room triggered him. Funerals always became family reunions, but he wasn't keen on the fact that his son had to die for motherfuckers to give a fuck. He was also aware that his anger was just a steppingstone on a long mountain of grief. It was best he stayed out of the way until he could gain more control over his emotions.

CHAPTER 8

To sit alone in a doctor's office as she anticipated hearing her child's heartbeat for the first time was torture. Charlie had never imagined this moment would play out like this. After all that she and Demi had been through...After the first abortion. After their breakup. After the begging and negotiating for her to give him a baby. She was sitting in this moment solo. In no world should this have occurred. Charlie was afraid to have her first child. Demi knew this. He had promised her that he would be present. He had vowed to always have her back, that her career wouldn't suffer, that her youth wouldn't be wasted. He had even promised her a pair of brand-new titties once she was done nursing. They hadn't even started parenting together and she was already feeling like a woman deserted. She wondered if these feelings of bitterness were just a part of the package of motherhood. It seemed that every woman she knew who gave a man a baby ended up full of pain and resentment once the baby arrived. Babies seemed to be the beginning of the end for happy Black couples. The commitment a baby represented seemed to scare Black men off. While women locked in on the new responsibility, their partners grew skittish as fleeting notions of boyhood sent them running back to the streets. She had seen it time and time again. She prayed her story wasn't more of the same. She had tried to reschedule the appointment, but this was the best OBGYN in the city, and her books were full for months. If she didn't squeeze in now, she wouldn't be able to get back in until halfway into her second trimester. Waiting for Demi to bury his son, unfortunately, wasn't an option. She kept eyeing the door, waiting for his arrival, because he had confirmed that he would be there.

"Charlize Woods."

Charlie stood and made her way to the receptionist's desk.

"Umm…I'm waiting for my fiancé. Can I have five minutes, please?" she asked. "I think he got turned around at the entrance. He's close."

"No worries, ma'am. I can send him back when he arrives," the friendly woman responded.

Charlie was stalling for time, hoping and wishing that Demi would appear, but her faith in him dwindled by the second.

"He's usually on time," Charlie added. It felt like she owed this woman an explanation as to why she was in this office alone when it took two people to make a baby. She didn't want to be another one of those women who proclaimed love aloud only to suffer in silence later. She and Demi were supposed to last. Her chapter of his story was supposed to be his last, but somehow it felt like she was simply the climax to a juicy love song. She wanted to be the couple that defied logic. The one that people looked at in awe because they were walking symbols of love and devotion. She felt that when she was with Demi. They always felt like they lived in their own world and spoke a language others couldn't quite grasp, but the distance that she felt creeping between them was telling. It was small. It wasn't even anything noticeable yet, but Charlie could feel the inevitable weft that was growing where awe used to be. Demi had been so enamored by Charlie when they first met, and he still was. Charlie had fallen before she could blink, and she enjoyed the breathless journey into his arms. A one-night stand had led to not being able to live without him, but this death in Demi's life left no room for anything else. It left no room for growth, and she could feel the seed they had carefully watered beginning to dry out. She could feel the nurse's impatience, but the woman was polite as Charlie anxiously hawked the entrance. Five minutes turned to fifteen, and when she could no longer stall the doctor out, she submitted and followed the intake specialist to the back.

She distractedly followed as she dialed Demi's number. The instant sound of his voicemail infuriated her to the point of tears.

She was too embarrassed to leave a message. She didn't want this nurse to hear her asking where Demi was. She didn't want to hear herself pleading for his attention. So, she hung up, took a deep breath, and prepared to face the day alone.

"What do you mean he won't be able to give the life tribute for my son?" Lauren asked. She sat in the office of her home church as Pastor Dean's secretary sat across from her. "I've been a member here for five years."

"Unfortunately, there is something on the church calendar, and we won't be able to accommodate the services," the woman said. "Revival is that week."

"My child is dead. This is our home church. Where else are we supposed to go?" Lauren asked. She was completely flustered. She was already overwhelmed with this new reality; she didn't need added stress.

"Easter Sunday hardly constitutes a church home, sister, and that public scandal with your husband and that young lady was anything but discreet," the secretary said, lowering her tone. "Can put the man in a church but can't put the church in a man, can we? Good for you for divorcing him."

Lauren's entire body heated as if someone could control her temperature with a knob. Embarrassment and anger took over, but she was stunned to speechlessness. This woman was bold. *I know this bitch ain't gossiping to me about my own shit.* Demi was a man she had called many names, but she was never going to sit by and allow somebody else to disparage him. That shit would always set her off.

"You're turning me away because my family isn't good for your optics?" Lauren scoffed in disbelief.

"Of course not!" The woman answered, feigning ignorance. "I'm sorry if that was too forward. I just remember when you were going through that public trial and your whole divorce, we wanted to see you in here. We were all praying so hard for your strength, sister. Listen, if I could help, I would, but the revival has been on the books for months. We have two other churches joining us. We are sorry for your loss, but our calendar just doesn't have the room to host your event," the woman said.

"Event?" Lauren repeated. The woman said it like Lauren was asking to throw a Sunday brunch. "Can I just speak to Pastor Dean? I'm sure something can be worked out."

"He isn't available right now, ma'am. I'll leave word for him to give you a call."

Lauren couldn't decipher the context in her current state. She couldn't tell if this woman was exceptionally callous or if she was just rubbed raw from pain. Either way, it hurt, and Lauren felt more hopeless than she had when she had walked through these righteous doors. She could admit that she hadn't attended service in person in quite some time, but she always tuned into the live services from her bed. She also paid her tithes faithfully, so to be denied in her time of need felt like a slight. To know that she had been the subject of the church grapevine was even worse. This was supposed to be a safe space. It was supposed to be where she could bring her burdens. Instead, it was a cold and sterile institution masquerading under the guise of godliness. Lauren tucked her pride in her handbag and walked out. Anything further would feel like begging, and she refused to do that. She wished Demi had come with her. He would have known how to handle the situation. He wouldn't have taken no for an answer, and he for damn sure wouldn't have let the disrespect slide unchecked. By the time her stilettos made it across the parking lot, she was falling apart. She remembered being the type of woman other women looked up to—some would even say envied. She had once been the total package. She was a woman with a degree, a successful career, a handsome and faithful husband, a beautiful child, and a breathtaking home. She wore the best fashions, carried the most exclusive purses, and traveled to the most desirable destinations. She lived "that life." She wondered if the women at this church were enjoying her downfall. Had she made them feel like she needed to be humbled? Lauren felt victory in the secretary's stare as she denied her in her hour of need. She wondered if she had done something to make her feel small once upon a time because the way that woman had diminished Lauren felt personal. On a day when she just needed support and a hug, she had been judged. Lauren couldn't stop herself from losing it. She hurriedly unlocked her door and sought out the privacy of her tinted windows as she cried. She called Demi, hysterical, as anxiety and stress forced sobs to flow freely from her lips. He answered on the first ring.

"What's up, Lo?" he answered.

"We have nowhere to have the funeral. Pastor Dean said no," Lauren cried.

"Fuck you mean he said no?" Demi asked in confusion.

"He wouldn't even come to speak to me. He sent word

through his bitch of a secretary," Lauren said, sniffling. "I've never felt so small. What kind of man of God turns a grieving mother away? I just really wish you could have come with me. I feel like I'm losing my mind. I can't process this right now, Demi."

"We've been members there for years. Fuck type of time they on?" Demi's tone was lethal. "I'm on my way, man. If that's where you want to have the service, then that's where it will be. Stop crying. You know what I taught you."

"Never let them see you sweat," Lauren whispered, as she sighed while hunting through her center console for Kleenex. "How did life get so bad for me, Demi?"

"Stop, Lo. Just hold tight. I'm turning around now. I'm on my way."

Forty minutes later, Demi pulled into the parking space next to hers. He was such a man. He never walked into a room without influencing the energy, and today was no different. The look on his face told her he was in a mood as he approached her door. He opened the door for her, and she climbed out. His presence relieved her. She didn't know why. She hated him. She hated him for what he did to their family, but somehow, he was the only person that she could lean on right now. How was the human heart so complex? To be able to love what hurt you and to hate what loved you was an anomaly. Life was a complicated puzzle that Lauren thought she had put together, only God had flipped the table on her. Now, all the pieces were scattered on the floor, some missing altogether, in fact. How was she supposed to put things back together?

They walked into the church side by side, and this time, she didn't feel so alone. She wondered how people made it through stuff like this by themselves. She was almost sure time alone would break her. She was being held together by a tiny thread, and it was threatening to snap at any moment.

Lauren led him right back to Pastor Dean's office door, and then she stopped.

"You know what, Demi? Fuck this church."

Demi frowned in confusion and scratched his temple. "You called me all the way here only to change your mind?" he asked. "If you want to have the service here, I'll make it happen."

"I know you will," she said. "But we shouldn't have to beg for support. This ain't no church. This is just a building full of judgmental-ass people. My baby deserves better. I want him to be laid to rest by someone who cares."

"And you couldn't come to this conclusion before I raced to your side, Lo? I put off something important because you said you needed me here," Demi said in frustration.

Lauren pulled back in offense. "Because I did need you here, Demi, but if it's that much of an inconvenience, then maybe you should leave. I'm not begging anybody for things that should come naturally. Not anymore. Not even you."

She turned on her heels and stormed out of the church. She would need to figure out how to deal with things by herself because it felt like no one else wanted the burden of helping her through it. She couldn't be mad at anyone for that, not even Demi. She knew she was responsible for her own emotions. She just had to figure out how to manage them. Simple things like remembering to breathe, climbing out the bed to use the bathroom, or even combing her hair felt like heavy tasks these days. Being accountable to regulate her feelings when all she felt was a daunting abyss of agony felt impossible. She would figure it out, however. She had no choice.

"Girl, turn around. Turn your ass around," Lauren whispered to herself. She hoped her feet would follow orders, but instead, she found herself on the front porch, pressing one hand to a queasy stomach as she contemplated ringing the doorbell.

When Nyair pulled open the door, Lauren stood there hopeless, and with nothing to offer but a shrug.

"If you ask me what I'm doing here, I won't be able to answer because I don't know," she said, voice cracking as her eyes misted.

"I won't ask," he said. "Come here."

He pulled her into his arms and hugged her so tightly that she couldn't help but release the rest of her tears. It was freezing outside, and he was shirtless as the wind whipped around them, but it didn't matter. He held her silently until she was able to look up at him.

"Can I come in?" she asked.

He stepped aside and welcomed her. He removed her coat, tossed it over the back of the couch, and then offered her a seat. "I'll be right back."

He walked out of the room and returned moments later fully clothed. His black joggers were now accompanied by a matching hoodie. He kept his distance. Lauren didn't miss his hesitation to cross the room. Instead, he leaned against the wall, arms folded across his chest.

"How can I help you, Lauren?" It was in his tone. The question was genuine, not a pleasantry that he had posed mindlessly.

"I feel bad, Nyair, and I'm not talking about the type of bad that a drink can dull or that sleep can wear off. I feel like I want to die," Lauren paused and rolled her eyes to the ceiling to try to stop gravity from pulling tears down her cheeks. "The reason I woke up in the morning... The reason I went so hard for everything is gone, and I can't stop my heart from breaking. Every time I think about it, it's like hearing it for the first time all over again. I've prayed. I've screamed. I've cursed. Nothing stops this pain."

Nyair's brow was low. She had his complete focus. He didn't speak, and she was grateful because she needed to keep speaking so she wouldn't lose her momentum.

"I know you're a man of God. I know you have things you should refrain from doing. I know we broke so many rules by even taking it as far as we did, but I need you to come take me out of this hole. I can't think here. It's dark, and I'm drowning, and I need you to make it all go away."

"I'm just a man, Lauren. I'm not God. I can't take it away, as much as I wish I could," he said.

"That's all I need you to be…" She swallowed the lump in her throat. "A man. Nyair, please take this away from me.

You're the only one I can ask. The only one I want."

Nyair crossed the room, and she stood, twisting the rings on her fingers nervously.

"I'm not clear on what you're asking me, Lo," Nyair said, brow dipped in confusion because she wasn't making sense.

"Fuck me, Nyair." It couldn't get any blunter than that. Lauren wasn't lust-filled. She wasn't unfocused. She was broken. She was numb. She needed to feel something other than this sinking, and when she was with Nyair, he made her feel like she could fly. She was desperate for the distraction, desperate for love, even if it was temporary and contrived. "It doesn't have to mean anything, Ny. I just need this. I need it with someone I can trust."

Lauren felt like she was disappointing him. The look he bestowed on her shrunk her a bit. Like she had performed under his expectations, but she didn't want to be on anyone's pedestal. She wanted to do what other women did when something hurt, when life ground them under its feet and snubbed them out like a lit cigarette. She wanted to search for fulfillment in all the wrong places. If she could smoke it away, she would. If she could drink it away, she would already be under the bottle, but she knew that this loss was mightier than all addictions combined. Sex, however, could outweigh it all. Sex with the right man, a man that made her feel like he could love her. Every touch felt like care, and she needed to be taken care of. The woman that had been strong for everyone else, now needed to be weak, but that was only allowed when you knew someone else was there to make sure you came out of the other side intact. Demi was trying to be that for her, and the part of her that still loved him wanted to choose him for this, but the part of her that mistrusted him wouldn't dare allow it. Nyair was a man of God. He was a lifeline. He was someone she may have fallen for if her world hadn't suddenly fallen apart. He wouldn't mishandle her. That she knew for sure. His attention would be keen. His hands purposeful. His dick masterful. His intentions self-less.

"Lauren, do you hear yourself?" he asked. "This ain't you."

He took her face into his hands, and her cheeks warmed in his hold. "Don't look at me like that. I'm not selling my soul. I'm grown. I know exactly what I want and why."

"You're not even in your right mind, and when I'm inside you, neither am I. I forget my responsibilities, Lo. As a man. As a leader. I'm supposed to be a man of the cloth. Ask for prayer. Ask for charity. Ask me for something I can give you without losing favor, and it's yours."

Rejection didn't feel like a rejection when it was delivered by an honorable man. Lauren leaned her head into his palm and closed her eyes as he pulled her into an embrace. Those strong arms hugged her so tightly that she wanted to escape there forever. The sigh she released contained anxiety that had nestled in her for days. "I don't have anything else to live for," she whispered.

"It will get lighter. It's heavy, and you'll never fully release it, but it will get easier to carry." He massaged the back of her neck with one hand and pulled her in tighter with the other. The light stroke to the small of her back as he held her caused her heart to thunder. "You can't hold me like this, Ny, and then say no." He smelled so good, and her throat felt like it was closing as she tried to swallow.

"I should let go," he murmured in her ear as his lips grazed her shoulder.

"Okay," she answered. Neither of them moved.

"I got to let go," he insisted.

"Okay."

Still, they stood there, unmoving, except for that hand. His hand moved from her lower back to her hip, and he kneaded into her flesh as she felt him rise.

"You haven't even called me. You didn't even check on me," she whispered.

"I couldn't," he replied. "I can't control myself with you, Lauren. I'm a disciplined man, and I have none around you."

"That's not a bad thing," Lauren whispered. "Maybe we can heal each other. Whatever's broken in you that you're afraid I'm going to hurt again…Maybe this can be good for us both because this is the closest I've felt to non-suicidal in days." He was hard for her. His need pressed into her so deliciously that it made her short of breath. Her hands caressed the back of his neck, and he tensed at her seduction. She wasn't even trying; her femininity just oozed from her and onto him. He wanted it. She felt it. She smelled it. She squirmed in his arms, desperate for contact, for these clothes to disappear so he could transport her to another dimension.

"This ain't healing, Lauren. This is gonna make it worse," he hissed in her ear before helping himself to a handful of her. He gripped her ass mannishly, pulling her into his girth, temptation pushing his morals aside, biblical decorum out the window.

"It can't get any worse," she panted as she kissed his lips. His tongue tasted like a green apple Jolly Rancher, and she sucked on it as she kissed him greedily.

"Shit's fucked up," he whispered.

"So fucked up," she moaned between tastes. Her hands were everywhere, pulling his shirt over his head and slipping her hand down the waistband of his joggers. His dick pulsated in her hand as she stroked him. He caught her wrist and pulled back suddenly.

"Lauren." The sternness in his voice brought a stop to her conquests. "This isn't going to help."

She pulled back from him, snatching her wrist out of his grasp.

"I'm really tired of people telling me what is and isn't going to help," she snapped. She snatched up her coat, and Nyair grabbed the other end of it, stopping her from walking away.

"Lauren!" he shouted. She stopped walking but refused to face him because now, on top of being horny, she was humiliated. "I've been a dog about women before. I've lied to them, cheated on them, told them what they wanted to hear, slept with multiple at a time, gaslit them, and taken advantage of their insecurities. I've weaponized sex before, trading their emotion for my satisfaction and then discarded them after I was over it. Trust me when I tell you this won't make shit better. I'm not that man anymore." He stepped up behind her and caressed her arm, running a finger down her skin, making goosebumps rise on the back of her neck. He reached around her body with both arms, hugging her from behind, and grabbed her hands. She held onto him for dear life as he kissed the nape of her neck.

"Pray with me, Lauren."

Lauren broke as she bent her head in shame as Nyair whispered the softest prayer in her ear. Her sobs were so loud that she almost couldn't make out what he was saying, but she trusted him to lead her.

"Amen," he said when he was done. She turned and hugged him, bawling, and he held her. He held her like he loved her. At that moment, no one could convince her that he didn't.

"I need to leave," she whispered. "I'm so embarrassed."

"Nah, you just need to rest." He removed the coat from her hands and grabbed her hand, leading her to his bedroom. He pulled her down onto his bed, and she laid her head on his chest. "Close your eyes."

"I can't," she said.

"You can. You won't get to see your son in many places. You'll always see him in your dreams. Your dreams are gifts. You deserve to rest and spend time with your son in your dreams. Sleep, Lo."

"That's really nice to think of it like that," Lauren whispered.

She wrapped her arm around his torso, and he tightened his grip on her. "I don't have a church for the service. My own pastor turned me away today. Apparently, my public divorce is too scandalous for the Christians," she said. "What kind of mother can't find a place to hold her child's funeral?"

"I think I know a place," Nyair said. The kiss he planted on her forehead ironed out the wrinkles that had settled there over the past few days.

"I can't ask you to…"

"You didn't ask," he said, settling the matter. "And your pastor ain't shit."

"Thank you, Ny." Lauren's sigh of relief was reward enough for Nyair.

"Don't mention it," Nyair responded. "Now sleep."

And that she did.

CHAPTER 9

Charlie couldn't stop staring at the ultrasound picture. She was both excited and terrified, but above all, she was enraged. Or was she disappointed? She was so many things. Demi had hit her with a "something important came up." Something important? As if she was asking him to come by on a whim for casualties instead of on behalf of the child he had planted inside her. Charlie wished she could get high right now. A little weed and her guitar would take all her worries away.

By the time Demi called her back, the appointment was over. She hadn't answered, and he had been calling her since. Charlie didn't know what to say to him, so she opted to say nothing at all.

"Bird!"

His voice boomed through the house, and Charlie didn't flinch. She tried to remain calm, but she could feel every step he took in her direction. So much anxiety filled her that it felt like she might faint. Her stomach tightened as she willed herself not to give Demi her tears.

"Bird, baby..."

He stopped at the doorway to their bedroom, and she could see the apology all over him before he even spoke.

"Please don't say shit to me." Charlie was seething. She flicked the ultrasound across the room. "There's the fucking baby you begged me to have." So much malice boomed off the walls that Demi recoiled. He grabbed his chest like his heart was attacking itself, but it was the daggers shooting from her stare that was piercing him.

"I can explain," Demi started.

"Fuck you and your tired-ass explanation. I don't want to hear it. I waited for you for almost an hour. Had me looking like a fucking fool in that doctor's office! Like a stupid-ass girl carrying another dead-beat-ass nigga baby!"

Demi's brow lifted in astonishment. "Word?" The nerve of him to be offended. "You gone let me get a word in, or you got more insults to throw at a nigga?"

"Why even ask me to have this baby if you're going to start off like this?" Charlie asked. She was trying her hardest to let anger prevail, but her feelings were as soft as butter. She was hurt, and he could tell. She couldn't even pretend to be hard for long. Her eyes were welling with tears, and it gutted him to be the cause.

"I had to handle something with the funeral. It was an emergency. I was on my way to you when Lauren called," Demi said. She was shocked at his honesty, but she almost wished he had lied. Being put on the back burner for Lauren felt all too familiar. It felt intentional, like a carefully analyzed chess move that Lauren had waited to play. "I wouldn't have missed it if it wasn't important."

"*This* was important, Demi!" She shouted.

"What would you have me do? You knew this week would be hectic for me. I told you I'd need to be around for Lo."

"And just completely abandon your responsibility to me?" Charlie asked, scoffing. She was flabbergasted. "Just forget about me, right?" Charlie challenged.

"I ain't say all that, Bird," Demi sighed.

"And you couldn't call? You couldn't text back?" Charlie asked.

"I thought I'd be able to make it on time. By the time I got wrapped up with Lo and that crooked-ass church, I forgot to call. When I was done, I called you. I knew the appointment was over, so I came right here. I can't be in two places at once, Bird. Give me some grace here. This is the hardest week of my life, baby."

Charlie felt like she was going crazy. Was she wrong for expecting him to be present? Did DJ's death absolve Demi of accountability? Were her expectations unreasonable?

"Give you grace? How much grace, Demi? Let me know. You want to sleep at your ex-wife's house. You want to skip out on our baby's first appointment to be there for her. You want to parade around as her shoulder to lean on all week while I'm banned from even being around. I thought me not bitching about that was grace enough. How much more you fucking want from me? Cuz at this point, you her nigga again, and I'm playing side bitch—*again*! You have me in the same fucking position I started in! When am I going to be put first?"

"You hear yourself? You jealous of Lo's fucking position? You don't want her position, Bird! She's losing her mind! She lost a son!"

"Fuck Lauren and fuck your son!"

Charlie wanted to chase the words back as soon as she said them. They felt wrong. They were wrong. She felt like the bad guy as soon as her temper pushed the malice from her mouth. She saw the words land like a knockout blow. Demi staggered a bit in his stance, and his face went cold. He changed in an instant, going from loving and remorseful, to irate in the blink of an eye. She had gone too far, and she knew it. Charlie motioned toward him.

"Demi…I didn't mean…"

"Stay your ass over there, Bird." His warning was real. She knew it as flashes of the past ran through her mind. He had a mean streak, and she had felt his wrath once before. He had vowed to never handle her with less than love again, and he hadn't, but in the back of her mind, she always wondered if he would ever lose his temper again. Her words, so callously spoken. The disregard for his loss. She could see them spark a dynamite stick of aggression.

He backpedaled from the room and panic spread through her as she rushed after him. "Where are you going?" she asked.

He kept moving toward the door, and he didn't answer. His silence stirred a panic in her.

Charlie was desperate for a minute of his time, for his attention. His focus had been altered, and rightfully so, but she couldn't help but feel like he was leaving her behind.

"You just got here! You're not leaving me here by myself! This isn't what I signed up for!" Charlie yelled at his back, following him, pulling him in an attempt to stop him. It felt like she was losing him, and she loved this man. She loved every single inch of him, and he was forgetting that he loved her. He was forgetting their obsession with one another. His sadness was all he felt, and it was infecting her. Their love was rotting on the shelf he had placed it on in the back of his mind. She just wanted to be acknowledged. She just wanted to be a part of his healing process, but she was restricted from being a part of that portion of his life. He spun on her, turning back so suddenly that Charlie's instinct was to retreat. She backpedaled, and he backed her against the wall, trapping her there, his hands pressed into the wall beside her head.

"I'm out of my mind, Bird. Do you hear me? I haven't slept. Can't eat. Can't get my mind right. Can't do shit but think about how I failed my son. Stop pouring salt in the wound. Just stop," he whispered. There was anger and desperation in his tone. He pulled back and pointed a finger in her face. "And watch your mouth."

She had only seen Demi this angry one time before, and that time hadn't ended so well for her. She trembled, anticipating what he might do next, and he noticed her trepidation.

"You're scared of me?" he asked, frowning. He knew why she was. He had thought they had healed from that place. He wouldn't dare take her back there again but seeing her anticipate punishment from him broke his heart. He backed up, giving her room, and she could see the disappointment on his face. She opened her mouth to say no, but nothing came out but sobs. She was so emotional. Pregnant, hormonal, and overwhelmed. She felt so many things, and they were hard to describe. If he could just stay with her. If he could just sleep next to her tonight, maybe none of her insecurities would exist at all, but the more time he spent away from their home, the more she feared his potential to break her heart. She wanted to apologize for what she had said, but before she could, Demi retreated.

"This is bullshit. I could have stayed gone for this shit. Rushing back to you to argue. I need some air, man."

This time, she didn't follow. Demi snatched his keys off the countertop and walked out the door, taking her heart with him. He didn't even know he had it in his back pocket. He wasn't even aware that he needed to be careful because it was fragile. Charlie wasn't sure if she could dial back the damage she had just caused with her words. She had crossed a line by mentioning his son, and she wasn't sure if Demi would be able to forgive her. They had been through their fair share of ups and downs, but she wasn't sure if they could survive this life change. This funeral seemed to be tearing them apart, and Charlie wondered if her karma would force her to watch the man she loved return to the woman she had taken him from.

"Thanks for meeting me, Stass," Charlie said as she slid into the booth at their favorite brunch house.

"You look beautiful. You're legit glowing," Stassi complimented.

"I don't know how. I feel terrible," Charlie replied. She reached inside her handbag and pulled out the ultrasound. She placed it on the table. "It's a girl." Her monotone announcement made Stassi stare at her in concern.

"Damn, Charlie, you could give me some excitement or something. No gender reveal, no nothing, just slapping the news on a dirty table," Stassi teased. Stassi frowned and reached across the table for her sister's hand. "Are you okay?"

Charlie shook her head. "No, Stass. I don't think I am." The dismal tone of Charlie's voice told Stassi all she needed to know.

"What do you need from me?" Stassi asked, instantly jumping into 'fix it' mode.

"I wish it was that simple," Charlie replied. "It's Demi. It's like we're not even together. He's sleeping at Lo's. He never calls. He doesn't check in. We got into the worst argument yesterday and I haven't heard from him since."

"Charlie, the funeral's tomorrow. I can see how he's been distracted. It will get better after it's over," Stassi promised.

"Will it?" Charlie questioned. "Because I'm not so sure anymore. It's like DJ's death is bringing him and Lauren closer together and tearing me and him apart. I feel like I don't belong."

Stassi sighed, and she debated if she should tell Charlie her true thoughts. As sisters, they had found their flow. Sometimes, they came to one another to vent, and sometimes they came for guidance. When it was a vent session, you weren't looking for a response. You weren't looking for the devil's advocate. Sometimes a girl just needed validation without challenge because the situation a bitch was facing was difficult enough. But on the days when you were open to growth, you wanted your sister to hold a mirror up to your face to tell you when you were wrong. A man could tell you his side of things and accuse you of being unfair until he was blue in the face, but if your best homegirl didn't agree, he had no wins. Stassi stared at Charlie, searching her eyes for preference on this day. Did Charlie want reassurance, or did she want the real?

"Why are you looking crazy? Say something!" Charlie urged.

"I'm trying not to hear you, sis. I'm just listening and trying to support you. I know how sensitive you are."

"Sensitive? The motherfucka ain't been home, Stassi! I'm not being sensitive! I'm not being hormonal!" Charlie was so emotional that she was yelling. The other patrons eyed the pair curiously.

"Girl, keep your eyes on your own damn paper. Your answers ain't over here," Stassi hissed at the nosy Black girl at the next table. She focused back on Charlie. "I saw Demi."

The way Charlie's eyes lit up at just the mention of his name reminded Stassi of an addict.

"Saw him where? How is it that you've seen him more than I have in the past week?"

Stassi hesitated, and Charlie could sense the reluctance.

"You were with Day, and y'all pulled up or something? Where did you see him, Stassi?"

Stassi took a deep breath and spit it out. "At Lauren's."

Charlie's confusion couldn't be missed. "Why would you be at Lo's?"

"I'm making the arrangements for the funeral, Charlie," Stassi admitted.

Charlie scoffed in disbelief. "So, I'm the only one who isn't invited? Lauren allowed you to help, but won't even let me pay my respects?" Charlie's feelings were crushed.

"Charlie, you're measuring yourself against a lot, and it's not about that right now. You haven't seen Lauren. You don't know how bad it is. Even for Demi. I've seen them, up close, and right now, they're connected by something nobody would ever want to be connected by. Even they wish they didn't share it. But it's strong. It's kind of beautiful. It's against their will. It's unconditional. It's everything you expect to see from a man and his wife."

"She's not his wife," Charlie whispered, eyes drowning in melancholy.

"When you look at them, you can't tell. Not right now. For better or worse, 'til death do them part. Everybody just assumes that God was talking about the bride and groom, but I don't think anyone thought to ask whose death. This is the worst part. Just give him until after the funeral. I'm not a fan of Demi's. You know that. But if he doesn't see this through, I'm not sure if you'll love the version of him that comes back to you. They need each other for this."

Charlie was so bothered that her hands shook as she picked up her tea.

"I've never wanted anyone the way that I want him. I've never loved anyone like this. I don't want to love anyone like this. Just him. He's not optional. Whatever I'm a part of is a part of him because I can't see myself without him. He's compartmentalized me, Stassi. He's giving people the option to take him, but not me. I understand they are in pain. I even understand that she needs him, but he's my fiancé. He's supposed to be my future husband. She shouldn't even have the option to have him without me. I'm not even able to hold his hand while he says goodbye to his son. I'm not able to pay my respects or even tell her how sorry I am—because I am, Stass! I'm so sorry for what happened to DJ. I'm so sad about it! I'm heartbroken that my baby won't have her older brother here. I'm devastated that every time we get to celebrate our child, we will have to mourn another. I'm aching, and nobody cares!"

"No, Charlie, nobody cares about you right now," Stassi whispered harshly. "It's not about you! You *are* his future wife, and Demi is crazy about you. I kinda hate him, but I'll give him that. He loves you, but in Lauren's world, you're the mistress that dismantled her life and sent her son into depression."

"That's not fair…"

"It's not," Stassi agreed, yielding sympathetic eyes to Charlie. "But neither is burying a little boy. Nothing about that is fair, and if you make him choose, even if he chooses you, you'll lose. They both need this closure."

Charlie sighed. "I just wish I could turn back time. I would have tried harder to connect with DJ. I would have fixed things with Lo sooner. I would have tried so many things to make this feel like one family instead of whatever this is now. I really wish I could change this or even just hug Demi's son. Do you know I've never really felt like myself around him? I always tried so hard, and it just never felt natural. It never felt like he was home."

"If it felt that awkward to you, imagine what it must have been like for him. You're an adult. You chose the situation. He didn't have a choice," Stassi said.

Charlie shook her head, forlorn, unsettled, and distraught.

"I want you to focus on growing my niece," Stassi said, smiling and trying to thrust the conversation in a positive direction. "That's your only job right now. Don't worry about Demi. I got my eye on him. You just make sure you and baby girl are doing okay. You can't afford to stress over Demi or anybody else. You just focus on what you can control, and that's bringing a healthy baby and a little bit of joy back into all our lives."

CHAPTER 10

Stassi stood at the front of the church, rearranging the flowers so that they sat around the casket perfectly. Her heart was heavy. She hadn't even known DJ, and the day still hung over her head like storm clouds in a torrential sky. His casket was small and golden. Remnants of his favorite things lay inside. His favorite video game, a stuffed bear that had been his since the day he was born. His favorite pair of hole-filled Pokémon socks that his mother had tried to throw away a thousand times and the Rolex watch that Demi had gotten him for Christmas. Demi and his son had matching timepieces. DJ's had been inscribed, and links had been removed just to fit his tiny wrist. It had been a watch that his son would be able to grow into, expanding the band as he got older, only now he would never get to appreciate the value of the timeless piece. Demi had made it clear that his son was to be buried with it. The time had been set to 4:55 AM, the time DJ had been born.

"I'll wake up every day to spend a few minutes with my boy until I see him again," Demi had explained. Stassi had made sure it was on DJ's wrist. Last, but not least, was a handwritten letter from Lauren that Stassi hadn't read, but she had made sure it was in the breast pocket of his designer suit. So many tributes to this little boy. So many small details that felt minor to the world but were major to these grieving parents. Williams Funeral Home had done a beautiful job with DJ's preparations. He still looked like himself, and as she stood in front of the casket before the family arrived, she couldn't help but feel sadness. He was so young.

"The family is en route. They're five minutes out."

She turned to the voice that had come up behind her.

"You're the pastor that saved the day," she commented. "Thank you."

"Just call me Ny," he said, extending his hand. He was in full robe, and Stassi was stuck as she took in his presence.

"You're young," she commented, searching for something else to say because that wasn't what she meant to say at all. He was fresh and debonair, poised and relaxed all at the same time. He carried an aura about him that made her feel he was trustworthy instantly. She had expected some old man to deliver the eulogy. Nyair was the opposite of what she thought of when she thought of a preacher.

"Nah, you're just used to God's hitters being old," he said with a charming half-smile. His cheeks sunk into deep dimples, and Stassi smiled.

"Sounds about right," she said, a bit in awe by how attractive he was.

"Better get to it. The family will need a lot of support today," Ny said. "I've got the local fire department ready to escort the procession to the burial site. That way, it isn't interrupted, and everyone will arrive in time for us to get DJ blessed before the rain arrives. The burial team needs to get him in the ground before the storm rolls in. It's supposed to get bad out there. Freezing temps and rain don't mix well."

"Not at all. It was nice to meet you, Pastor Ny," Stassi said.

"Just Ny," he corrected. "And the pleasure was mine." He held out his hand, and she shook it but sucked in air as he held it with both hands and brought her knuckles to his lips. "God bless you. Stay strong today." He walked off, and she gawked in intrigue because damn it if her hand wasn't tingling. He was magnetic, and Stassi had to suck in a deep breath to shake off the butterflies she felt. Some men just had a presence like that.

Stassi beelined for the door so that she was visible when Demi and Lauren arrived. Minutes later, a string of Black SUVs pulled into the parking lot.

Stassi was in sync with the theme. Her off-white sweater dress and thigh-high, cream boots were covered by a nude-colored blazer. She was professional, patient, and polished, but most of all, she had been present for this family. The paparazzi were present, standing along the barriers that Stassi had set up to keep them out, using zoom lenses to narrow in on the processional.

Demi emerged from the back of the truck first, and Stassi could see the turmoil hanging on him. Demi was a powerful man. Everything about him said so, and he was appealing in a way that made women feel like he was out of their league. Rugged and mannishly attractive, it was apparent that he had earned his position in the field, fighting one battle after another, until he sat on the throne. He was kingly, and Stassi understood how Charlie had fallen for him. His posture was strong in his taupe-colored suit as he reached out his hand to help Lauren from the car. Lauren Sky was so beautiful that Stassi gasped. She looked like his rightful queen, and Stassi's stomach ached knowing that Charlie was trying to fill big shoes. Stassi couldn't imagine how left out her sister felt. The intimidation of coming after a woman like Lauren was real. Stassi felt it, and it wasn't even her situation. The family had shown up in style to say goodbye to their baby boy. Despite how well they had pulled themselves together, Stassi could see their burden. Day emerged from the back of the second SUV, and he was dapper as ever. His red eyes told her that a combination of weed smoke and tears had consumed the car ride. He pulled designer sunglasses over his eyes before approaching. Stassi wanted to wrap her arms around him, but this was a job for her, and she wanted to be professional. When Kiara Da'vi emerged from an SUV behind Day's, Stassi's stomach hollowed. She cut her eyes as she watched him turn to the songstress, greeting her. The kiss on her cheek could have been polite or intimate. She couldn't decipher the intent, but it put Stassi in her feelings. Feelings she would hide well because she was working. She acknowledged Demi and Lauren first.

"I've prepared everything for you. I want to escort you to the sanctuary. I've reserved a half hour for just you two with DJ. The doors will be locked, and the curtains pulled for privacy. After that, the rest of the close family can come for the remainder of the family hour before I open the doors for everyone to be seated as we start the service."

Demi nodded and Lauren lowered her eyes to the ground as Stassi motioned for them to ascend the steps. Day was next. He motioned for Kiara to walk ahead of him, and Stassi rolled her eyes as the singer bypassed her without even a hello. Day stopped briefly.

"Thank you for all this," he said. She didn't know what she wanted him to say, but she was bothered.

"Just doing my job," she replied shortly.

"Can I pull up on you after this?" he asked.

"Day, we better get inside!" Kiara called from the top of the steps.

The look of impatience Stassi gave the girl was deadly. "You better get in there," she said sarcastically without looking at Day.

"It's just business, Anastassia," Day reassured. "We're just standing behind Demi today, as a company, a united front."

Stassi nodded but refused to meet his stare as she smiled and greeted the people coming up the steps behind him.

"Sure," she said. She turned and walked away, heading inside, ignoring Kiara Da'vi as she passed her.

Stassi had never quite heard death until she entered the sanctuary and shared space with Lauren as she said goodbye to DJ. Pure agony emitted from the deepest tunnels of her throat. It could be heard all the way to the door. It was a distinctive cry, a desperation, a pleading for more time, and it was earth-shattering. It almost felt too intimate to witness. It was, in fact, because when Demi gripped the edge of DJ's casket and lowered his head, Stassi knew he was crying. It was a moment he couldn't stop. He had hidden his vulnerability well until now. He turned to Lauren and pulled her into his arms, or did she pull him into hers? Stassi couldn't tell. All she witnessed was beauty as Demi's tall, vast body shrank into the safety of Lauren's shoulder as they held onto each other for dear life.

My God, she thought dismally.

Stassi was so full of their woe that her vision blurred. Stassi, Day, and Nyair were the only witnesses to this farewell, and even that felt intrusive.

The way Lauren held onto that man. The words that they couldn't hear that were being whispered in his ear and the way he buried his shame in the shadows of her neck. This couple shared this child, and this child was made from love. This loss was being handled with love, and if Stassi didn't know their situation, she would swear she was witnessing a dutiful husband and his beautiful wife. She may even envy it if she didn't know any better.

Stassi heard the door to the sanctuary open, and when she turned to see Charlie, her stomach plummeted. Demi and Lauren were so engrossed they never heard the interruption. The sight of them so intricately engaged with one another froze Charlie. When Demi finally pulled away from Lauren, he cleared his face, swiping a large hand to erase the evidence of this breakdown.

Charlie stood like a deer in headlights until he finally looked her way. Stassi knew this was bad. She just didn't know how to stop it. Stun was written all over Demi's face when he realized Charlie was present.

"She needs to leave," Lauren said in a low, monotonous tone.

"Lo…" Demi protested.

"Lauren, please," Charlie said as she made her way halfway up the aisle. "I just want to pay my respects. I'm so sorry. Lauren, from the bottom of my heart, I am sorry."

"The woman who disrespected my marriage now wants to pay respect. You're respectable now? It took me to lose my son for you to show me some fucking respect?" If looks could kill, Charlie would be eulogized next. Lauren was so full of resentment, so maxed out on sorrow, that she couldn't receive anything from Charlie. She didn't want anything from Charlie. She would rather die than be the recipient of Charlie's condolences. "I won't ease your guilt for you. You want to be here? You were never supposed to be here! If you weren't here, my baby would still be here! And you march in here pregnant on the day I'm putting my son in a hole in the ground! You audacious, mindless, thoughtless, selfish, childish bitch!"

"Lauren!" Demi's voice boomed through the church, disrupting whatever peace they had come to terms with just moments ago. "That's enough, man," Demi stated as he hooked his finger around the tie that was choking him.

"It'll never be enough," Lauren sneered as she turned and made her way back to the front of the church.

Demi went to Charlie, who stood shell-shocked. She was covered in the filth that Lauren's words had left behind. They weren't untrue, and that's what had hurt her most.

"I'm sorry," she whispered to Demi, crying.

"It's okay," he said as he cradled her face in his large hands. He pressed his forehead to hers. The connection gave him a slight refill, like he was a dead car battery and she had given him a boost.

"Go home, Bird. You shouldn't have come," he whispered.

"Demi-"

He swiped away her tears with his thumb. She needed him. He knew it. She wanted to be here so badly, but he couldn't be her strength right now. Her presence made this loss more painful for Lauren, and he couldn't ignore or override that fact. He motioned for Stassi, and Stassi stepped up to intervene. "Charlie, you can't stay," Stassi whispered softly. "And he can't leave right now. This is the last time they get to see DJ. This isn't the time or place, Charlie. You can't be here for this part. Come on, sis. You have to go."

Demi loved this girl, but he couldn't access that chamber of his soul, not today. He could see the look in her eyes, and he was trying to muster up any other feeling than this despair he was feeling, but he couldn't. She was pleading with him, silently beseeching him with her eyes to save him, or at least to join her in Charliezonia, but Demi was too injured to take one step in her direction. She was falling down a rabbit hole of impossibility. She was worried about the wrong things, concerned about losing him, when in his mind, it would never happen. He was lost right now, but Charlie was like the North Star. He knew how to find his way back to her; he just needed to be able to carry her when he returned. Right now, he couldn't carry himself. The battle was lost against the emotions that came with telling DJ farewell. Stassi pulled Charlie toward the exit as Demi made his way back to Lauren's side. Stassi got Charlie all the way to the parking lot before Charlie broke down. She was hysterical, and Stassi couldn't say she blamed her. It was a fucked-up situation for everyone involved, where no right or wrong existed. Stassi felt guilty for being able to attend the funeral when Charlie was banned, but at the same time, she understood why she symbolized pain. It was unfair, but it was understandable. Human emotion couldn't be measured against morality at this moment. Not when the death of a child was concerned, and unfortunately, Charlie was an easy target to blame. She didn't belong here. She was an outsider, and Lauren had all the power.

The fact that Demi hadn't protected Charlie made Charlie feel worthless. They lived together. She had let him inside her heart, mind, and soul. He was growing in her body at this very moment. Charlie felt like she should be able to enter any room at his side, but he didn't even try to make room for her. Lauren's word was bond. She felt like trash, like he had used her up and set her out on the curb. Men had hurt her in the past, but never had it cut so deeply. This was an emotional lashing like no other. She admired Demi. She loved him. She would do anything for him. She *was* doing anything for him because having a baby was a gift he had begged her for. He couldn't even carve out a seat beside him for her. Charlie had never felt more alone. Even when they first met, and he was married, she hadn't felt this secluded. It was like he was hiding her to tap back into his life with Lauren. The ring on Charlie's finger didn't hold significance at all if it only held weight between the walls of their home. Charlie's world was shaken. Every decision Charlie had made since meeting him, she now questioned. She had given up her independence. She had cut Justin off, who had been a good friend at one time. She had distanced herself from her disapproving father. All because she was placing her chips on Demi. She was betting on love. This was a slap in the face, and Charlie wasn't sure how they could ever find their way back to a good place after this. It seemed that love no longer mattered.

Demi felt like the world was sitting on his shoulders as he walked back toward his son. He was worried about Charlie, but his capacity to do anything about it was limited. He walked to the casket, leaned down over his child, and kissed the top of his head.

"I'ma miss you, big dawg," he said. "Daddy loves you, man. Daddy loves you so much. I'm sorry for everything. I'm so sorry. It's me and you, forever, baby boy. These your eyes now, man. Everything I see, everything I do, is in honor of you. I wish you could be with me. Don't be mad at your old man, but I can't do this crowd. I can't share this pain with these people. I'ma come see you when they're all gone. Look over me, DJ. Watch over your mama, too."

Eyes flooded and burning, Demi couldn't take anymore. He couldn't sit and listen to the sermons; he couldn't bear to hear the sad songs. He couldn't greet the people who had come from near and far. He wanted no parts of any of it. None of it would make it better. It was all for show. He stood upright and walked out of the side door of the church. He was done.

"Yo, Demi!"

Day's voice followed him as he stepped out into the cold air.

Demi wished Day hadn't followed him. He just wanted the privacy to cry in peace for a little while. He hadn't been granted that since he found out about his son. He wiped both hands down his face and sniffed away his emotions before turning to face his friend.

"Don't leave her side, Day. Whatever she needs. I just can't be in there."

"I know you need to get to Charlie but leaving don't feel like the best idea. I don't know if anybody is worth missing this," Day said.

"I can't be there either," Demi admitted. "When you lose your kid, being here when they ain't just don't feel right. I don't know where I belong. I don't even know how I'm standing. My son is about to be put under the dirt. Do it even matter where I am after this? Who am I without that little boy, bruh?"

Day couldn't comfort Demi. God couldn't even do that. There were no reassurances to make because no matter how many people told him it would be okay, Demi knew it would not. He just wanted to go somewhere and fire up. To be alone with a blunt and his woes was his only option.

"A'ight, get up out of here. Clear your mind. Feel what you keep trying to stop yourself from feeling cuz I know you ain't gon' do it in there with all them eyes on you. But don't do nothing stupid, my nigga. I don't know what losing a kid feels like, but I imagine it make you feel like leaving this here shit behind. Lauren can't lose nobody else, and you're still responsible for another kid. One foot in front of the other."

Demi nodded but couldn't find words. He simply walked to one of the awaiting SUVs.

"Where to, Mr. Sky?"

"Anywhere but here," Demi said. "You mind if I light up?" he asked.

"Handle your business, sir," the driver said. Demi had been working with the car service for years with his company. He was grateful for the understanding. He found himself at the graveyard anyway, and he just stared at the hole in the ground where his son would rest. He trapped himself in that car, smoke filling the air, mind floating, heart sinking until he was numb. He was the first one there because everyone else was sitting through the pomp and circumstance of the funeral. He got good and high in the back of the SUV.

"I'm sorry for your loss, sir," the driver said.

"Appreciate it, potnah," Demi replied. "People think it helps. They say sorry, but it doesn't change a damn thing. It just reminds a nigga that he down bad."

"I've been there. I lost my son ten years ago. He was gunned down off Pierson Road. Hanging out in the streets and caught a stray bullet at the car wash right there off Clio Road. I still remember what it felt like when I got the call. It's a club that I wouldn't wish on no man, but when I see another brother join up, my condolences are from the heart, young buck. Sometimes you two seconds off checking out of here, and the random interruptions be the only thing to interrupt the insanity."

A renegade tear broke free, but Demi's thumb made magic of it, instantly causing it to disappear.

"Thanks, man."

They sat there in silence as Demi watched the gravediggers clear the plot in preparation for his son. Two hours passed before he saw the processional enter the grounds. He exited the truck and watched as the pallbearers, Day included, carried his son toward the hole in the ground. Demi tapped Lauren's cousin and took his place as he and Day led the way toward DJ's final resting place. The casket wasn't that heavy, but it felt like he was carrying an elephant. Every step felt like he was trudging through mud. It was the slowest, most torturous journey he had ever taken. It was below zero outside, but Demi couldn't feel the frigid temperature. He was already frozen before stepping out into the elements. They placed DJ on the platform that hovered above the grave and then stepped back so that Nyair could give the final eulogy and prayer.

"Why would you leave me to do that alone?" Lauren hissed as he took his place beside her. "You're never there when I need you. Where were you when he needed you? You take care of every other person around you. What happened to taking care of home? I'll never forget the way you moved on me, Demi. Leaving my baby here, in this hole, when he should be alive and well at home with us. I'll never forgive this."

"I'll never forgive myself, Lo. What else you got? What other fucked-up shit you need to get off your chest? Today of all days."

Lauren lowered her eyes, and when she looked back up at him, he saw her plight shining in her eyes like it was playing on a movie screen.

"We have to leave him, Demi," Lauren bawled. "This is why I didn't want to bury him because I knew I wouldn't be able to walk away." She wasn't the type of mom who spent a lot of time away from her child. She hadn't done the babysitting thing. She had never spent any real time apart from DJ. She was hands-on. From the day he had been born, he had become her little best friend. Where she went, he would follow, and when he wasn't in her eyesight, he was with his father. Driving away from this cemetery was going to feel like abandonment.

"I know," Demi answered. He took her hand in his and she cowered against him as they said their final goodbyes.

CHAPTER 11

Stassi stood off to the side. Somehow, seeing Demi holding Lauren's hand, doting over her so tenderly, made Stassi feel like she was complicit in a conspiracy against Charlie. She couldn't say that they were doing anything wrong. Their pain, this day, just felt like theirs. Like it was one they would mark on their calendars like a wedding anniversary—this death date was reserved for them. They presented like family, and she didn't blame them for that, but it was awkward. She was straddling a fence, and it didn't feel good. Her eyes landed on Day, and her stomach sank when she saw Kiara Da'vi discreetly wrap her pinky finger around his. He gave her a hug and then whispered something in her ear before the popular singer moved along. The body language was telling, and Stassi couldn't unsee it. *He's definitely fucking that bitch,* Stassi thought. This wasn't the time and place to address it. In fact, she wasn't sure she had any cause to address it. He wasn't her man, but Stassi made a mental note. Day was too famous and too used to his routine of rotating women. She didn't have time or the desire to play games. She could feel herself becoming disinterested, just off the assumption that he was involved elsewhere. The last thing she needed was to have her business blasted all over the blogs again. Kiara was a young artist. She lived for internet clout. Stassi preferred to keep her happenings private, especially anything concerning Day. He was too high profile, and too many women lusted after him. As soon as she posted any indication that he could possibly be on her roster, the hens would come pecking. There was nothing that could humble a bitch more than posting a nigga on social media. She had a feeling that if the world ever got wind of whatever it was they called themselves doing, that hoes would come out the woodwork to burst her bubble. For that reason alone, Stassi kept her distance. There were too many relevant faces at this funeral, and she was determined to retain a level of privacy.

When the service was over, Lauren approached. Stassi was taken completely by surprise when Lauren hugged her tightly.

"Thank you so much. I will never be able to repay you for the kindness you've shown me this week. You didn't owe me this. You did a beautiful job for my baby," Lauren said. She was still so emotional that her nose ran. Lauren sniffed and dabbed at her eyes with a handkerchief.

"You don't need to thank me. I'm glad it met your expectations," Stassi replied.

"You're welcome to come back to the house for the repass. The least I can do is feed you," Lauren offered.

"I'm sorry, I really do have somewhere I need to be, but I've made sure everything at your house is prepared. The caterer, the housekeeper…all that. You and your family won't have to worry about anything for a few days."

"We should get back," Demi said.

Stassi's eyes searched the crowd for Day only to find him climbing into the back of an SUV behind Kiara.

She scoffed. One minute, he was begging on stage for her time, the next, he was entertaining someone else. One thing was for certain, she wasn't chasing him, and she wasn't going to compete for his time. She believed in letting a nigga choose. She would react accordingly.

She sighed and made her way back to her car. Demi and Lauren were so well respected that there were over a thousand people in attendance. The number of cars coming in and out of the church was ridiculous, and the one-road cemetery was even worse. She climbed into her car and dialed Charlie's number. The phone rang through her blue tooth as she pulled into the line of traffic. She saw the fire truck and one police car ahead. "Thank God Nyair pulled some strings to help with this traffic."

When she saw him, their eyes connected instantly, and she hit her brakes abruptly. She wasn't quite sure why or how the smile formed on her face, but the one he returned made her giddy. He walked over to the car, and she rolled down her window.

"Grayson, right?"

"She remembers," he said as he motioned for the cars behind her to go around.

"What are you doing here?" she asked.

"The stations work in the community with the local churches when high-profile funerals take place. Police presence, first responders. It's a lot of people out here. Traffic and roads are bad. Plus, I guess this group is known for a level of violence. Rappers or something, so having a presence stops one funeral from turning into two," Grayson explained.

"They aren't violent. Just Black men making money," she said.

"Were you close to the little boy they buried today?" he asked. "My condolences on your loss."

She shook her head. "I wasn't. I used to work for his mom. Just felt appropriate to pay my respects. It hits differently when it's a kid, you know?"

"I'm very fortunate to not know what that feels like," he answered grimly.

"You don't have kids?" she asked.

"I do. Proud dad to a 16-year-old son," Grayson said.

"Oh!" Stassi said in surprise. He looked damn good. She hadn't expected him to have a full-blown teenager.

"I was a high school senior. Slipped up. Became a dad early. He's the best thing that could have happened to me, though," Grayson replied. His pride shone brightly as he spoke about his child.

The driver behind Stassi blew his horn, leaning on it impatiently.

"Okay, damn!" Stassi shouted as she peeked in her rearview mirror.

"Aye, my man, relax on the horn. Go around!" Grayson shouted sternly. "I guess this isn't the time or place for life stories." He chuckled, and Stassi smiled.

"I'm sorry. I'm distracting you. I'll let you get back to it," she said.

He leaned down into her window so that they were eye to eye. "Can I take you out, Stassi?"

It was so random and sporadic that Stassi's mouth fell open and nothing came out.

She had just accepted a car from Day. She knew it didn't mean they were together. Clearly, they weren't. He had left the funeral with someone else, but she didn't want to be messy. She needed a little clarity from Day before she answered this question.

The next car honked at her.

"Okay, okay," she said. She pulled out her phone and handed it to him. "Put your number in."

"Is that a yes?" Grayson asked.

"It's an 'I'ma let the fine firefighter call me so I can get to know him.'"

He entered his phone number and pressed send so that he had hers as well. He tapped the side of her car and she put it in drive.

"Don't wait too long to call. Girls hate waiting to see if a man is really interested."

She pulled away, and within seconds, her phone rang.

She answered with a smile. "Can't call too soon either, sir. You don't want to look thirsty."

"I'm a grown-ass man. When a woman crosses my mind, I

call. Actually, I prefer to pull up, but I ain't been invited yet. I ain't worried about looking thirsty. I am very interested, though, Stassi."

"Never knew I was so captivating," she joked.

"Somehow, I think you know better," he replied with a laugh. "I got to get back to work, but I'ma hit you up later."

"Enjoy your day, Grayson."

"Today was the hardest day of my life," Lauren said as she sat across from Demi at the dining room table. Everyone was gone. Just like every other funeral, after the official burial, the others went back to their lives. Their regularly scheduled programs continued while the people closest to the deceased were left to endure.

"I'm just glad it's over," Demi stated. "All those fucking people. My skin is crawling." Demi had shaken so many hands and received so many hugs that he felt like he was infected. His OCD was working in overdrive, and his mind was exhausted. "Feels like I been running uphill all week. A nigga can't even catch his breath. I'm mentally exhausted."

"I know," Lauren whispered.

"What happens now, Lo?" Demi asked.

He sat tilted back in the chair; legs open wide, handsome, and solemn as folded hands rested on his abdomen. Stress was his most consistent accessory these days.

"You're looking to me for answers?" she scoffed. "I don't

know, Demi. How am I supposed to know what comes next? So much of my identity was tied to being a wife and mom, then, out of nowhere, I am neither of those things anymore. What am I going to do?"

"You're going to live, Lo. We're going to live. I don't know how, but we have to."

"That's easy for you to say, Demi. You have something to live for. You have a life and a home, and you have a child. I have nothing."

"You've got me," Demi answered swiftly.

"Oh, Demi," she whispered in exasperation. She shook her head, eyes watering. "You're so dependable. You're so present. So accommodating. You've wiped my tears this past week. You've held me. You've wiped the snot from my nose. You've ignored every single instinct that makes you want to disconnect. You were warm with me. You coddled me. If you could have been that way when we were married, we would still be married."

"I thought I was a good husband, Lo. I gave what I thought you needed."

"You provided and protected, but you didn't let me in, Demi. You were hard with the world, and then you came home and remained hard with me. You weren't a bad husband. I would be lying if I said that. You were great in so many ways. You just never softened. You weren't intimate with me. And at first, I thought it was because you just couldn't be that way. You and your OCD and your issues, I just thought you weren't capable of intimacy, but now you're intimate with someone else. Now you're having a baby with another woman, and our baby is gone. Do you know how resentful that makes me?"

"It's the same resentment that put the blade in DJ's hand," Demi huffed. It took everything in him to admit that. "And because of that, I'll never forgive myself. I know I can't make it right, but what can I do? What do you need me to do?"

"I don't know!" she feigned. "Don't you think if I knew, I would tell you? A part of me wants my lick back. A part of me wants to tell you to come home because I can't let my old life go completely. I can't be alone in this pain. I'm terrified for this to close the chapter on us. We have no connection, no reason to continue to be in one another's lives. And I really want Charlie to feel what it's like to have another woman take what you think is yours. But the other part of me knows that we have to let go. The familiarity is a crutch. It's a fake comfort, and eventually, the resentment I have towards you will destroy us anyway. Would you leave her if I asked you to?"

Demi sighed.

"I will stay here if you need me to stay, Lo. I'll protect you. I'll take care of you. You ain't got to lift a finger, but I can't ever leave her. I know she triggers something in you, and I understand why you couldn't have her at the funeral, but Charlie is important to me, Lo. And I'm not saying this to hurt you. I don't want to cause no more hurt. I've done enough. I'm indebted to you, and I'll give you everything I got, but I need you to be tolerant of her. I won't flaunt her. I won't rub her in your face. I want to be here. You're my family. I don't want us to end with our son in the ground…"

"It sounds like you're asking me to let you have your side chick in peace," Lauren said in disbelief.

"Don't call her that, man," Demi replied. It felt like such a reduction of Charlie's value for her to even be thought of as a side anything. Even when it was true, she had been so much more to him. He didn't know what the fuck he was asking. He was grasping at straws, trying to be everything for everybody. He was responsible for Lauren, and he had a fiancé at home. He didn't want to lose either. He had taken Lauren for granted even after their divorce. He hadn't known how much he cared for her until they lost their son. They had too many years in each other's lives to not know each other for the rest. He felt it in his bones that he didn't want that. He didn't want DJ's mother erased altogether.

"That's what she is. You can put a ring on her finger. You can put a baby in her stomach, and she'll still be the woman who slept with my husband. I'll still blame her."

"Blame me," Demi countered. "I'm to blame, but now she's here, and she's pregnant, Lo."

"You should leave, Demi," Lauren interrupted. It was hard for her to hear him profess such devotion to a woman he hadn't even made vows to. Where was this devotion with her?

"Lau-"

"Demi, get out of my house!" Lauren shouted.

Demi didn't move. He couldn't move. He wanted to commit her face to memory, just in case Lauren walked out of his life for good. The fact that he wasn't motivated to leave infuriated Lauren.

"There is no being family with me and keeping your life intact with her. You can't be that self-centered!" She exclaimed. "Life doesn't work that way, Demi! You don't get to be in two places at once. There is nothing here with me at all if she's a factor. I loved you, and I would be lying if I said this past week didn't make me miss what we had. I was loyal to you. I did everything for you for fifteen years, and you betrayed me. You gave the best of you to that girl, and my son felt that shit. He felt it every time he walked into your office, and it was empty. He felt it every time he called, and you didn't answer. He felt it every time he had to pack his shit up and go to a weird house with your weird-ass bitch. You're the reason he's gone, and now you're still asking me to make room for her? Fuck her! Fuck you," she cried, shaking her head. "We are done. We are dead. This entire family is destroyed because of you."

Her words were bullets because he owned what she was accusing him of. He had spent plenty of nights feeling the burden of the home he had broken. He had wanted full custody and had even gone as far as to file for it, but he eventually withdrew because he couldn't see himself taking DJ from Lo. She was too good of a mother. They just hadn't been able to see eye to eye over the little things. Visitation and scheduling were a nightmare because DJ never wanted to visit. He wanted Demi to come home. His son hadn't taken the divorce well at all. All he knew was a world where his parents lived under one roof. The separate homes had taken their toll, and Demi had noticed. He had tried to overcompensate with things, with money, but it never made up for his presence, and in the end, it had cost him greatly. He stood and squeezed the bridge of his nose as he stared silently at Lauren. He nodded as he convinced himself to take steps toward the door. It took everything in him to walk out. He felt his disconnection from Lauren as soon as she slammed the door. There would be no more grieving together, no more leaning on one another for support. He had to process this alone, and for the first time in his adult life, he was terrified.

The smoky club was filled. It didn't surprise her. As she squeezed her body through the standing-room-only juke joint, she felt an immediate healing. She hadn't attended in a while, and it was still the same. That was the beauty of low-key spots like this one. The audience changed nightly, but everything else seemed to be frozen in time, recreating a vibe of 90s R&B that just made you feel good inside. It was the nostalgia of the music that lit a small fire in her broken heart. She appreciated it as soon as the notes from the piano keys hit her. The live band was legendary around town. They had been packing out this very spot for years, and Charlie had been lucky to fill in for the backup singers on more than one occasion. She wasn't even sure how she ended up back here. She had gone home after the funeral, hoping that Demi would come immediately afterward, but he hadn't. She sat in that empty house, crying all day, until the walls started to feel like they were closing in. She didn't even know what made her come here, but she was glad she had. Music brought her peace, and in the middle of this storm, she needed a little sunlight.

She found a random seat near the corner of the stage, and she sat.

Her heart seized when she recognized Justin on the stage, playing with the band. She didn't even need to see him. She'd recognize his playing anywhere. He was a musician through and through. He could play the drums, piano, and guitar. Tonight, his fingers strummed the bass guitar with expertise, and it may as well have been calling her name through the strings. A slight panic pulsed through her body because she knew Demi would have a fit if he saw Justin even staring her way. They hadn't seen one another since the fated night when Demi and Justin had fought. She was almost sure Justin hated her after that, but the smile he gave her when he saw her face told her there were no hard feelings. After what he had endured because of her, she had expected him to harbor a grudge. Still, she felt like she was betraying Demi just by being in Justin's space. It was a slippery slope that Charlie would rather not be caught on. They had indeed slept together while she and Demi were together, and Demi had every right to dislike that man. She felt conflicted being in his presence while Demi was off burying his son. It felt like the makings of bad decisions to come.

The cover of Anita Baker was played so expertly that Charlie felt her soul stir. Her eyes watered, and Charlie took a napkin, dabbing the emotion away. Her hormones were all over the place. Up was down and left was right. She was so overwhelmed that she almost couldn't process who was right and who was wrong. The sensitivity of death clouded her judgment, and everyone in the world seemed to be against her. This singer, crooning about apologies, felt appropriate. The band went into a medley of 90's R&B, and Charlie's head fell into an effortless nod. Justin walked off the stage while playing his solo, and the women in the crowd stood out of their seats. It truly was an erotic scene to witness. His Kravitz-esque essence was real. Leather jacket and designer jeans were balanced out with Timberland boots. His talent couldn't be denied. His fingers on those strings were legendary. She hoped he wouldn't come to her. He could go to anyone but her, but sure enough, he brought his solo over to her obscure table. All eyes were on her as he played in front of her, showing out in a way that only a virtuoso could pull off. Waterfalls by TLC. She recognized it instantly.

"Oh, what a treat!" the lead singer called out in shock. "We have Charlie Woods in the building, ladies and gentlemen." The announcement put her on blast. "Somebody give my girl a mic."

She shook her head to decline but gave a gracious smile as the crowd clapped.

"Okay, let's see if we can give her something she can't say no to," the lead singer said as she cued the band to play something else. "Justin, play us something."

The lead singer and the backup vocals crooned. "Myyyy lovveee, do you… ever… dreammm of."

By the time they sang through the first verse, a microphone was in Charlie's hand, and a spotlight was on her. She smiled as she joined in softly.

"My loveee, do you…ever…dreammm of, candy-coatedddd rainnnnndrops."

"Good girl," Justin whispered in her ear as she rolled her eyes and blushed, then joined the band on stage. Charlie's range was ridiculous. She flipped the entire scale of the classic. If she didn't know how to do anything else, Charlie could find a note and pick it out of thin air. Her musical inclination was top tier. For the first time in a week, she felt free of worry, free of angst and sadness. On this tiny stage, she released it all, and she was having fun. The lead singer beckoned her.

"Alright now, Ms. Charlie, let's see if you remember this one," she said. The band transitioned effortlessly into another hit.

"Don't walk awayyyy boy..." Charlie sang.

"I'm not gon' hurtttt you," the woman sang back.

Charlie laughed and then went into the first verse. This was a test of her musical history. They were cutting to songs Charlie had heard playing in her mom's house back in the day.

"Tell me if you want me to, give you all my time. I wanna make it good for youuuu."

The crowd cheered as the band played *Groove Theory*. *Groove Theory* transformed to Brandy, and Charlie was singing about being down. There wasn't a song they could play that Charlie wouldn't make her own. Her skill was honed, and it was obvious. The crowd was singing right along with Charlie, hyping her up so loudly, standing out of their seats, snapping their fingers, catching their groove. Charlie laughed, as she handed the microphone back so the band could get back to their set. She had caused enough distraction. She remembered the days when no one knew her name. Now, she was a recognizable artist. She would never claim to be famous, but people thought of her talent when they saw her, and she had to admit that it was Demi who had made sure of that. He had changed her life from the very first hello.

"Give my girl a hand, ladies and gentlemen," the singer said. Charlie lit up as the crowded club showed her love.

She sat through the rest of the show, thoroughly enjoying her time. It was truly what she needed. She had been worried all week about the negative emotions pulsing through her body. Nothing had felt good. She hadn't held down a bite to eat since DJ's death, and all she did was worry. She had cried her days away and let anxiety keep her up at night. She couldn't help but wonder what this energy was doing to her baby. No amount of sage or meditating could clear what was haunting her. Nothing could impact a woman like a man who was supposed to be her man switching his energy. She and Demi had a flow. Their cadence was passionate and steady. He had been a consistent source of stability for her soul, and suddenly, things were different. Things were unstable, which made her mentally break down. She was overthinking everything, and it was debilitating.

It made her feel like she couldn't breathe. Her every function had become dependent on Demi, and Charlie felt lost without him, like her days held no purpose. She knew now that there was a such thing as being too in love. She had been through hell in her lifetime, but no fire had ever felt like this. This waiting. This sitting on a nigga's back burner was torture because she had no idea when he would be back. His actions were threatening to burn their house down, but Charlie was the only one in it. He was under another woman's roof, caring for her and providing for her needs, while Charlie was suffering.

Just thinking about it ruined her mood. She sat and enjoyed Justin's entire set, and once it was over, he came to her table.

"It's been a long time," Justin said. They hadn't seen one another in years.

"I'm really sorry about what happened," she replied.

"You sorry for another person's actions?" he asked. "You weren't responsible for that. You still with him?"

Charlie stared down at her hands and the huge diamond ring she was wearing. His eyes followed.

"You're too good for him, Charles," Justin said, shaking his head. The old nickname made her cringe. It felt inappropriate.

"Don't do that," Charlie replied softly. "You don't know him."

"You right," Justin admitted. "Once upon a time, I thought I knew you, though, and the girl I knew would never be possessed by anyone. I guess I was wrong."

Charlie shook her head because she knew he held some reasonable resentments toward Demi. "He doesn't possess me. You make it seem like I'm trapped. I want him. I know he flew off the handle with you. That's not who he is with me."

"Then explain why I see fear in you. I've known you for a while, Charles. That fear wasn't there before," Justin said.

"The only thing I fear is losing that man. You don't see me being afraid because I'm with him. I'm terrified to be without him. I'm pregnant, and I'm terrified to do this alone. That's what you see," Charlie defended.

"Look, what you got going on ain't my business. You ain't got to explain shit to me. I just hope you're okay. You were my friend, and I overstepped back then. It didn't take an asswhooping to regret the way I pushed up on you. I lost a good friend over a mistake, and I apologize to you," Justin said. "I knew you weren't into me like that, and I still went for it. I don't care for your dude, but I respect you. I just hope you're happy."

Charlie hadn't known how much she needed to hear this or how much she missed Justin until this moment.

"I really appreciate that, Justin. And I'm so sorry you were hurt over me."

"Don't even mention it again," Justin said. "The past is the past. Come here."

Justin had no idea how much she needed the hug he offered. She fell into his arms, and before she knew it, she was crying. Forgiveness and human compassion were missing in her life. She had been denied that lately, and she was thirsty for it. Justin was forgiving what the average person could not, and she respected him for that. Charlie wasn't perfect. She had made many mistakes in her life. She had moved poorly with Demi at the beginning of their relationship, and because of that, she had become the source of Lauren's pain. She didn't want to be. She hated that Lauren looked at her with contempt. She had tried to seek atonement. She wanted to be Lauren's ally, not her enemy. Charlie was a young woman who didn't know love from a lot of people, and if she was truly honest with herself, she would admit that she admired Lauren. She was everything Charlie wished she could be. Successful, independent, driven, focused, and incredibly smart, but most of all, she was a natural nurturer. She could tell that Lauren provided love and a foundation for the people she was responsible for. She saw that in DJ, and she saw it in Demi. To this day, even after conflict and divorce, Demi held great pride in Lauren loving him once. Charlie didn't want to be enemies with Lauren. She wanted to be family. She wanted to be a part of a situation so healthy that maybe one day they could even consider themselves friends. That's what co-parents should be, but with the death of DJ, she had been shut out of that equation forever, and it bothered her. Lauren was a huge part of Demi's world. To be shut off from that made Charlie feel like she didn't truly know Demi. He was being put in a position where he could only share himself in seclusion, but the world didn't work that way. She wanted all of him, and that included accepting a past that involved an ex-wife and a child. Why couldn't Lauren just forgive her? Lauren had forgiven Demi, but Charlie was still being crucified. It didn't seem fair, but life was life. It wasn't always easy.

"Don't cry," Justin soothed, rubbing her back. Charlie held onto her friend for dear life, and it felt so safe to be covered, even momentarily. When she opened her eyes, her entire body turned to stone.

She pushed away from Justin as her gaze landed on Demi. She could see the flames emanating from his body and almost read the look of devastation on his face as he witnessed this intimate moment. She had never seen this look of disappointment in Demi before. It was like someone had deflated him and enraged him all at the same time. The weight of his current predicament stuck to him. Physically, she could see the toll DJ's death had taken on him. She could see him assigning meaning to her being in Justin's arms. He was misunderstanding, and she knew it.

"Demi," she whispered. Justin turned and tensed at the sight of Demi. "Ayo, get security in here. Escort that nigga out the building."

At first, Demi's gaze had only been trained on Charlie. When Justin spoke, Demi lost his cool.

"My nigga, what?" He was crossing the room, and Charlie felt like she was stuck on a railroad track as a train was barreling in her direction.

Charlie met him halfway, placing a hand to Demi's chest. "Demi, stop. Baby, it's not what you think. It's not what it looks like," she pleaded.

Demi couldn't even hear her. He saw her mouth moving. He felt her hands, but he was zoned out. He put his hands under her underarms and picked her up, moving her aside like he was rearranging a piece of furniture that was in his way.

"Demi, no!" she shouted as she pulled on his shirt, trying to stop a second altercation between the two. Justin didn't move. He stood there cockily as security intervened.

"Don't get mad because she keeps coming back. Check your bitch! That pussy fire, though, my nigga. I understand!"

"Wait, what?" Charlie shouted as Justin switched up, distorting the truth and turning into someone she didn't recognize before her very eyes. "Justin!"

Justin chuckled from behind the protection of the club's bouncers.

Demi scoffed and bit on his bottom lip like he was out for blood. He nodded his head. "You got it. Remember where you at, though. There's a whole city outside these walls, and I'm heavy out here. Remember that."

"She keeps coming to me! I ain't your issue!" Justin shouted. "Get that nigga up out of here."

"Baby, let's just go, please," Charlie begged. "Demi, please, before they call the police."

Demi nodded and snatched away from her before storming out the club. He pushed the door open so violently that it dented when it hit the brick wall outside.

Charlie chased after him. She hadn't expected for him to check her locations and find her. She hadn't even expected him to think to come home. On the one night when she had found a piece of solace, he had popped up, and it was a disaster.

"Demi!"

He turned around abruptly and faced her. He was so angry that he looked ten feet tall as he hovered over her.

"You fucking that nigga?" he asked. "After all this time, this nigga still in the picture?"

"No! Demi, no!" she cried.

"I'm out here putting dirt over my son, and you sneaking off to clubs with your side nigga?" Demi accused.

Charlie could see him building a case against her in his head. He could be crazy that way. He turned molehills into mountains when he had time to overthink. His eyes were clouding, and her heart was breaking because she knew this assumption was tearing his heart in half.

"Demi, please," she pleaded. "I haven't seen you. I don't want to fight!"

"Nah, you just want to be hugged up with niggas and give my pussy away, then cry when you get caught," he accused. "I will kill that nigga!" he barked. He put his hands on both sides of her face, and she held onto his hands as she cried. He squeezed her face slightly, and grit his teeth as he showed restraint, pulling her forehead to his. It wasn't until then that she smelled the cognac on his breath. He was drunk, and this was bad. It was really bad. "With my bare fucking hands!" The scary part was, she knew he would. She knew he was probably making plans for Justin right now that were deadly. He released her and stormed to his car.

"Demi!"

"Stay the fuck away from me, Bird!" he warned.

And she did. She planted her feet right in the middle of the parking lot as red and blue lights pulled onto the scene. She was certain that Justin had called the cops. He knew better than to walk out of that building because Demi had already planned to catch him outside. The officers didn't even ask questions. They got out of their vehicle, guns drawn.

"Sir, close the door and put your hands above your head!"

"Wait! He didn't do anything! Officers! Please, just let me explain!" Charlie asked as she rushed over to the scene.

The officer who wasn't trained on Demi brought his aim to Charlie, and she froze, raising her hands.

"This is a misunderstanding! He hasn't done anything!" Charlie just wanted to get to him. She was panicking. For a week, all she had wanted to do was see him, to touch him, to hug him. She just wanted to breathe a little bit of Demi's air, to spend a little of the nigga's time. Finally, he was within reach, and he was about to be carted off to jail.

"Bird, go home!" Demi barked. It was the way he said it that broke her heart. She would be walking away from this night, while he would not have the choice. They both knew it. "My man, she's pregnant. Put your fucking gun down!" Demi's temper was barely controllable as the officer forced his hands behind his back and cuffed him.

"No, you don't have to put those on him! He didn't do anything!" Charlie cried, nose running from the freezing cold.

Justin waltzed out into the night, and the look of satisfaction on his face infuriated Charlie.

"Justin, please! This is too far!"

"Thanks, officers. We hate to call you out in this weather, but we want everybody to make it home safe. You know it's been a few shootings in the area. We just want tonight to end with everybody alive," Justin said. "I'm pretty sure he's armed."

Demi scoffed as the officer began to pat him down. Sure enough, they pulled a 9mm Ruger off his waistline.

"It's registered. Paperwork is in the dash, and I got a

license to carry," Demi said sternly as he stared Justin down. Demi was always strapped, but he was no dummy; it was registered. "Pussy," he said with a deadly smirk. "I'ma see you, my nigga. Don't even worry about it. These cuffs gon' come off, then what you gon' do?"

"Demi, stop!" Charlie pleaded. She knew he was in another zone. Not even the cops could filter the threats coming out of Demi's mouth, and she knew more than anyone that he meant every word.

"We're going to take you down to the station while we figure all this out," the officer informed. "You might want to listen to your wife and stop talking before you get yourself in more trouble."

Demi's sneer was locked on Justin as Charlie broke past the second officer.

"Officer, please. He lost his son a week ago. The funeral was today. Please, just let me take him home."

"If all of that is true, ma'am, then he'll be fine. We're taking him downtown. You can follow us if you'd like," the cop responded. Even in handcuffs, Demi wasn't easily rattled. He stood, head up, biting the inside of his jaw in irritation while thoughts of murder filled his mind.

"Go home, Bird. Just wait for me there," Demi instructed.

She nodded, stomach in knots and heart racing as she watched them put him in the back of a squad car and carry him off into the night.

The look of vindication wearing Justin infuriated her.

"When he gets out and I can't stop him from coming to see you, remember you could have stopped it," Charlie warned.

"Making him think this is something it's not is lame as fuck."

Charlie never saw the slap coming. Justin hit her so hard that her lip split and the impact sent her to the ground. To add insult to energy, he hawked up as much bile he could muster and spit on her before stepping over her like trash and leaving her in stun. Charlie was shaking as she crawled to her feet. Her blood stained the snow, and her legs trembled as she rushed to her car.

When she pulled down her visor, she saw the damage. His ring had cut her nose, and her lip was bleeding from the inside.

"Bitch-ass nigga," she shouted angrily. She had never pegged Justin as the type to hit women. His aggression had blindsided her. She didn't know how she even made it home, but as soon as she walked through the door, she peeled herself out of her clothes and hopped in the shower. The moment his spit touched her, she was taken back in time to all the abuse she had endured at the hands of men. She felt low and dirty as she let the water run so hot it turned her skin red. By the time she felt clean, the water ran cold. Charlie stood in the mirror, wrapped in nothing but a housecoat, and she didn't recognize herself. Her scars would heal. The swelling would go away, but this past week had created emotional wounds that she didn't know how to heal.

She reached for her phone. Demi hadn't called. She wondered if she should dress and go get him, but he had given her clear instructions. She was home. He had said to wait. So, she did. It was all she had been doing for days, and she wondered if she was waiting for nothing.

CHAPTER 12

"Yo, I don't really appreciate the strong arm," Day said as he followed Kiara Da'vi inside her home studio. "Today of all days."

"I know it's bad timing, Day, but it can't wait," Kiara said. "My album comes out in a week. You haven't even listened to it all the way through."

"The team says it's strong. Just cuz my eyes ain't on you, don't mean my eyes ain't on you," Day responded. "I'ma always keep tabs on my money."

"Well, the plan was to give me leverage," Kiara combatted. "People don't really care about good music these days. They want to support the girl that's wearing the most exclusive shit, the girl that's with the flyest nigga, and who's on the scene. That was your plan. We popped out at a few little events, and I got some traction, but then you just stopped calling altogether. I see you all in the blogs with this new bitch, then she showing up at my shows bossing me around. Meanwhile, you sending me a company car. What was that? A consolation prize? Like, what's really good with you?"

He had known it had been a mistake to gift her one of the Hondas. She had been trying to force her way into his space. She would do whatever was needed to gain clout, and it was starting to annoy him.

"Look, man, I know the album's coming. I ain't go ghost on you, my fucking nephew died," he stated harshly. The distaste building in his mouth was strong. She was worried about something trivial on a day when he could care less. "I sent you the car because you earned it. The pre-orders went crazy. Consider it a gift from the company."

"So, not from you?" Kiara asked, frowning.

"What you want from me, man? I'm not your nigga, Da'vi. You gave up a little pussy, I spent a little paper on you and let you get some shine. You not my girl. That was never going to be a permanent situation for you. This whole conversation taking up too much time," Day stated. He was so nonchalant. His heart was in the gutter. The funeral had taken its toll on him, and he didn't have the energy to cater to someone else's emotions. He knew Kiara Da'vi wanted to remain attached to him. It was the company's PR who came up with the idea to bring her out on his arm, boss her up, ice her out, and step out onto the scene together. Any woman he had ever been linked to, caught the public's eye, and Kiara Da'vi was no different. Day had influence, so whoever he chose automatically became relevant. Kiara was one of the 'it' girls by proxy. All it took was for them to be photographed courtside at a Piston's game, and social media ate her up. The culture was predictable that way. If he wanted to make a woman famous, he knew how, and he had done that for Kiara because it was in his best interest. Now, she had a few million followers, several brand deals, influencer friends, and an album that he had produced on the way. He was into her for a little while, but the conversation was too shallow to keep his attention long. She didn't make him work for it, and Day was a man who enjoyed a chase. He had grown bored fast. He wished he had never indulged at all because she was clingy, and demanding, territorial women had never tickled his fancy. He had gotten rid of women before her for less. He had invested a lot of money into her album, however, so he knew he couldn't just write her off like all the rest. He also felt a bit of allegiance to her on behalf of her brother.

"I want you to let me do that thing you like," she said seductively.

Day sighed and winced as he scratched his temple. See? Shallow shit. "I ain't really in the mood. You know? Funeral and all." It was like her emotional intelligence was non-existent, and he was more annoyed than anything.

He went into his inner jacket pocket and pulled out a pre-roll. He had been grounded all day. He needed to get high so he could float away from the bullshit; all of it— dead kids, grieving potnahs, and women who chased him for clout. The only bright spot of his whole day had been the 30 seconds he had spent in the shadow of Stassi's Prada perfume. The scent still lingered in his nostrils.

He took his time blazing up and inhaled deeply before blowing out a cloud of smoke. He deadpanned on her. "Why you fuck with me, Da'vi?" he asked.

She let off a nervous giggle. "Because you're that nigga, Day. The fake humility is cute, though, but be for real. You're the boss."

"What makes me that nigga? Cuz I know plenty niggas with paper out here. Plenty guns. Plenty cars…"

She sucked her teeth. "That's not why I like you," she said.

"So, if I ain't have none of that?"

"I don't know, Day. It's just something about you." She was reaching, and he was letting her because the shit was comical. He wished it got deeper than this, but in his experience, it never did. The standards of women were so easily met these days. It took no effort to get them into his bed. The threshold was non-existent, and while Day appreciated an easy win, he respected a hard-fought one more. Still, business was business, and the six figures he had put into studio time and brand-building with Da'vi had to bounce back.

A few public appearances can't hurt, he thought. *I still got a job to do.*

"PR got the press run already lined up. They lined up a performance at the Hip Hop Awards in LA, and the company is hosting a brunch the day after. We'll put you on the stage, something dope and intimate. Let you do your thing while everyone is locked in. Like an unplugged vibe. Put Charlie around you, have her open with an a cappella joint," he explained. He could break an artist in his sleep.

"Charlie? Ehh. Nah, I ain't feeling that. Why can't I just do it by myself?" Kiara responded.

"Da'vi, it's your name on the marquee, but it's my name on the checks. I wasn't asking for feedback, just your participation."

"Don't forget my brother's name is on those checks, too. I really shouldn't even be begging for anything in this bitch, Day. A part of this company technically belongs to my family. I could be coming for that. Treat me right, and I ain't got to take it there, but it can go there. Those checks you and Demi sending monthly didn't make me forget Duke helped start this," Kiara Da'vi said.

"Is that a threat?" Day asked, bending his brow. The moment a motherfucker felt like they were owed something was the moment they became an opp in Day's mind. Kiara Da'vi didn't know shit about the business that Day, Demi, and Duke had indulged in. They were paying his mother out of loyalty, not necessity. Sure, Duke had helped fund the company, but upon his death, he was owed nothing further.

His tone of voice and the change of his mood were enough for her to backtrack, but Day made a mental note that this could become a potential problem. He would be contacting their lawyers tomorrow to ensure Duke had been removed from all shareholder documents upon his death.

She rolled her eyes and folded her arms across her chest. "No, I don't have no smoke. I'm just saying, remember that we're family, and look out for me. If Duke was alive, this wouldn't even be a conversation."

If Duke was alive, you wouldn't be asking to sit on my dick, either, Day thought.

"I would be a priority. I don't understand why I have to share the limelight with Charlie," she pressed.

"Because Charlie can sing a cappella. You need a track and autotune. You really want to get up there by yourself?" he asked. "It's hard to grab attention from celebrities. Especially from people who do the same thing as you. Niggas who think they the biggest star in the room don't look at the sky. Got to give them a shooting star for them to notice. Nobody's doing what Charlie does. She'll make them notice, and you'll keep their focus once she sets the tone. Besides, Demi owns half of this company. If you used your head a little more, instead of being jealous of every artist you see as competition, you'd see it as a smart move to hitch your cart to Charlie's horse. Charlie's performance will have the highest budget, her tours the most support, and her promotion will have no limit. If you're co-headliners, you reap the benefit of his love for her."

He could see the idea blossoming in her simple mind.
"Yeah, I guess that makes sense," she said, yielding. "And we're going together, right? I still need that look, Day." Her persistence was exhausting. "We were vibing, and then all of a sudden, we fell off, and you were out with these other bitches that ain't got shit on me." She huffed her displeasure. "And I really, really miss the dick."
Day hit the blunt. Did he miss her? He couldn't say he did. Day was never alone long enough to miss anyone. Women were everywhere in his life. His phone was full of first-round draft pics that most niggas would kill to be in contact with, including Kiara Da'vi, but Day had become immune to their beauty. He required a little more to keep him tuned in.

"You just talking, Davi. You ain't about that life. You a runner. Don't act like you can handle a nigga now." He had turned her pretty little ass inside out when she was in his bed, and she could barely take the dick. The culture had labeled her music *Sex & B*, which was the title of her impending album, but she wasn't truly the siren she claimed to be. She talked big. He smirked as he remembered the way his name had bounced off the walls of their hotel rooms.

She smiled mischievously because, for her, his words were a challenge. She approached him, pressing her body into him as she kissed his neck. The voluptuous woman was made in cookie cutter image. She looked like every other Instagram model these days. The aesthetic was pleasing, but nothing about it was unique. That ass was fat and beautifully done. Her artist development budget had contributed towards that, and her doctor had given her dangerous curves. Her face was caramel in hue and stiff from the Botox shots she had indulged in, and those titties sat up at attention. Everything about her was manufactured. From the body to the 30 inches of hair sewn into her head, and the claw-like nails on her fingers. She was stunning, but he had seen it before. She straddled him. The discovery that she hadn't worn panties made his dick jump simply because he was a man, and his dick was going to dick whenever it was in the vicinity of wet pussy. She was throwing it at him, and he contemplated breaking her off one last time. It had been a rough week. Days had been long and hard. Something easy felt warranted, but there was something nagging in him all the same.

"You can't do stuff like buy me brand-new cars and think I ain't gonna want to sit on this dick to thank you, Day."

A man was a man on every day of the week, and her words aroused him. That was the one thing a girl like Stassi couldn't provide. Ho shit. Kiara Da'vi used seduction as currency. He had clout; she wanted to buy it, so that pussy was for sale. He would be lying if he said it wasn't good as fuck. She was wet and tight and clean. He palmed her ass with one hand, pulling her into his dick. He pulled in a long toke of the weed and blew the smoke slowly into her face. The fact that she giggled instead of correcting him made him shake his head. She went to kiss him, and he lifted his head to avoid her lips. He brought his hand up once more to hit the blunt.

"Promise me that we'll hit LA together. The awards, maybe an after-party or two, then the brunch the next day? I can come in with you on the PJ."

"I might let you and your little crew take the jet. I'll be out there later, though."

"Dayyy," she whined. "You know the cameras won't flick the same if I walk in by myself."

"I'ma be there," he said unconvincingly. "I got business to handle before I come out, though. I'll put my card on file with the company stylist. Get yourself right so you're ready. I got to talk to Demi. See where his head at. See if he fucking with it. I doubt it, but we'll see. If Charlie performs, I doubt he'll send her alone."

Kiara wrapped her arms around his neck and leaned in to hug him. "Thank you, Day," she sang it so sweetly he knew the wrong nigga would have fallen for the trap of the faux worship. She didn't love him. She loved his caliber. There was a difference. He tapped her on the ass, and she stood in confusion. His decision was made. He wasn't hitting anything tonight.

"You're not staying?" she asked.

"Another time," he said. "I'ma get up with you, my baby."

Day knew it would take some convincing to get Demi to agree to the Dynasty Brunch, but it was necessary for both Kiara Da'vi and Charlie's projects to thrive. Their family had taken a devastating hit, but the business couldn't go unmanned. Even if Day had to captain the ship alone until Demi came back to work, the show had to go on. They had poured too much into their company to neglect it when they had two burgeoning stars on the horizon. He thought about asking Stassi to plan the LA event, but he had a feeling that Kiara Da'vi would buck against that. He had heard her subtle shade while referring to Stassi, and Day didn't feel like running interference between the two women. Kiara wasn't one to play her position. She was only interested in the top spot, and if Stassi felt like a threat, Kiara wouldn't play nice. He would throw the job to someone else, maybe even see if Lauren wanted to distract herself with the task, just to make sure he didn't put two trains on the same track. He knew that Lauren would need a watchful eye on her for a while. Keeping her close would be a good idea. His only other concern was figuring out a way to detach his name from Kiara Da'vi's without kicking a hornet's nest. The subtle power she had tried to assert by mentioning Duke's ownership didn't sit well with him. He had a feeling if things didn't go her way, she would become a problem. He was trying to get to know Stassi, but he couldn't do that by playing the same old games he was accustomed to. Kiara Da'vi was the same old game, and women like Stassi wouldn't give him a pass. She would expect him to be all the way in or all the way out. Day wasn't sure if he could commit to someone so seriously, but he had to admit that Stassi had done what no other woman had been able to—keep his attention. Even now, after a day of heartbreak and after an offer most men wouldn't reject, he just wanted to ring Stassi's line. If he was honest, she was the only reason he was leaving without taking Kiara Da'vi to bed, and it bothered him a little that Stassi had him so preoccupied. A woman had never been a distraction to him, but Stassi, with her generous spirit, her infectious smile, her stubborn nature, and unreasonable boundaries, had him looking forward to jumping through hoops.

Lauren's heart was beating. She felt it. She heard it as it thundered in her ears, but she had no idea how it was still working. She had been sitting in her car for hours. She had rushed to her car after Demi had left because she hadn't wanted to be alone. She couldn't remember where she had planned to go. She wasn't even sure if she had a plan. She had just needed someone, but as soon as she had closed her car door, the privacy and solace that the lonely car provided was perfect to let out her screams. She sat there, shivering and bawling. So much snow had fallen that her windshield was covered. The only evidence that she was even inside was the barely-there footprints in the snow. That's how he had found her. She was sure of it.

"Lauren! Lauren, what you doing out here? Come on. I got you."

She wrapped her cold hands around his neck as he hoisted her from the car.

"You're freezing," he stated as he carried her inside.

She didn't realize how cold she was until the heat of her home hit her skin. She didn't realize how lonely she was either until he sat down with her in his lap. Nyair felt like God himself. He felt like an altar she could pray at. He felt like a pillow she could rest her head on, and she curled up in his lap as he rubbed warmth back into her body.

"What were you trying to do, huh?" he asked. "What if I hadn't come over here?"

She would take his scolding as long as he kept holding her. She closed her eyes and sniffled as he held her tightly.

"Today was hard," he said.

She nodded, and she wasn't sure if her frozen tears were thawing or if new ones were coming down her cheeks. Either way, he was ready, wiping them away.

"Tomorrow will be hard, and maybe the day after that, and the one after that."

She choked on a sob.

"And I'm sorry for that, Lauren. I truly am. I wish there was something I could say or do to make it easier," he said.

"But this is the body part of it. The flesh. The part that makes it hard to understand. The spirit isn't worried because the spirit doesn't die, but the part of you that needs proof that your son is still with you. The part that's grieving the body hurts. You got to have a little faith, beautiful. You got to feel Him even when you can't see him because that's where DJ is. He's with God. He's not hurting. He's safe. He's also here. You can't see him, but you can feel him if you let go of this grief. This grief will kill you, Lo. You hear me?"

She nodded. This man was such a motherfucking man. He placed his hand on the side of her face, and Lauren gripped his collar for dear life as she gritted her teeth.

"I hate this, Nyair. Why did this have to happen to *my* baby?" she whispered.

"I don't know," Nyair answered. "But I'm right here."

She nodded, and she panted like she was desperate for a bit of his air. His breath smelled sweet. "Ny, just make it better," she whispered.

"I don't know how," he said in a low tone that held so much regret. "If I knew how..."

"You know how," she pleaded. "Just make me feel better."

"You're a problem for me, Lauren Sky," he said, pulling his face back so that he could look her in the eyes.

"And you're an answer for me."

Lauren kissed Nyair, hesitantly because she expected him to stop her. She felt his entire body tense. Every muscle contracted as she paused to stare at his lips.

"I get addicted to shit like this," he said as she placed another timid peck on his lips.

"I want you to," she said in an airy breath that was full of intimidation and curiosity. He fisted the back of her hair, and she kissed him deeper, swallowing his entire tongue as her moans filled the air. She needed this so badly she could feel her body screaming for him. The clothes were in the way. She unbuttoned his shirt, pulled the wife beater beneath it over his head, and then stood between his legs. He ran his hand up her leg and then leaned in to kiss the softest part of her thigh as she frantically pulled the dress over her head. She stood there, in her panties and bra, vulnerable, trembling as he planted soft pecks on her body. He was still seated on the couch, and he was taking his time. She could feel his breath on her center as he came close, and when his finger pulled the edge of her panties to the side, she siphoned in air through pursed lips. He licked her with a flat tongue, placing his entire mouth over her pussy lips before sucking on them like they were dipped in honey. His hands gripped her ass, and he sat back on the couch as he pulled her toward him. Head resting on the cushions, he relaxed and pulled her right on top of his face. He ate Lauren from her clit to her crack as she held onto the back of the couch for dear life.

"It feels so good," she moaned.

"It tastes better," he mumbled. This man was an eater. He savored her like he had spent hours in the kitchen preparing this meal. She was at his mercy, and it felt so good that she had to squeeze her eyes tight and bite her bottom lip to allow him to continue. This wasn't a quick bite. This was five courses. His tongue did tricks she didn't know tongues could do, and her pussy pulsed in satisfaction. She came all over his tongue, and Nyair just kept going and going, and, oh my God, why was he still going? The way her stomach was contracting as she jerked from the orgasm should have told him he could stop, but they were nowhere close to the finish line. Her clit was so sensitive she couldn't take it. She was losing her mind as she tried to run from the sensation.

"Mmm hmm," he groaned, denying her as he eased up from full pressure to delicate licks.

"Yes, like that," she groaned. "How do you know what I need?" she asked in amazement as her face twisted in an ugly sneer. "Baby, I'm about to cum." But the sensation was so strong it felt like her bladder was full. "Wait, I think I have to pee."

"That ain't pee, Lo. Just enjoy it. Let it go."

Lauren couldn't take anymore. She pulled away from him, standing and backing up as she placed her fingers between her lips. She was stupefied as her legs shook so much she could hardly stand. Her pussy was so wet her fingers were glazed when she pulled them back. He stood.

"You can't handle it. We can stop," Nyair said, his tone a bit disappointed, like he had expected more.

"I can't stop," Lauren damn near shouted. "I can handle it. I can take it." He unbuttoned his slacks and stepped out of them. Designer drawers for a high-class man. His dick print alone sent a sensation through Lauren's clit. He gripped his blessing with one hand and waited for her to approach.

Lauren rushed over to him, tongue kissing him, tasting herself as she slid her hands into his underwear. She had never felt a man brick like that. Every vein, every inch, even the rim of the head of his dick was defined.

"I don't have condoms. I didn't come here for this," he whispered.

She paused, but the lust was so potent it wasn't enough to stop her. They both stared at one another, chests heaving, as they weighed the risk in their minds.

"I don't think I care," she whispered. He sat back on the couch, and she straddled him, easing onto his dick, inch by inch. The ride was spectacular. The way that pussy squeezed as she rose and the wetness that saturated him when she lowered was earth-shattering.

"Ooooh, Nyair, I really have to pee," she moaned. Only it felt good. It felt like he was pressing on her bladder and her clit at the same time.

"Let it go," he whispered. He wrapped one hand around her neck and pulled her close to his face. "Wet this dick."

He bit her bottom lip and then pulled her bra straps down, freeing her titties so that he could bite softly on those too. He pushed them together as she bounced slowly and winded her hips intensely. He went from one nipple to the other and back again.

"You're perfection, Lauren. Every inch of you," he whispered. She was crying, this dick was so good. She pressed her forehead to his as she whimpered. "Anytime you're sad or lonely, let me come get this. Every time you need it. I'll put my face in it any time you want me to make it better, Lo. I promise."

"Ahhh!" She exploded. Lauren squirted all over Nyair, flooding everything. Him, her couch. He came right after her, lifting her from his lap and pumping his dick slowly as he got rid of every drop. Lauren didn't know what came over her. The sight of his fist milking his dick just did things to her. She straddled him again, this time backward, and swallowed his dick.

"Ohhh, shit," Nyair moaned as he filled her throat. He lifted her hips onto his face again and spread her cheeks before licking her ass as his middle finger stroked her stiff clit. Lauren was sucking him dry. She was swallowing dick and balls and nut like it had the power the heal her ailments. She felt him grow hard all over again. Nyair focused on eating her ass while he took three fingers on an exploration of her wetness as his thumb focused on her pearl. It was too many sensations at one time for Lauren to handle.

"My God, Ny!" she screamed as her pussy convulsed, creaming.

He smacked her ass gently and then moved her cheeks in circles before kissing one pussy lip, then the other. His toes were curling from the job Lauren was performing. Never would he have ever looked at Lauren and predicted that she got down like this. He laid his head back.

"Fuck, baby. You sucking the shit out that dick," he moaned. He never stopped circling her clit with his thumb. He knew how sensitive a woman's clit was after orgasm. Lauren had cum twice. He knew that pussy was raw with pure, exposed nerves, and his thumb was the perfect amount of pressure to keep her aroused. The way her juices were flowing, it felt like just his touch was enough to make her cum a third time. It was pretty and pink and coated, and Nyair was greedy. He lifted his hips slowly, grinding into her mouth, and lowered his head to suck her clit.

"Mmmmm," she moaned, mouth still wrapped around him.

"Fuck," Nyair hissed as he came. She came up for air and cuddled under him as he welcomed her into his body. They were both heaving.

It was the nastiest sex Lauren had ever had and the best. Two simultaneous truths. She could barely catch her breath.

"I apologize, Lo. I'm out of line," Nyair said. She could see a sense of shame and guilt wash over him as their high faded. He was so remorseful.

She shook her head and climbed back into his lap. "You're exactly where I need you to be and exactly who I need you to be. I don't care if this is wrong because everything is fucked up anyway. I don't care if it's an unhealthy way to heal. Don't feel guilty, Ny. Don't feel guilty for making this better for me. I'm a big girl. I know what I'm doing."

Nyair sighed. "I'm taking advantage, Lo. Of my position… Of your hurt. This ain't where a man of God supposed to be."

"Well, you're the only thing that has me not questioning God right now. You're the only thing making me think He's even real because He sent you, and everything that hurts, stops. I don't care about anything else. Nobody even has to know, Ny, but you can't not give me this. I need you to fuck me, Nyair. Keep fucking me and keep eating my pussy, and making me call your name…and…"

The more she talked, the harder Nyair became until she was sliding him right back inside of her.

"Yes, just like that," she moaned. "Keep doing this." She wasn't even sure how he was hard again, or why her body still craved him, but they were on it, and she wasn't complaining.

Nyair turned her over and delivered back strokes that had her clawing at his skin.

"Fuck!" she shouted. Lauren knew this was a distraction from the pain, but she didn't care. She was grateful for it; she praised him for it. The stamina of this man. Ain't no way God didn't want him to use it. Nyair and Lauren fucked for two hours straight and only stopped because Nyair couldn't rise again for round four. Even then, he didn't stop. They showered, and he ate her as the water washed the evidence of their indiscretions away.

He climbed from the shower, frowning in concern as he came up behind her while she stared at herself in the mirror. She rubbed her hands together, moisturizing them as she stared at her reflection.

He kissed the back of her shoulder.

"I want to ask if you're okay, but I know you're not," he whispered.

She turned to him and lowered her head to his chest as he enveloped her in a hug.

"It feels like I need you, Ny, and I don't want to need you. I don't want to need anybody, but it really feels like I need to fall in love with you to get through this."

Nyair pulled back slightly and took in her facial expression. He had never heard anyone be so technical about the act. It was like she was ordering a prescription for heartbreak.

"I know," she cried softly. He didn't need to tell her that she sounded like the clingy girl or the crazy chick that would key your car for not answering a call.

"You don't know. Don't presume to know," he replied seriously. She could see his deep thoughts like he was writing them down on the lines of his creased forehead.

"If we fall in love, I want it to be because you're happy. I want it to be because you've tried your hardest not to, and you just can't resist it. I want you to not be able to exist without your thoughts wandering over to me. I don't want it to be out of desperation, Lauren. Love out of desperation won't last. It's mean and aggressive and possessive."

Her face was in his hands again, and she decided then and there that he might as well cut them off and leave them with her because it was her favorite place to be. Staring in his eyes felt like security. "I want you to love me because God places you here, not because grief forces you. And this…" Nyair blew out a breath of exasperation. "I'd have to step down from so many things to do this."

She shut her eyes as her chest rose because he was rejecting her. He was about to take away her one source of relief.

"Why can't we have both?" she asked, opening her eyes again.

"Because this is lust, Lauren. The way I want this again, this isn't…"

"So, fall in love with me. It can't be lust if it's love," Lauren reasoned. Or was she unreasonable? She couldn't tell. All she knew was if she lost one more thing, she would lose it.

Nyair was lost in her stare. If only it was that easy. "You're beautiful," he complimented. He sighed. "So damn beautiful."

"Let's fall in love, Nyair," Lauren said.

He pulled her close, holding her like she was a baby. She needed his heartbeat to calm her. Neither knew what they were getting themselves into, but it was too late to turn back. They would have to figure it out along the road to wherever they were going.

Lauren's landline rang, and she frowned because only a few people had the number. Her mother. Demi and her son's school. Whenever it rang, she knew it was an emergency.

"I'm sorry. I need to get that," she said, regretfully breaking up a moment that she could have lived in forever.

She rushed to the nightstand and picked up the phone.

"Hello?"

"You have a call from the Genesee County Jail. To accept this call..."

She pressed pound before the automated voice could even finish because she knew it was Demi. It was the only person it could be. The worst-case scenario ran through her mind.

"Lo, I need you," he said as the line connected.

"What the hell are you doing in jail?" she asked.

"I just need you to come get me, man. Day ain't answering and..."

"I'm on my way," she said. "Is there a bond?"

"Twenty-five hundred, and I can walk out tonight. Bring cash," Demi said.

"Fine, hold tight."

She hung up and turned to Nyair, who had begun to dress.

"I need to go. I have an emergency that I have to take care of..."

"Your husband, right?" Nyair asked.

"Yeah," she said, then shook her head. "I mean, no. He's my ex-husband, but it's complicated. With what happened to DJ, it's all so complicated."

Nyair nodded. "I'll see myself out and let you get to it."

Lauren was moving around the room, pulling open drawers, throwing on sweats and a t-shirt as quickly as she could. Just the mention of him leaving froze her.

"Demi is not an issue for me, but he's family, so I do have to go. You could stay?" she proposed.

"Picture that. Me laying up in your crib, Lo," he chuckled. "I ain't that type of man. I also ain't worried about what a man before me did, cuz it ain't gon' compare to what I'm trying to do with you now. So go ahead and handle your business with your family."

The worry lines faded from her forehead. There was nothing like a confident man. Nyair didn't form assumptions or insecurities about her dealings with Demi and she appreciated that. Every exchange with this man was so refined. He was just a grown-ass man, and she couldn't handle anything less right now.

She didn't want to go. She didn't want to tap back into reality and remember her grief. Coming down off this sexual high would do that. Seeing Demi's face would do that.

Nyair recognized the dilemma in her, and he pulled her into his space. The kiss to her forehead was intimate. The one to her lips left no confusion. He kissed her like it was his only form of communication, and he was dying to be understood. Lauren wasn't really into swapping spit with humans. Demi had trained her not to even expect to. For years, they just didn't kiss at all, besides, the occasional peck of the lips. Nyair kissed like he was born and bred in France, like it wasn't just the precursor to fucking, but was a form of it all by itself. He was seducing her, and it was working. She couldn't believe she was wet for him again.

"Good night," he said, before walking out.

Lauren was so bothered that she had to freshen up again before she could leave. She rushed out the door and hopped in her car, headed to pick up her bothersome-ass baby daddy.

"On my motherfucking nerves," she complained, battling the snow as she pulled out of her driveway. She would have to brave the elements for 60 miles to get to him, but she couldn't leave him on stuck. It wasn't a coincidence that he had been arrested the day of their son's funeral. She knew he was in emotional turmoil, and whatever he had done was a result of that.

CHAPTER 13

"Sky, you're out of here."

Demi stood and sauntered out of the jail cell he had been held in for hours. He had called Lauren hours ago, and he knew they had purposely made her wait to get him out. The police played games that way, and he mugged the officer as he bypassed him, while walking out. He stopped at the front and retrieved all the items they had taken from him. His phone, wallet, keys, belt, and shoestrings. He was a disheveled mess when he emerged to find Lauren waiting in the lobby. She was barefaced and dressed down, which was unusual for her, but even in this state of distress, with her eyes red and swollen from crying, she was gorgeous. Even after their divorce, her presence felt like an answered prayer. Lauren had been his partner for years. Any time he was uncertain, in trouble, or something heavy was weighing on him, she came to his rescue. They would sit and discuss a problem for hours and game plan together until Demi worked out whatever dilemma he had brought home with him that night. She was always his right hand, and tonight was no different. He couldn't pay for loyalty like hers. Despite the hurt he had put on Lauren, she had still shown up.

"Thank God," she sighed in relief while shaking her head. "Are you okay?"

"Yeah, man," he answered. He put himself back together, lacing his shoes and all before he followed her to the car.

They settled into the car before either of them spoke.

"You want to tell me what happened?"

"Not really," he said.

"Well, tell me anyway, Demitrius," she ordered.

"This some bullshit," he drawled. She wasn't even his wife anymore, and he was still reporting to her bossy ass. He rested his elbow on the door and rubbed the top of his head. "I got into it with this nigga Charlie fuck with."

Lauren scoffed. "Wow," she said. "Karma gon' do her big one every time. That explains why you called me instead of her."

Demi knew that Lauren felt a bit of victory in his situation.

"So, you cheated on me only for her to turn around and cheat on you," Lauren stated. She shook her head. She laughed, and Demi grimaced because she was gloating like a motherfucker. "I'm sorry. Shit is funny, though."

"Nice, Lo. Real fucking nice," he said.

"Where am I taking you?" she asked. "You going home?"

"Yeah," he huffed.

The ride was silent and extremely long because the roads were getting worse by the minute. By the time they pulled up to Demi's house, she could barely see out of her front window.

"You not gon' be able to drive in this," he said.

"I'll be fine," she stated.

"I know you will because you not driving nowhere in this shit." He took her keys from the cup holder. "These on me."

"Is *she* here?" Lauren asked.

Demi glanced up at the house and saw that the light in their bedroom was glowing. "Looks like it." He knew that Charlie didn't turn out the bedroom light at night if he wasn't home.

"I ain't coming in there," Lauren protested. "Give me my keys."

"You can stay in the guest room or in DJ's room. They'll have the salt trucks out by morning," Demi said. He popped open the door, and Lauren lingered behind for a second before submitting to the circumstance. She really didn't have a choice.

"This is bullshit. I should have left your ass in jail," she hissed.

"Pretty much," Demi agreed.

They entered the house, and Demi motioned for the living room.

"Let me talk to Charlie. You can make yourself at home," he said.

Lauren shook her head. "I'ma stay right here until you give that girl the heads up."

"Lo, we buried our boy today. Of all days for it to be okay for you to be under my roof, this one is it," he said. He couldn't even reference the occasion without his eyes betraying him. He was having a badass day, and he felt every minute of it. "Wait for me in there."

She nodded.

Demi made his way to the bedroom, and as charged up as he was, he softened as soon as he saw Charlie. She was curled up on the bed, squeezing a teddy bear he hadn't seen before as she slept. The bawled-up tissue strewn around her told him she had cried herself to sleep.

She was almost angelic. Her locs fell around her face. Demi sat on the edge of the bed and bent over onto his knees. The weight of his body awakened her. When she turned to him and cleared the locs from her face, his entire body stiffened. Her lip was swollen, and her face was bruised. She saw a fire start in his eyes.

"It's nothing, Demi. I'm fine," she started before he could even speak.

"Who am I killing tonight, Bird?" he asked calmly. She would have felt better if he had yelled. The calm meant it was already decided.

"You want to go back to jail? Is that what you want?" she asked. "I need you to let this go. It's not as bad as it looks."

"Did the cops do this? Or did that bitch-ass nigga put his hands on you?" Demi asked.

Charlie's eyes watered because if she told him, it wouldn't do anything but push him right back out the door.

"You're protecting him?" Demi asked.

"No!" she shouted, eyes watering.

"So he did do this?" Demi asked. "Let me see my baby's face."

She stopped avoiding his stare and looked him square in the eyes. He took in every inch of her face, and she could see his rage. He nodded his head like he had just made a complicated decision.

"What are you going to do?" she asked.

"That's not for you to worry about, Bird," he replied.

"Can you just talk to me? Stay here. Don't go out there. Don't go after Justin. Just talk to me. I feel like I haven't talked to you. I feel like I don't know you," Charlie cried. Demi knew he wouldn't be able to leave her tonight, but he had an appointment tomorrow. It was an appointment he wouldn't miss either. Tonight, he would ease her mind. Just the sight of her face set him off inside.

"I had a real bad day, Bird," he said, face twisting as the weight of everything he had been carrying suddenly hit his shoulders. He was fighting himself. Demi just wanted to cry. He needed to cry, and when Charlie sat up and put her hands on his back, he almost allowed himself the privilege to feel her. Then, he remembered Justin. He pictured her hands touching another nigga the way she touched him, and he tensed. She didn't miss it.

"You fucked him, Bird? Have you been fucking that nigga?" Demi asked.

Charlie scoffed in disbelief and jolted her body from the bed. She kicked off those covers with so much aggression that Demi's eyes widened in surprise.

"You really got to ask me some shit like that?" Charlie screamed. "After you've been gone all week! Living with your ex-wife! Caring for her! Completely shutting me the fuck out! Noooo," she shouted like a mad woman. I didn't fuck Justin! I didn't even know he was going to be there! I went searching for music because I was lonely and hurt! I didn't know he was going to be performing there! I couldn't be here because you weren't here, and I was depressed! I was miserable because you gave her the authority to put me out of your life! Like I'm nothing! Like I'm fucking optional. Oh, I'll take Demi, but leave Charlie at home! You made me feel unwelcome in your life, and you got the nerve to ask me if *I'm* the one fucking somebody else! Nigga, are you?!"

Demi had never heard Charlie snap like this. The animosity in her voice and the tears raging from her eyes rattled him, and he stood.

"Nah, nigga, sit your ass down! You not towering over me with all that pent-up fucking anger and grief! I'm tired! I'm fucking exhausted from trying to make you want me. Trying to make myself less offensive to that bitch you used to call a wife!"

"Mannn," Demi interrupted, knowing that Lauren was under this roof, listening to every vicious word that was said.

"No, fuck you! And fuck her! You didn't even take up for me! You didn't even pretend like you wanted me there! You treated me like you were ashamed of me. Like I didn't even belong."

"You didn't!" Demi shouted back. His words stunned her, and she physically recoiled. "I know you wanted to be there. I might have even needed you there, but you didn't belong there, Bird! My son hated you! His mother hates you! I left them for somebody they hated, and you wanted me to flaunt you in her face while we said goodbye to our only child? I'm the only one who wanted you there. I needed you! I always need you. From day fucking one, I looked at you, and I wanted you. Had to have you. Wasn't nobody making me come up off you because you were all under my skin. All in a nigga heart. In my head. That voice. Those eyes. I needed all that. All it took was one night with you to take me away from 15 years of a life I had somewhere else. And I was serious about you. I left my family to keep you, and now I got to live with that shit! I got to live with the fact that I chose you over my son's mental health. He killed himself because I left! It didn't matter if I wanted you to be there. Lo didn't, so you couldn't be there, and I'm sorry for that, baby. I'm sorry, but today wasn't about you."

Charlie was bawling. Neither of them was wrong. That was the hard part about it. Two things were true. No lies were told. It was a harsh consequence of the fact that their relationship was birthed from an affair. Their love injured people. It was so potent that it had become poisonous.

"This is my fault," Demi said, lowering his voice and bowing his head, breaking down. "I love you, Bird. I'm obsessed with everything about you, and it cost me my son."

"That's not fair," Charlie whispered. His tears and hers made a river of love, and they couldn't swim.

"It's not. I know. It's not. None of this shit is fair. His body was so small in that casket, Bird. How am I here, and he's under the ground? That's what's not fair. You feeling a little left out is the small price to pay in all this."

Charlie was so hurt. Demi felt relief oddly. So much emotion had been pent up inside him, and this fight was like the draining of an infectious wound. It hurt so bad, but it was the only way he could even start to heal. "I'm in love with you, baby, but this is all I got to give you right now, though, and it might not be enough. My baby boy broke me. I just got to get through this."

"You will and I'm praying for you, just like I been praying all week," Charlie whispered. She removed the ring from her finger and set it on the nightstand. "But we won't."

It was like Charlie was moving in slow motion as she made her way to the master closet. When she pulled out a suitcase, he realized that she had thought about this. This wasn't a spur-of-the-moment decision that had come during this argument. She was leaving him. He was losing her, and as she walked down the hallway, Demi felt the world narrowing in on him. How the fuck had this happened? They were just happy. They were just celebrating their engagement and their pregnancy. She had said yes to marrying him. They were supposed to be stronger than this. He was going through one of life's toughest seasons. Why was she throwing in the towel so easily? Demi felt betrayed. He felt abandoned.

"Bird! Fuck you mean? Put your shit back, baby," he said, pulling the suitcase from her hands. "You not leaving me, Bird. Just listen to me."

Charlie shook her head. "Fine, keep the clothes. You bought them anyway. I don't want anything else from you."

"What the fuck, man?" Demi was having a meltdown. This couldn't be happening to him, especially not right after the death of his son. His life was unraveling more and more as each day passed by. "What I'm supposed to do without you?" Demi asked as he damn near chased behind her. He couldn't even believe these were his words, but he loved her too much to let her leave without a fight. "What do you want me to do, Bird? Just name your price!"

When Charlie rounded the corner and found Lauren sitting awkwardly in their living room, her feet stopped moving.

"You have got to be fucking kidding me," Charlie scoffed. "What is she doing in my house?"

"Believe me, I don't want to be here," Lauren said.

"Lo, mind your business!" Demi said sternly, but he couldn't even lend her a gaze. His eyes were locked on Charlie.

"Why is she here?!" Charlie shouted. "She has free rein to walk into my house whenever she wants, but I can't come to pay respects at a funeral?" Charlie was so mad that she jabbed Demi's ass. "Are you fucking kidding me? You see how you let another woman just make the rules for you? That's not supposed to fuck with me?"

"She got me out of jail, Bird. It's at least two feet of snow on the ground. She couldn't drive back home," Demi explained.

"So you invited her into *my* house?" Charlie asked. "After she humiliated me today? After you both made me look like a fool?" Charlie was so emotional that she was hyperventilating from crying so hard.

"Bird, I'ma need you to calm down, baby, you're pregnant," Demi said, lowering his voice and grabbing both of her hands. Charlie sobbed as he pulled her into his body. "I know, baby. I'm sorry. I'm so fucking sorry, Bird." Lauren rolled her eyes as Demi embraced Charlie.

"You make me feel like I'll never measure up to her! Like I'll always be the side chick that comes second to your family!" she shouted, pushing against him. "Just let me go!" She snatched away from him, embarrassed and frustrated, retreating to the half bathroom.

Demi blew out a breath of overwhelm. He knew the situation was tense and a bit inconvenient for Charlie, but he didn't know it would turn out this badly. He expected to have some ass-kissing to do, some spoiling to indulge in, and some reassuring to provide, but had he done enough for her to leave him? His son had died. She was too emotional to reason with. Or was he too emotional to empathize with her? He couldn't tell at this point. They were both on different ends of the spectrum of crazy, and they were out of touch with each other's emotions. The heightened stakes that had been thrown into their lives had turned them into enemies. Death did that. It uprooted every piece of normalcy that existed in a person's life. It picked off scabs to wounds that were supposed to be long healed. DJ's death had unearthed an insecurity in Charlie that he didn't even know existed.

The locked door made him panic. His son had cut himself in secrecy behind a locked door just like this, and in the state Charlie was in, his mind went to the worst-case scenario. "Open the door, Bird!" he shouted. He rattled the door handle. He wanted to snatch the door off the hinges, but instead, he leaned his head against it. "Bird, just talk to me, baby. You said you been wanting to talk. I'm right here."

Lauren sighed and came to Demi's side. They shared so much passion that she couldn't help but feel resentment. She also felt pity.

Lauren knocked on the door lightly.

"Charlie, I know I've been hard on you. I want to be sorry for that, but it's just so fresh. I can't apologize because I'm not sure if I should be apologizing or not. All I can do is be real with you. Woman to woman. I didn't want you at DJ's funeral because…" Lauren paused and swallowed the lump in her throat. Demi looked at her bewildered, unsure if Lauren was making things better or worse. "Because of so many reasons. I blame you for breaking up my family. I blame you for my son feeling like he lost his daddy. I'm so damn jealous of the way Demi is with you…"

Shock cut across Demi's face and Lauren shook her head. "I hated when I found out you were pregnant, and now that my son is gone, I can't even look at you. It feels like he's replaced. It feels like you're living the version of a life I should have had with Demi and that hurts. I didn't want to be the only parent grieving our son at his own funeral. Demi gets another chance at parenthood with you. I needed him by my side today. I couldn't let you be there. I couldn't stomach it. I'm not saying it's right; it's just how I felt, and I hope you never have to experience it to be able to relate. I needed Demi to be my child's father today, not yours. It was harsh, and I'm sorry if you were hurt by that, but it's a mother's worst nightmare. I know I need to work out my feelings somewhere else because Demi is who I should be having these hard conversations with. It's not on you. I know it's not on you, deep down. You are just a trigger for me. This is your house. You're right. I shouldn't have come here after the way I treated you. If anybody should go, it should be me. You're pregnant, and I'm not trying to be the reason anything happens to another woman's baby. Please come out of this bathroom. Locked bathroom doors feel very fresh to us right now. It's too soon. I don't want anyone else to get hurt."

Demi damn near held his breath as nothing but silence filled the air. When he heard the lock turn, he breathed a sigh of relief.

Charlie pulled open the door, and Demi was there.

"You're welcome," Lauren said as she turned to make her exit. She collected her bag from the couch.

"I'll brave the snow," Lauren said. "You two clearly have some stuff to work out in private."

"Nobody's leaving here tonight," Demi stated. "I should have handled you better," he whispered to Charlie. "Bird… look at me…burn me, baby," he whispered.

Charlie refused to look at him. She was still so angry. "Lauren, you can take DJ's room," Charlie said. She turned to Demi. "And you can sleep on the couch."

"We got a whole guest room," Demi said.

"And your ass still gon' sleep on the couch," Charlie snapped as she walked by him and headed back to her bedroom. The door slammed so hard that Demi flinched.

Lauren gave him a knowing look. "Guess she told you," she said, shrugging before retiring for the night.

"She know this couch gon' tear my ass up," Demi complained.

"I think that's her point," Lauren called out over her shoulder as she disappeared down the hallway.

Demi had never thought the three of them would be sleeping under one roof, but tragedy made a mockery of their circumstances. He didn't know how to split his allegiances without offending one or the other. Tonight, he was just grateful that neither Charlie nor Lauren had left. He would take the couch, and he prayed for clarity in the morning. All he knew was that he didn't want to lose Charlie while honoring his son, and he didn't want to abandon Lauren and disrespect his son's memory. He felt responsible for both women. It was a balancing act beyond his ability, however, and it felt like he was failing them both.

CHAPTER 14

Charlie didn't sleep. She couldn't. Between the nausea and the relationship drama, Charlie couldn't get her body to relax. She climbed out of bed and crept out toward the kitchen. She didn't turn on a light. She knew the house by heart. She didn't want to wake Demi up because she wasn't ready to face him again. She rounded the corner, and the glow from the open refrigerator shined on Lauren.

"Oh, I was just…grabbing water," Lauren said as she took a bottle out of the refrigerator and moved aside.

"Sure, make yourself at home," Charlie said sarcastically. An awkward silence fell over them as Charlie opened the cabinet and pulled out a box of tea. She filled her kettle and placed it on the stove. It clicked as the fire ignited.

"DJ's room. It's nice. All his favorite things are here," Lauren said.

Charlie reluctantly replied. "Yeah, I wanted him to be comfortable. I wanted it to feel like home…" Charlie's eyes watered, and she quickly gained her composure. "I cared about him, Lauren. I hate that I never really got a chance to show him, but I was excited to be a part of his life. You could have at least let me walk to his casket to say goodbye and that I'm sorry. He was just a little boy. I was so afraid of him. Like, afraid to say the wrong thing or do the wrong thing. I just wanted him to like coming over here."

"I painted a bad picture of you, Charlie. For a long time," Lauren admitted. "Being mad at you is a deflection from being mad at myself."

Charlie looked at her in shock.

"I'm sorry you didn't get to say goodbye. Anybody who loved DJ deserved that chance," Lauren whispered.

"You really do have Demi eating out of the palm of your hands; you know that, right?" Lauren asked.

"Are you fucking him, Lo? Are you taking him back? Like, is this what this is? You're being nice to me to set me up for the gut punch? I know he's been staying at your house. I know he's practically been playing the husband role. Did you get your lick back?" Charlie asked.

Lauren's silence made Charlie ill. "I fucking knew it," she whispered dreadfully.

"No, Charlie," Lauren answered. The relief that filled Charlie pushed a breath of angst from her soul. Lauren could see it. "The only thing Demi and I have done is parent our boy. No lines were crossed. Emotions were high, and I'll always love him. We spent 15 years together, and even after his bullshit, he's still important in my life, especially now. But I know Demi isn't the man for me. I don't think he ever was because he ended up here with you."

"Only he's not here. He's there with you. I'm here alone,"

Charlie whispered. The kettle whistled, and Charlie turned to take it off the stove.

She retrieved two mugs and then prepared tea. She held one out for Lauren.

"It's the middle of the night, and we're stuck here together in the middle of a snowstorm on the night you buried your son. Can you just not hate me until morning? It's just tea, Lo."

Lauren sighed and grabbed the cup. "Let me show your young ass how to make a decent cup of tea," Lauren said. She walked over to Charlie, took her cup, and poured both cups down the drain.

"Hey!"

"Girl, pass me some Henny. I know you got some cuz Demi keep a full bar," Lauren said. "I need something stronger than tea."

"Lauren..." she paused. "I can't."

Lauren froze. She shook her head like she was clearing cobwebs from her mind. "I'm sorry. Of course, you can't. I'm not in my right mind." Lauren turned to leave the kitchen but then spun back to face Charlie.

"You're not alone, Charlie. Because of that baby you're growing, you'll never ever feel alone again. You're in here worrying about Demi. Fuck Demi. Fuck everybody, except yourself and that baby. All the tears, all the stress you've been taking yourself through. It's not worth it, Charlie. You're carrying the most precious gift a woman could ever receive. You're not alone. I would give anything to go back to the beginning and do it all over again. I would have held him tighter. I would have watched him closer. I would have loved him harder."

Charlie's heart was weighted because she could feel Lauren's anguish. She remade her tea and then fixed Lauren a real drink.

"I hope you find peace one day, and I am sorry for your loss. I know this doesn't mean anything to you, especially coming from me, but I've prayed for you every day since this happened."

"You are so hard to hate," Lauren said, crying and laughing at the same time.

"So don't hate me." Charlie shrugged. "Good night, Lo." Charlie took her cup of tea and headed back to her room. Apparently, the conversation with Lauren was just enough to allow her mind to ease so she could get some sleep.

Morning came, and Charlie heard the knock at her bedroom door.

She was already dressed. When she went to open it, Demi stood on the other side.

"Can we talk?" he asked.

"No, Demi, I don't think I have anything left to say, and I was going to leave, but I'm not leaving my home. I will raise my baby in this home. I packed you a bag instead," she said. She went to the bed, grabbed the duffel bag, and set it down near his feet.

"This is bullshit, man," Demi mumbled. His exasperation wasn't missed. "How long this supposed to last? How long a nigga supposed to pretend like he letting you have your way? Because hear me clearly, Bird, I ain't never coming up off you."

"You don't have a choice," Charlie stated firmly. "This isn't a game. I'm choosing to end this. I'm not looking for attention. Me and my baby…"

"Our baby," Demi interrupted. He placed a hand on her stomach. "That's me growing inside there, Bird."

"Me and the baby will be staying here and you're leaving."

Demi usually knew when Charlie was bluffing, but the serious expression on her face told him that this wasn't a ploy. "You're punishing me for going through a hard time? That sound right to you?"

"No punishment. I'm making a choice. The same way you made a choice. You secluded me from the most intimate moment of your life. I'm supposed to be who you find safety in. I'm supposed to be your retreat. I'm supposed to be your safe place, and you don't see me that way. You see Lauren that way, and I'm coming to understand that whatever this is that we have…" She paused because it hurt to even diminish their bond. It hurt her to think that it was small. He was the biggest thing in her life. He brought about big energy, he made her soul shake in a big way, he gave out big love, gave her big goals, big dick, big emotions, big everything. Lauren's energy, apparently, was larger if it distracted him from their entire life. "I can't compare to a lifetime with her. You still take pride in that life. I think you miss that life and still crave a presence there. So, I'm letting you go. No harm. No foul. No ill feelings. I just need what I give, and I give you everything. I'd never make you feel like a small part of my life. I give you every single emotion."

"And what the fuck I give you, Bird? I didn't cheat on you! I lost my fucking son! I barely touch Lauren. I'm all over you! Only fucking you! BUT WE LOST OUR SON!"

"You went through the worst moment of your life without needing me. How can we do life together if you don't even allow me to be a part of the important moments? I expected animosity from Lauren. I get that. I deserved more from you, though."

"This isn't happening, Bird. You can punish a nigga. You can throw your fits. You can do whatever you got to do to prove your point. You ain't leaving a nigga, though. I'm completely fucking smitten with your little ass. You hear me? I fucked up these past few days. If you say I did wrong, fuck it, I'm wrong. I ain't gon' argue 'bout it. Just tell me what you want me to do to make it right."

"You can't," Charlie said. "I can't forget how you made me feel." Demi was so blown, he felt like tearing the roof off the entire house. She was dragging him over the coals on this one, and it didn't seem fair. Little bitty Charlie felt like a motherfucking bully, and he wanted to cry. How the hell she had this much power over him, he didn't know. "No matter how I moved, it was going to disappoint someone…"

"Nigga, and you picked meee!" she shouted in frustration.

"I need you to give me some grace, Bird. I'ma lose my mind behind this shit here. Baby, I feel you. You're mad. I know; shit you got it. Can you love on a nigga anyway? Cuz I need it. I'm not perfect, but I ain't mean to hurt you. I ain't held you all week. I just want to close my eyes with you on my chest, Bird. I just want you to sing me a song and make all this disappear. Come on, man."

"You can leave, or I will," she whispered. He was wearing her down because God knows she loved this nigga. She knew Demi wouldn't want her to leave. It was only then that he bent down to grab his bag. He snatched it up forcefully, full of attitude and disdain.

"This is bullshit," he grumbled as he stormed for the door. He stopped abruptly and turned back to her, snatching her up by her waist, pulling her into his body, and pressing his forehead to hers.

"Demi, stop," she whispered.

"I'm never stopping, Bird," he said. He kissed her lips and then walked out, tapping the door frame as he departed. "Take care of my baby."

"Can I speak with Anastassia?"

Stassi squinted as the bright glare from her phone irritated her whole being.

"It's six o'clock in the morning. Who is this?" she groaned as she fell back onto her pillow in pure distress.

"It's Grayson. My bad if it's too early. I guess I'm programmed to rise before the sun. I thought you were, too," he answered.

"I'm a rise against my will type of girl," Stassi said grumpily, closing her eyes, trying to hold onto a bit of sleepiness because she was headed straight back to dreamland as soon as she swerved this call.

"Can I take you to breakfast?" he asked.

She opened her eyes.

"Breakfast?"

"Yeah, you eat, right?" he asked.

She giggled. "Yeah, I eat."

"Then meet me for breakfast. I'll send you the address," he replied.

"Yeah, okay…I guess," she said reluctantly.

It took Stassi two hours to pull her life together. She didn't know why, but she was giddy at the thought of meeting this man for breakfast. It was a simple request, and she didn't know if she would even call it a date, but it felt good to be the first thought on his mind, especially when she was still waiting for a call from Day.

She expected to pull up to a brunch house or a restaurant, but when she got to the address Grayson had sent, she frowned. She called Grayson, and his phone went straight to voicemail. The fire truck sitting out front told her that he was likely inside. She climbed out of her car and flung her handbag over her shoulder as she made her way inside.

She signed in at the office. "I'm looking for…umm…one of the firefighters. His name is Grayson. He asked that I meet him here for breakfast."

"Oh, yes! He's right in the gym! Down the hall, make a left, and then follow the commotion," the secretary instructed.

Stassi nodded. "Thank you."

She walked with determination, heels echoing in the hallway until she located the gym. When she stepped inside, she saw him. He and what appeared to be his entire firehouse. They were serving breakfast to a gym full of kids. She didn't want to interrupt. She stood near the door, leaning against the frame, arms folded as she watched him. There had to be at least three hundred kids in the gym. When he looked up and noticed her, he handed his duties off to someone else to greet her. He was casual today in jeans and a Flint Fire Department fitted t-shirt.

"This isn't what I expected at all," she said, smiling.

"Breakfast with a hero," he said. He pointed to the sign hanging above her head. "We come out every week to make sure the kids in this neighborhood have a hot breakfast on Saturday mornings. It's the poorest area in the city. If we didn't, some of them wouldn't eat until they came back to school on Monday morning."

Her heart melted.

"Wow. That's really..." She paused as she looked around the room in awe. "Needed."

"Mr. Grayson! Mr. Grayson! Can we play the games now?" A little boy ran up to him and had ten kids behind him as they awaited an answer.

"You know the rules. Breakfast then 30 minutes of homework or reading, then it's fun time. Because why?"

"We handle the business first!" the little boy screamed.

"My man," Grayson said, extending his hand for a shake. "Do me a favor. You can start picking up any paper plates you see on the tables that need to go in the trash."

The kids ran off, and Stassi swooned.

"They love you." She laughed. "This is probably the best breakfast date I've ever had."

"I got to feed you first before we can call it a date," he shot back. "You hungry?"

"I am, but I want to help! I'll eat later. Put me to work!" Stassi was so excited. The energy in the room was infectious. She just wanted to contribute to it.

"You know how to make pancakes?" he asked.

"Boy, I'm the pancake queen," she bragged.

"Okay, well, I'ma put you at the pancake station with me," he said. "Come on. I'll get you an apron and show you where you can put your stuff."

She followed him to the kitchen, and they washed their hands before he slipped a plastic apron over her head.

She couldn't stop smiling.

"Never saw anybody this excited to make a couple hundred pancakes," Grayson snickered.

"I've never seen a man this intuitively conscious of the needs of children that don't belong to him. That makes me proud. Like, this is amazing," she said. "Good job, Black man."

He blushed, and Stassi did too, just out of reaction to his humility.

"Thank you," he said. He led the way to the station, and Stassi got to work. The first little girl in line was a little snaggletooth, brown skin girl with braids and barrettes. She was so intrinsically Black that Stassi fell in love instantly.

"Mr. Grayson is this your girlfriend?" the little girl asked.

Grayson flipped one of the pancakes on his griddle and then put it on the little girl's plate. "She's a girl and she's a friend. Does that count?"

Stassi laughed as the little girl shook her head. "That's not the same thingggg."

They spent the entire morning engrossed in these kids. Stassi served pancakes, wiped down tables, tied shoes, played kickball the best she could because she had worn heels, and helped with homework. She had been so tuned in to the event that she forgot to fix herself a plate. It was such a good time that she hated to see the morning come to an end, but when the last kid left the school, it was time to say goodbye.

"This was the most fun I've had in a long time," she said. "Thank you for inviting me."

"Thank you for not running for the door as soon as you got here," he replied.

"If this is what a date is like with you, I'm going to have to get creative when it's my turn to plan," she said. She felt awkward as soon as she said it.

Oh, you desperate-looking-ass bitch, she thought. She hated to look thirsty or to be one of those girls trying too hard too fast, forcing a square into a round hole.

"I'm not that difficult to please," he answered. "I live out the station, and my DoorDash bill is crazy, so a good home-cooked meal would do it for me."

"I most definitely can accommodate that," she replied. Stassi felt like her cheeks would fall off, she was smiling so hard. Grayson was genuinely nice, and not just to her. She noticed how he treated others around him. The kids were a given. They loved him. His colleagues loved him and looked up to him. She could tell just from their interactions, but also, he was kind to the little people in the room. The people most wouldn't even acknowledge. The janitor, whom he spent ten minutes with just inquiring about his family and his day. The secretary, who unlocked the building each Saturday, who he made it a point to take a plate. His spirit was soothing. Not to mention, the selfless job of being a firefighter. She didn't mind feeding a man like that.

"Just let me know when," he said jokingly.

"How about tonight?" she asked.

She could see his surprise. She shocked herself at how easily he had earned an invite to her crib. They walked toward the door, and he held it open for her.

"Just let me know what you'd like," she offered. *Oh, bitch, you really like him,* she thought. Most men would get shrimp alfredo, salad, and breadsticks because it was quick, good, and one of her favorites. She was giving Grayson options.

"I get to pick my poison, huh?" he asked.

"Unt uh, not you think I'm gon' poison you," she laughed. "I don't get to cook often, but I'm actually kind of good at it. I know my way around a kitchen. You say you don't get home-cooked meals often, so make it count. What would you like? If you could choose any meal to eat tonight, what would it be?"

He was digging the conversation. He was already rubbing his stomach. "Not going to lie. I haven't had an old-school pot roast in years. With the gravy and the carrots and some mac and cheese, cabbage. A little cornbread on the side."

She laughed.

"I can do that," she said. He went into his back pocket and pulled out a leather wallet. The logo told her it was Tom Ford.

The firefighter has good taste, she thought.

He pulled out two-hundred-dollar bills. "Will this cover it?" he asked, holding it out for her.

"Grayson, you don't have to give me money. It's my treat," Stassi insisted.

"You cook, I'll provide.

She looked at him in awe. It was a simple statement that held an old-school sentiment. He was a classic man, apparently, and he believed in traditional gender roles. She didn't know if she loved or hated it, but she knew better than to argue.

It could be a red flag for a man to believe in chauvinistic ideals and who has misogynist expectations, or it could mean security. It could mean that forever kind of love with a man who would go to work and come home every day, never cheating, never lying, never complaining, until the end of days. She wondered which type he was.

She took the money and stuffed it in her pocket. "If you insist," she said.

"I do," he countered.

"Seven o'clock," she said. "You know where I live."

"Whoa! Hey, where are you going?" Lauren asked.

"She needs space," Demi huffed. "I need you to stay here, Lo. Until she lets me come back, I need you to be here."

"Boy, what?" Lauren hissed. "You're running out, Demi. This girl is not my responsibility."

"You really want to be in that house by yourself? I risked my shit with her to be there with you. I can't lose her, Lo."

"You aren't thinking clearly, Demi. She and I aren't friends," Lauren protested in a hushed whisper. "This is her house. I can't babysit her just because she's mad at you."

"If I lose her, that's going to be the end of me," he admitted.

Lauren looked at him sympathetically. "The way you love her… Like the depth of it. It's almost scary. You're not supposed to risk it all for another human being, Demi. You're supposed to be able to live without them. Maybe give her a bit of space to learn how to live without you. Let her figure out how to love you without needing you to breathe. You took a week to grieve your son, and she completely unraveled. You both need to come down to reality because the love is too potent. It's so high that even the two of you are having a hard time reaching it. Too much of a good thing can be bad. You need time apart. That way, when she does come back, this time you know it's because she wants to, not because she needs to. You'd be smart to learn to do the same. I'm not smothering her. I'm not guarding her for you. She's grown, and I have my own shit to work out. Get your shit together."

Demi walked out, and Lauren sighed before gathering her things and leaving, too.

CHAPTER 15

"Don't walk into this church unannounced. He did not invite you here," Lauren whispered. She heard herself. She wanted to be the levelheaded woman who waited respectably for a man to call her first, but Lauren was pressed. Nyair was the only positive force in her life at the moment. He was like that hint of light that peeked over the storm clouds. Dare she say he might even be the rainbow after the storm?

She got out of the car and walked inside the church. She knew he was there because his car was in the parking lot. She was on some real-life dick-stalking shit, and she was so ashamed. She was being a hussy in the house of the Lord, but she wasn't shamed enough to turn around. Going home alone felt like a looming terror. She didn't want to face the new solitude of her house. She had half a mind to sell it. It was where she lived as a wife and a mother. Both those roles were stripped from her. She didn't need the big, empty house to remind her that she was alone.

"It's a blessed day in the house of the Lord. I haven't seen your face around here. How can I help you?"

A woman in a purple skirt and ivory blouse greeted her.

"Umm, yes, I'm looking for Pastor Ny," Lauren said.

"Do you have an appointment?" the woman asked.

"I don't. I'm a friend. Do I need one?" Lauren asked.

"Well, normally, but I can let him know you're here. He's in his office with one of our members now. You can wait right here," the woman said, pointing to a chair. "What's your name?"

"Lauren," she answered.

The woman disappeared inside the church offices, and Lauren waited in the hallway nervously. She pulled the Mario Bros. Amiibo from her coat pocket. She had taken it from DJ's room at Demi's house. It made her feel closer to him just to carry it with her.

"God, please help me through this," she whispered.

Before she could fall down a well of sadness, the door opened, and she stood as Nyair and his brother, Ethic, walked out. Lauren had seen Ethic before. His son, Eazy, played on DJ's football team as well. She wanted to say she had even seen his family at the funeral. She couldn't even remember because the funeral had felt like a blur. His presence felt grand, however, like she was supposed to acknowledge him.

"I'ma get with you, G," Nyair said, hugging Ethic goodbye.

"Sounds good," Ethic replied. Ethic turned to her and nodded a silent greeting. "I'm sorry for your loss."

She nodded. "Thank you."

It seemed odd to thank him for his sorrow, and she wondered how long people would feel obliged to say something when they saw her. She knew it was meant to be supportive, but it was exhausting. Any millisecond of relief she was able to capture when her son's death wasn't on her mind would be stolen every time someone shared their condolences. Ethic made his exit, and Lauren focused on Nyair.

"Come in," Nyair said. He extended his hand so that she could walk by, and he followed before closing and locking the door behind them.

"I been here all morning questioning if I even have a right to lead this church, Lo," he said in a low tone. "This thing with you." He stopped and shook his head.

"It's wrong?" she asked.

"It is," Nyair admitted as he leaned back onto his desk, sitting slightly. Lauren loved the way this man hung this suit. He was just so fucking solid and strong. He filled out every inch of the designer threads.

"It doesn't feel wrong," she answered. "It feels..." She stopped talking, and her breathing deepened as she literally felt his aura penetrate her body. Just being in his presence made every nerve in Lauren's body awaken. "Electrifying. Like my body just wants..."

"That's sin, Lauren," Nyair interrupted. "I'm standing up in front of my flock in the mornings and fucking you at night. That's lust."

"Why does it matter? I'm single. You're single..."

"You're also grieving..."

She shook her head. "Not when you're inside me. You're too big to leave room for anything else."

Nyair had to pull on his tie. She could see him trying to stand tall. He was trying to stick to the rules. If she could, she would, but who was she being good for anyway? For God? For a god that took her son away? She had no qualms about putting pussy on Nyair to calm the burn of her broken heart.

"Can I come closer to you?" she asked. She hadn't missed that he had retreated from her as soon as they stepped inside.

"That's not a good idea," he said, head tilted back a bit, one hand clasping the opposite wrist. It was almost like he was trying to shackle one hand to imprison himself from committing a sin under this roof.

"Nyair, please," she said. It was the need in which she said it. Nyair's dick was growing by the second. His hands covered the evidence of his lust for this woman. "You can't tell me you don't want this too. Am I being desperate? Am I feeling this by myself? Why would God make you fit so good if he didn't want you inside me?"

"Get over here," he said, tone low, guttural and demanding.

She stepped toward him, and he grabbed her hand, snatching her forward, then placed her hand on his dick. "You got to stop doing this," Nyair said. Lauren gasped at his hardness. "You can't come here, Lo."

"I'm sorry," she replied. She rubbed him through his pants, and Nyair swiped a hand down his face. He was overwhelmed and tempted, bothered, and fucking attracted. She was too. She was growing dependent on the euphoria he provided. It was like a high. Their draw to one another was magnetic, and the allure was extremely hard to dismiss.

"Lo, you're killing me," he whispered. "I'm in my flesh." He was trying to remind himself that he had a greater responsibility, but even as he said the words, he pulled her face to his and kissed her. Between every kiss he chastised her. "This what you want?" His tongue in her mouth, sucking, pulling, invading. Lauren loved it. "This what you came here for?" He moved to her neck. "I'ma fuck the shit out of you."

"Oh my God, yes, please," she moaned. Her pussy was drenched. He knew it, and he got on his knees, sliding her pants down and her panties aside so he could kiss her there, too. The fact that they weren't supposed to be doing this, especially here, especially now, made it that much better. Pure adrenaline coursed through her as he sucked her clit, gently. He went from her clit to her inner thigh, to her stomach, and back up her body until they were face to face.

"Why do you taste so fucking good?" he asked.

"That's a lot of cussing for a pastor," she teased.

He blushed, and she pinched his goatee. "I'm all over you," she whispered. "Give me what I need, Ny. I swear I'll take it so good. I promise I won't scream."

"Yeah, you will," he said.

"I won't, Ny. I won't," she was damn near whining she wanted it so bad. Her hands fumbled at his belt buckle, and she undid his slacks. By the time she got her hands on it, he was ready to burst. She stroked his dick, and the wetness from the pre-cum that rested on his tip astonished her. "You have no idea how neglected my body has been. I love this dick, Nyair. I love what you do to me."

"You have no idea what you're getting yourself into, Lo," he admitted. "I fucked you for hours last night, and it still wasn't enough. I went home and the thought of how good you feel had me out my mind. I wanted more. I'ma keep wanting more."

"What did you do?" she asked, her eyes widening in shock at his confession. "Did you stroke it, Ny? That makes me so wet, just thinking about you stroking your dick."

"Stop, Lo." He was growing weak.

He walked her backward until the back of her feet hit the couch. When he smacked her ass lightly, she knew it meant turn around. He bent her over the arm of the furniture, and when he entered her from behind, she moaned. His dick was so damn satisfying. It was just thick and long and full. He got up under that pussy, beating it slowly while lifting her hips and then lowering her down onto him. He wanted to beast on her, teach her a lesson about showing up without calling, but he knew she wouldn't be able to contain herself if he did, so instead, he fell into slow motions. Nyair was breaking every rule known to his religion, but this pussy was too enticing. She had put a bow on it and dropped it off at his front door. He didn't know how to turn it down, and if he was honest, he didn't want to. She had been right. He had stroked his dick at the thought of her last night, but there was nothing like the real thing. Her warmth. Her wet. So tight. Goddamn.

"Don't run from it," he said. "Take it, baby. Wet this dick up."

He reached around her body and played with her clit while never missing his stroke.

"Fuckkkkkk, Nyair, baby, don't do that like that. Oh my… sssss…" she sucked in air through clenched teeth. "What are you doing? I'ma cum. I'ma cummmmmm; oh my Goddd."

"I know," he whispered. He squeezed her meaty clit while flicking it, and Lauren lost her mind. Why was he strumming her love like this? She was writhing beneath him like a fish out of water because her body was so stimulated. "Save that nut for me. I ain't done eating yet," he whispered. "Come here," he said as he redirected her to the cushion and pulled her thighs to the edge of the seat. He got on his knees and went right back to work, worshiping between her thighs. This woman's work was lethal. He was eating her right into ecstasy. It felt so good, too good. "I taste you, baby; keep cumming." He had different tricks because he was handling her body differently than he had last night, and she couldn't choose a favorite. This orgasm was so strong that she spread her legs further.

You classless, nasty, trashy-ass bitchhhhh! She screamed in her mind as she put one hand around the back of his neck and pulled him in deeper. She wondered if he could even breathe. She was drowning this man, pussy all on his nose. The part of her that couldn't take it pushed him away with the other hand. She didn't know if she was coming or going.

The smug look he glanced up at her with told her that he knew he had destroyed her.

"That's what you came here for, miss lady?" he asked.

KNOCK! KNOCK! KNOCK!

Nyair was reminded where they were, with the interruption at his door.

"Give us a few minutes. We're in worship!" Lauren shouted.

"Pastor, your next appointment canceled," the woman called through the door.

"Give us a bit, Alicia," he called out. "And cancel the rest of my day!"

Lauren sat up breathlessly as they adjusted their clothes.

"I need to know that everything I'm doing to you is of your free will, Lauren. It's important that you say it. I don't want to feel like I'm taking advantage in any way because I want to test your body and your limits in ways I'm sure you haven't experienced before," Nyair said. He was bashful, speaking in a tone so low it felt like a warning. Her breath hitched, and her lips parted slightly in panic.

"In what ways?" She was taken. Mentally enslaved. Emotionally void. Physically bound by the possibilities. Were these ways he spoke of more of what they had been doing? Was he holding back? How could he be? The shit they had been doing was the most pleasurable sex she had experienced in her life. There was more after that?

"I know a whole lot of ways to satisfy you, baby. You got to be willing, though," Nyair said. "And brave."

"I'm brave," she piped up. She sounded like a motherfucking child trying to prove that she could be big and strong.

He smiled and licked his lips at her enthusiasm.

"You're not in your right mind, though," Nyair whispered.

"I'm not," she admitted. "I'm all over the place. Except when I'm with you. When I'm with you, I know exactly where I am." She sat on the arm of the couch, and he towered over her. His hands were in her hair, caressing her face. "I'm going to have to grieve, Ny. I just prefer to do it next to you."

"I shouldn't be compelled by you like this, Lauren," Nyair stated, shaking his head. "Your frame of mind should be a red flag, but it's stunning to me. Your grief is…" He paused as he searched for the right words. The teardrop pooling in the corner of her eyes was like art. The worry lines in her forehead, like sketches under da Vinci's pen. "It's proof that God is an architect, Lo. He's making a masterpiece of you, but it's a messy job, but still so beautiful. You're a work in progress."

"You see God in me?" she asked.

"I feel God in you," he replied. "When I'm inside you, I feel the universe He created inside you. A nigga want to live there, Lauren."

Mind blown. Lauren didn't even know what to say. She just knew what she felt, and she felt like fucking this man. "Nyair, you got to stop talking to me like this," she whispered.

"I'm sorry you're hurting," Nyair said. "I'm sorry you've lost so much."

"Is it possible to find something through the grief?" she asked. She placed a delicate hand to his chest, pausing him as she glanced up and into his eyes. "Someone?"

"Feels like it, don't it?" Nyair asked. She kissed his lips, and the tension and apprehension she felt in his strong back literally melted in her hands. He was so intentional in the way he handled her. This wasn't a leisurely peck. It was a consumption of her soul. This was romance. His hands were everywhere. She leaned back in his arms, and his tongue explored the flavors of her mouth. This type of kissing led to lovemaking that didn't end.

"I need you in my bed," he groaned. "Damn it, woman, it's the middle of a workday."

"So, put in work," she answered. "Take me to your place."

Day walked into the office of Dynasty Records.

"Yo, get me on the phone with that bitch that own the hip-hop tea blog. Why the fuck they keep posting me with this bitch? I told y'all I ain't want no cameras at my nephew funeral," Day barked into the phone as he scrolled through the hundreds of notifications on his phone. Social media had him linked to Kiara Da'vi again. He had been recorded leaving the funeral with her, and then she had posted some cryptic-ass stories, insinuating that they had rolled up the partition on the driver. It must have been a slow news day because social media was eating it up. The fact that Kiara was leaning into it and fanning the flames made it worse. She had even posted the brand-new car Day had given her to add fuel to the fire. The fact that Stassi had liked the blog post made him feel a way. She was letting him know she had seen it without saying a word. She wasn't his girl, but bullshit like this would make it even harder for him to get her to trust him. He was fed the fuck up with the antics, especially when the shit was manufactured. The smell of weed lured him into Demi's office. No way had he expected him to be here. He could tell Demi was a wreck. Demi was a creature of habit. Anytime he felt shit was out of control, he would find solace in work. A blunt to the face and Jeezy's debut album on low while he ran plays in his mind was Demi's routine. A disturbed Demi was a dangerous Demi. He hoped niggas walked straight until the freshness of this loss passed and time made the pain bearable.

"What up, boy? What you doing here?" Day asked.

"Establishing an alibi," Demi answered as he turned slightly in the swivel chair, blowing smoke in the air. "Besides, business don't stop."

"Nah, man. It should stop. It's okay for things to stop for a little while, while you get your mind right, brody," Day sympathized. "And if it's smoke, you know we got that handled. What's this about an alibi?"

"Nothing nobody else needs to handle. I got it. Just wanna make sure my ID badge is scanned in, and these cameras catch me on a loop for the night before I go body me a nigga," Demi stated.

"Why you ain't home with Lo?" Day paused, realizing his misstep. "My bad, I mean, Charlie," Day corrected. "You out here talking about killing niggas and shit. You need to be where your peace is. You're unfocused. Now ain't the time to settle no old debts."

Demi groaned as he sat up and swiped his face in frustration. "Shit's all fucked up, man."

Day sat in the chair across from Demi's desk and reached for the blunt.

Demi passed it and shook his head.

"How bad was it when you made it to the crib?" Day asked.

"Nigga, she put me out," Demi stated. "Put me out my own shit. Figure that."

"That's rough," Day snickered. "You real soft on Charlie girl, my boy. She got you whipped."

"I'm too old for this shit. Lo ain't bring a nigga these kind of headaches," Demi stated.

"Young pussy, young problems. That insecurity a mu'fucka," Day stated. "But she got a point. She ain't coming from left field with the shit."

Demi frowned. Men could be so obtuse when they wanted to be. Day continued. "I can't lie. With everything that's going on, you and Lo been looking like the good old days. I never knew y'all to be anything other than a great team. Y'all were 'that couple' for a long time."

"Lo's a partner in life, man. The shit is hard to explain. I thought that part of my life was over. I thought Charlie could be that, but Lo was more than my wife. She was literally 50/50 with me on everything but the street shit. If I made the deals, she followed up with the paperwork and the enforcement, you feel me? From everything like a nigga dentist appointment to seven-figure brand deals. She made the home complete, but she covered a nigga whole life too. From these events to networking with these fake-ass niggas in the industry, to making sure the suits were pressed each week and the guns locked tight and cleaned in the safe. She was just my partner, man. That's all I can sum it up as. I lost my wife…this week, my partner needed me."

"And Charlie can't be that?" Day asked.

"Charlie only needs to be one thing," Demi stated matter-of-factly. "She don't got to do anything else except keep a nigga heart in those hands. She wants to be all over the place, doing what Lo do, competing cuz she thinks that's what a nigga expect. I had that kind of wife. I left that kind of wife. I want her, but I can't just ignore all that I owe to Lo. She's not my romantic partner anymore, but we partners in this loss. We in debt on this shit together, and Charlie's young. Her feelings so fucking soft, man. She can't really understand where I'm coming from."

"One woman only being able to give one thing sound like a woman that's easily replaced," Day stated. "I can see why she's intimidated by Lo."

"Nah, my nigga. I don't want her hands in a million places. She only needs to be an expert on me. Keep them hands on me. I'ma handle everything else for her. I want her to live the softest fucking existence in life, on God. Her and my baby. They won't ever have to worry."

"Damn," Day stated. It was all he could say. He couldn't relate and didn't want to ever be that in love. That type of love scared him. That type of love was risky. That type of love had a rich-ass nigga sitting in the dark, putting one in the air after hours instead of falling into the next option. Whipped. His homie was whipped. Demi was a grieving father and a whipped-ass nigga. Day never thought he would see the day.

"So, it would be a bad time to ask you to get Charlie on board for a showcase with Da'vi, huh?" Day asked.

"She's pregnant," Demi said, frowning.

"She can't sing while she pregnant, my nigga?" Day countered. "I ain't gon' overwork your girl. That's my niece or nephew growing in there, but the public loves to be a part of them nine months. If she goes ghost, she gon' lose her momentum."

"I'm fighting for my life over here, and you talking about a performance," Demi groaned.

"We all need a distraction," Day said. "This last week felt like it ripped a nigga stomach out. We can host the Dynasty Brunch and add a cause to it in honor of DJ. Maybe something tied to mental health in children. Find a worthy foundation, get all these industry niggas to come out they pockets and donate. We can't change what happened to nephew, but we can honor him, and maybe prevent it from happening to the next kid. Raise some awareness. Have you and Lo talk about it. Nobody talks about shit like this, dawg. I thought cutting was some white shit, to be honest. His death doesn't have to be for nothing, bro."

Demi leaned onto his knees, pushing the rolling executive chair back slightly. He squeezed the ducts of his eyes with two fingers as he held back emotion.

Day was silent. He knew to remain still. He couldn't say or do anything, or else Demi may flee.

"Set it up," Demi stated simply. "All of it. The interviews. The promoting Charlie's pregnancy. The showcase. The foundation. I'm with it. Put Stassi on it."

"I was thinking Lo, give her something to put her mind on," Day responded.

"Stassi will get Charlie on board. If I put Lauren in Charlie's face one more time, a nigga never coming home," Demi said. "It's too sensitive right now. Put her sister on it."

"Consider it done. You want me to have flowers sent? You know that's the first step to an apology, my G. The money flowers always a nice touch."

"It's gonna take a lot more than that this time," Demi stated, shaking his head. "I really fucked up."

Patience was a virtue when you were stalking prey. Demi sat inside Justin's crib for hours, waiting for him to arrive. He had left his car parked at the studio. His phone had been left there as well, so that it could bounce off the cell towers, marking his presence. These were necessary precautions in case he lost control tonight. He had borrowed a car from his mans who ran a chop shop to transport him to this place on this dark night. A hoodie had concealed his identity from any neighborhood cameras that may have picked up his presence. He tried to reason with himself and tell himself that all he needed to do was teach Justin a lesson, but the longer he sat there, the more he thought of the bruises on Charlie's face, the heftier the fine became.

He knew Justin would walk in late, after a set, more than likely. He lived a night owl's lifestyle. It didn't matter. Demi wouldn't grow tired. It had killed him to see Charlie's face bruised and he would wait all night to avenge that. He wasn't a fool, however. The confrontation at the club had been put in a police report. He had to be careful about the way he moved, and he needed to have his alibi airtight. Justin had probably swept the incident under the rug, but Demi had been brewing.

He saw the glow of headlights as a car pulled into the driveway, and he moved to the edge of the couch. He sat, legs wide, elbows meeting knees, gun gripped in one hand. Justin entered the door unsuspectingly. He closed and locked it behind him. It was the lock that would fuck him up. He had just trapped himself inside with a monster. When he flicked on the living room light, Demi flipped his hood back and stared Justin in the eyes. Justin turned to pull the door open, trying to run, but that lock…oh, that lock. The millisecond it took for him to turn it was all it took for Demi to be on his ass. He yanked Justin backward by his collar and then dragged him across the room, kicking and screaming before he shoved him onto the couch.

"If you scream, I'ma blow your fucking head off," Demi said calmly.

"Man, you got it. I'm done with it. I don't want no trouble, man. I didn't touch her. I haven't seen Charlie in years," Justin admitted. "I lied, man, just to get under your skin. I lied!"

"If you fucked my bitch, that ain't my bitch," Demi said. "And that's her pussy, so that's her business. She gets to decide how to slang that. That's neither here nor there. But them marks you put on her face? That's my business, and I'ma square that business, my nigga."

The look of dread that crossed Justin's face amused Demi. "Nothing to say? You said a lot the other night at the club. I told you them cuffs wasn't gon' hold me," Demi stated.

"Please, man. I'm sorry. I'll leave it alone. I'll never go near her again. I'll apologize," Justin stammered.

"Put your motherfucking hands on the table," Demi barked suddenly. He snatched Justin out of his seat, forcing him to his knees.

"Please, man! Please!" Justin begged.

"You fucking with the wrong nigga," Demi whispered in his ear as he hovered over Justin, digging the gun into the back of his skull. Demi pulled a driver's license out of his back pocket and tossed it on the table in front of Justin. "Who is that?" he asked as he pushed Justin's head down violently. His eyes were so close to the table that he couldn't quite get a glimpse at it.

"I don't know! I don't know!" Justin cried. He was shaking so badly.

"Nah, nigga. You wanted to bait me when you thought it was safe. Had some heat on your chest with them officers around. Where your heat, nigga?" Demi asked. "You put your hands on her. You must have lost your mind. You lucky that license is the only thing I felt like taking. Could have been her life. Look at it, pussy."

Demi eased up enough for Justin to lift his head to view the license. His mother's license. The one she had told him that she must have misplaced.

"I'ma let you keep your life, nigga, but I'ma take that hand you play with, and if you breathe a motherfucking word of this to anybody, I'ma use that address. You hear me?" Demi asked.

Justin was so terrified he peed himself.

Demi rounded the table and placed the tip of his gun next the Justin's hand.

"Please, man. My hand is my life," Justin sniveled, his lip trembling violently. "I'm sorry. I'll do anything, man. Demi knew he played with that hand. He also knew it was the hand he hit Charlie with because it was his dominant one. "Don't shoot me. You'll never hear from me again. I'll never bother Charlie again."

Demi smiled like he was a good guy and a change of heart had come over him. "I ain't gon' shoot you, man, relax."

Justin felt some relief as he trembled. "Come on, man, get up. I just want you to apologize. I just needed to put some fear in you. Come take a seat at the table. I'ma call Charlie and you gon' tell her you're sorry."

"Yeah, man, whatever you say. I really am sorry. I swear I am. I'm sorry," Justin repeated as Demi walked him into the kitchen. Demi pulled out a chair.

"Sit down, man," Demi said. "I ain't got my phone. Call Charlie, put her on speaker."

Justin pulled out his phone and made the mistake of dialing Charlie's number. The fact that he even still had it stored in his phone infuriated Demi. Demi grabbed the hammer he had found in the drawers before Justin arrived, and he brought it down over Justin's hand.

The scream Justin let out was animalistic as his bones shattered. Demi gripped Justin's hand by the wrist, forcing him to withstand every blow as he beat that hammer into Justin's hand with all his might. He didn't stop until he was sure that the hand was irreparable. Demi had not only taken his hand, but he had also taken his dream. Justin would never be able to play his guitar professionally again.

"Lucky I ain't take your life, pussy. Consider us square. Breathe a word of this, and I'ma put that address to use," Demi said. "I'm up two. I have to come back again, and I'ma finish the game." He didn't need to wipe the hammer down because he wore gloves. He simply tossed it on the floor as he flipped the hoodie over his face, tying it tightly to conceal himself as he walked out the back door.

Bitch-ass nigga, Demi thought.

Stassi scrolled through the comments on the popular blog, and she couldn't help but be in her feelings. Receipts of Day and Kiara Da'vi's "budding romance," as Black social media was dubbing it, made her feel foolish. One of the cars he had purchased had been gifted to the singer, and pictures of them were circulating online. She clicked out of the phone and put it face down on the countertop. "Fuck him," she said aloud. The timer on her oven went off, and she looked around the kitchen in satisfaction. The aroma of the homemade meal filled the air. She thanked God that she knew how to cook. She didn't do it often, but when she did it, she did it well. Years of helping her mama cater to different men before she finally married Charlie's dad, gave her some know-how around a kitchen. She could burn a little bit. The fresh flowers on the table and the formal place settings were appropriate to feed a man. One thing her mama taught her was not to feed a man off of a paper plate, so Stassi pulled out the real dishes for Grayson. She would regret it later when she fucked up her manicure washing them. She didn't want to set the wrong vibe for the night, so she opted out of a candle on the table. She would keep it casual. The doorbell rang, and she took off her apron and stopped in front of the mirror by her front door to make sure she hadn't spilled anything on her dress. She looked cute, but not too cute. A taupe sweater dress gave off the impression that she was comfortable in her own home and that she hadn't tried too hard, even though she had spent an hour trying hard as hell to pick the shit out. Her makeup was subtle. Her hair curled and swept up lazily in a clip. She left out just enough of a side bang to sweep behind her ear occasionally. Stassi liked Grayson. Surprisingly, she liked him a lot. She didn't realize how much until she found herself overthinking all day to prepare for this evening.

 She opened the door and smiled as she took Grayson in. Handsome-ass, traditional-ass man. He was clad in denim and a sweater with a nice Chelsea boot. She wondered if he had changed three times like she did or if this was effortless. He held a plant in one hand and a bottle of wine in the other.

 "Most men choose flowers. I'd like to linger in your thoughts a little longer than that, give you something that grows. I don't know if that's corny or not, but my grandmama told me to always choose plants instead of flowers," he explained.

"Not corny at all," she quipped as she took it from his hands. "Thank you." She stepped aside. "Come on in."

He stepped inside, and she closed the door, turning the lock before placing the plant on her living room table.

"Nice place," he complimented, looking around. "And the food smells amazing. My stomach literally just growled."

She laughed. "Good because one thing I haven't mastered is how to make small portions, so I hope you brought a big appetite."

"Yes, ma'am, I brought that," he chuckled.

It was the small things like his manners that charmed her. Her experience with hood niggas had lacked that. This felt so normal, but it wasn't the norm at all. Where Day almost love-bombed her with extravagance and over-the-top gifts, it almost felt like he thought she was for sale. His money could easily influence her will—or so he thought. Something as simple as a plant felt valuable because it took some thought to execute. A cheap plant measured up against the car, in her mind.

She motioned for the table, and Grayson walked to one of the chairs and pulled it out for her.

See. Mannerable as fuck, she thought.

She sat, and then he took his seat. He surprised her and sat at the chair beside her instead of rounding the table to sit across from her.

She wasn't surprised when he lowered his head for a quick beat to say a silent blessing of the food. She took note and did the same. It was a step she normally skipped, but she liked that he didn't.

He rubbed his hands together and said, "Okay, I don't know where to start."

"Let me," she said. She fixed his plate and then fixed her own. "Now, don't get used to this."

"I'll consider it a privilege every time, miss lady," he responded.

"Good, because this took me hours." She laughed.

She picked up his fork and cut it through the roast. She had to use her free hand to catch the drippings as she lifted it to his mouth for a taste. He took it in, and instantly, his face melted into satisfaction as he nodded his head.

"Aww man, that's good," he complimented. She smiled in satisfaction.

"Yeah?" she asked.

"Nah, like for real, for real. It's good as hell," he confirmed. She beamed. It felt like the nigga had given her a gold star. She handed him the fork. "Well, dig in," she invited.

Grayson ate her food like he hadn't eaten all day, and she felt pride in watching him enjoy the meal. She had always hated to cook, but watching someone be so appreciative after slaving over the stove, really did feel purposeful. She kind of understood why some women loved to do it.

"Did you save any lives today?" she asked playfully.

"We had a fire on the Eastside. Somebody thought it would be fun to set an abandoned building on fire. The building is known to have homeless people inside this time of year. Pulled out one of the neighborhood winos. The shit people do never surprise me. Just destroy their own neighborhoods for nothing," he said.

"Oh, wow. I was joking, but you really did save a life today," she said.

He chuckled. "It's not like that every day. Yesterday I did a dry run to an old lady's house who calls 911 every time she gets lonely. Makes up a different emergency every time. Said she smelled gas. When we got there, nothing was wrong. We stuck around for a few hours. Fixed her sink, changed the light bulbs, and shit. She just likes to talk."

Stassi swooned. "That's kind of superhero shit, too, Grayson," she said, chuckling. "Might not be exciting, but I'm sure that old lady really appreciates it. She probably doesn't have anyone else to call that she knows will come."

"I guess you're right," he said. "Never thought of it like that." He reached for the bottle of wine and stood. "Do you mind if I grab an opener?"

She folded her hands under her chin and rested her elbows on the table. "Sure, it's on the counter."

He filled her glass and then his own. "I don't know a lot about wine. The lady at *Cooper's Hawk* said this was a good choice, though."

More effort. This man had put out a fire and had still taken the time to stop at a plant shop and a wine shop before coming to her door.

She picked up the glass and took a sip. "She didn't lie," Stassi said. "Tell me why you're single. Or am I assuming that? Are you single? Cuz niggas be lying these days. You could be here with me and have a wife or girlfriend waiting for you at home."

"Man, that seems like a lot of lies to keep up with. Niggas really have that type of time on their hands?" he asked.

"You would be surprised," she answered.

He shook his head. "I'm single, Stassi," he said. "My job makes it real hard to date. Women aren't typically patient with me on that. It's a lot of overnights, a lot of interrupted dates, and missed moments because I'm a first responder. I work a lot of holidays. It can be a lot, I guess. What about you?" he asked as he raised his glass to his lips.

"I had a thing that I thought could be something, but men play a lot of games. I'm not quite sure where that stands, if I'm honest," she said. "It's still kind of fresh."

"You're playing the same type of games you hate it sounds like."

"I mean, am I? I like for things to be clear. Like, if we're dating and you don't want me to date anyone else, say that. That's the type of time I'm on. Men sometimes do all the things that scream relationship, and then as soon as you start to feel like you're important, they act like you're not in a relationship. The guessing games get exhausting."

"So, the last guy you liked fucked up, basically," Grayson presumed.

"He just sends mixed messages, and now I'm here cooking for you," she said, shrugging her shoulders. She raised her glass. "To keeping shit clear."

"To keeping it clear," he replied, tapping her glass with his own.

The wine made Stassi loose, and her head spun a little.

"It's strong, right?" Grayson noticed her eyes had lowered a bit.

"It's so good. It sneaks up on you."

He turned in his chair so that he was facing her. "Definitely," he chuckled. "I appreciate all this."

"Yeah, no problem. I have something you can wrap this up in if you want to take the rest down to the station for the rest of the guys," she said.

"Should I take that as my cue to wrap this up?" he asked.

Her eyes widened in alarm. "Oh my God, no!" she said, laughing. "No," she repeated sternly. "I'm having a really good time. Are you not? Are you, like looking for a reason to duck out?"

"Not gon' lie. A little bit," he said. She covered her mouth with one hand, and her eyes widened.

"Oh my Godddd. That's so bold!" she exclaimed, laughing.

"Nah, I'm bullshitting. I'm bullshitting," he said, joining in her laughter. "This is smooth. Not too much pressure. Good food. Easy conversation. It's a good night."

"Go easier on me, Grayson. My heart can't take too much rejection," she teased.

The conversation was easy, and Stassi appreciated that there was no pressure to this date. The comfort of her home made her feel like she was in control—home court advantage and such.

"I think I'm the one who should be worried about rejection."

Stassi leaned against the back of her chair and faced him. Her thighs were between his as they stared at one another.

"Why don't we just make some rules to this thing right here and now? That way, we're on the same page, and nobody ends up feeling a way," she said.

"A dating contract?" he asked.

"An understanding," she corrected.

"I like that. Let's do it," he agreed.

"Rule one," she started. "We will be honest with each other, even when it's hard."

He nodded and refilled their glasses.

"Well, that works for me, but you've already started off bad on that. Your word ain't good," he said.

She frowned and jerked her neck back. "I ain't even known you long enough to have had the opportunity to lie," she said.

"Well, you did," he said, shrugging nonchalantly.

She was so offended that she placed her glass down. "What are you talking about?" Stassi asked.

"It was you who said I could choose my menu tonight, right? Have whatever I wanted," he said.

"Nigga, I know you not talking about me substituting the cabbage for greens. The store was out of cabbage, and that's petty," she argued. She looked around the table at a loss for words, trying to figure out what she hadn't delivered. "And a little ungrateful. Do you know how long it took me to cook this? What else do you want to eat?"

He leaned into her space. "Wouldn't mind tasting you. If we are following rule number one and keeping it honest."

Stassi forgot to exhale. She was speechless. Her cheeks warmed, and she just knew they were red, giving away her embarrassment. She bit her bottom lip as his hand trailed up her thigh. Her chest heaved in anticipation as he reached her panties. He slid her panties aside, and a slight hint of recognition flashed across his face when his finger connected with the silky wetness between her legs. He found her clit and then trailed that finger down her slit before pulling his hand back. As if he had just swiped his finger through a freshly iced cake, he put it in his mouth. Her whole pussy jolted as he tasted her.

"Ain't nothing left to do after that, but fuck," she said.

The laugh that erupted from him was contagious and she laughed too.

"I'm patient. I just wanted a sample. Give me something to look forward to," Grayson said, smiling. "Don't want to apply no pressure."

"A little pressure might be okay. Likeee, so a little dick would definitely be something I'd overthink in the morning, but a little head, I wouldn't even think twice about," she said playfully.

"A little head, huh?" he shot back in amusement as he got down on his knees. She pinched her fingers together.

"I'm just saying, if you want to give your compliments to the chef. That's the currency I heard she accepts," Stassi said.

He lowered his head and lifted her dress, pooling it around her belly. He pulled her panties between her slit and shook his head as she wet the fabric.

"A woman's body is amazing. You know how inaccessible water is? And you make it. Like magic. All a man got to do is know how to turn the faucet on." His baritone was laced with lust as he pulled her panties down, removing them. It was his pace. He didn't rush. He was eager but not thirsty. He made her wait for his touch, and it was torture. She felt every nerve ending on her body as it begged for attention. Her clit pulsed. She could feel it jumping all over the place. He had her in a desperate way. He pulled her onto the edge of the chair and lowered his head to blow gently on her clit. The sensation of cool air against her wet center made her clit pebble hard. "Pretty as hell everywhere," he complimented.

The knock at the door was like an alarm clock crashing into a wet dream.

"What the entire fuck?" she shouted in frustration as he lowered her dress.

"You expecting someone?" he asked.

"Not at all," she fussed. She stood, practically stomping her way to the door in protest. She was pretty sure he was about to deliver the best fucking head of her life, and the moment had been ruined.

Grayson took a seat on the couch as she went to the door.

When she peeked out the peephole, her heart sank. Day stood outside her door, hands in his pockets, waiting impatiently like the arrogant asshole he was.

"Anastassia, open the door. I know you're home. The car I bought you is sitting right out front."

"Shit," she whispered, shaking her head as she glanced back at Grayson. He stood.

She didn't know why her heart was racing. She felt like she had been busted; like she was caught up, cheating on her man.

"I'ma let you handle your business," Grayson said as he picked up his phone and wallet from the table.

"No, you don't have to leave. I want you here," she said. "Just give me a second."

Fuck that, I don't owe his ass no explanation, she thought. She pulled open the door, and instead of inviting him inside, she stepped into the hallway.

"You need to leave, Day," she said, crossing her arms and side-stepping him as he tried to reach for her.

"You know I can't really figure out the hold you have over me," Day said. He shifted nervously and stared down at his Prada boots before meeting her glower.

Stassi scoffed. "You're so full of shit. You barely spoke to me at the funeral, and then you left with someone else. I ain't heard from you. You're so hot and fucking cold, and I don't have time…"

"That was business," he said.

"Sure, business," she answered.

"I fuck with you, Anastassia," Day said.

"What does that mean? Do you even know?" she asked.

"Man, why we doing this out here? Can we go inside and argue? You can cuss a nigga out. I can say I'm sorry, and I can proceed with making you call a nigga name," Day stated. His arrogance was such a fucking turn-on. "Because we both know where our fights lead to. A nigga fight with your ass on purpose just to get to that." He backed her against the door. "Nothing happened with me and Da'vi. My head is fucked up. I lost my nephew. I just want to be under you for a minute. Or inside you. Just let me, Anastassia. Let's just fuck and forget the world."

"No, Day," she said, putting her hand to his chest and

softly pushing him away. "No."

He stepped back, and she could see his bruised ego. The audacity for him to be confused pissed Stassi clean off. "Go and play with somebody else, Day. Like, for real. You think I didn't see the little blog post about the car you gave that girl? She posted it, and the blogs ate it up. She posted you or what looked like a silhouette of you. I don't know. I'm sure she snuck the picture, but it was you. You're there, you're here, and who knows who else is in rotation. Nigga, you out here everywhere. And I'm not interested. You can have the car back…"

"Don't play with me. Ain't nobody taking no fucking car back from you, Anastassia. That girl is business. She just wants a little clout. I'm not fucking her. I haven't fucked her. Damn near don't even like the girl," Day said. Neither Stassi nor Day could believe he was even doing all this explaining.

"Doesn't even matter. You clearly don't like me either," she responded.

The door opened behind her, and she ceased to exist. Somebody may as well have dug a grave because she died in that very spot. Grayson emerged from her place.

"Stassi, I'ma go. Just want to make sure you're good," Grayson said.

"Fuck is this nigga, man?" Day asked.

"You don't have to go," Stassi said.

"Nah, bruh, you should. Like now, before shit get thick, dawg," Day stated in irritation.

Grayson scoffed. He wasn't moved or intimidated, but Stassi prayed that Day had left his gun in the car. She didn't see an ounce of bitch in Grayson, and she knew exactly how

Day got down. This could go bad quickly. "Rule number one," Grayson said to Stassi. "When you wrap this up, you know where to find me. But before I go, are you good here?"

"If she ain't good, I promise you can't do shit about it," Day stated. "Get the fuck gone, nigga, before I lose my shit out here."

"I'm fine, and I'm so sorry," she said, stepping between them. "I'm so sorry. I promise I'll call you later once I handle this."

"Thank you for dinner." He kissed her cheek and then walked by Day, stopping in front of him. "Might wanna look a nigga up before you let your temper get you into something you can't get out of." With that, he left. He was a grown-ass man. No need to beef with Day. No need to cause a scene. He didn't even seem upset. He just left them to handle what was clearly a pressing situation.

"He's a fucking city official, Day! What the fuck is wrong with you? Popping up here! Causing a scene? After the shit you pulled at the funeral?"

"I don't give a fuck who that nigga is. You fucking him?" Day asked. "Cuz I promise, I'm taking issue with any nigga falling in that. It's that good, my baby, and that's how I'm coming behind it."

Stassi hated that his toxic ass turned her on. She had just been entertaining a perfect gentleman, but God, this street shit made her wet.

"Let me be clear with you, Day. I like you. I may have even thought I had feelings for you, but every time I let my guard down, you fuck up. So, nah, we're not doing this."

"It's just a lifestyle, Stassi. It's not real. The shit is smoke and mirrors. I'm a rapper and a music mogul. It's gon' be a lot of speculation. You got to be able to handle that."

"I can't handle it. I'm telling you now. So, let's just not. You have a good night, Day," Stassi said, shaking her head. "And thanks for ruining mine."

"Proudly ruined that shit," Day stated unapologetically. "Corny-ass nigga. Sleep tight. Good and lonely. Let me know when you done being mad. Stubborn ass."

She was annoyed that he was annoyed because how dare he feel a way about a game he started.

He walked into her space and gripped her face, kissing her lips. "I swear you give me a fucking headache, Anastassia. Fix your attitude."

"Nah, how about you fix your fucked-up actions that's making me catch an attitude," she shouted. He backpedaled and then pushed out of the door that led to the stairwell. He was too mad to even wait for the elevator. She shook her head. Her life was a mess, and she knew she would have to hold on tight to her boundaries because Day had a way of finessing her. He was so charming, so good at seduction. She wanted him. Even now. Even still. She knew all it took was a night in his bed to make her feel better, but she needed more from him. She needed consistency, and she wasn't even sure if he was capable of that. A man like Grayson stood on that. No way was she settling for less.

CHAPTER 16

I need you to burn me, baby.

Charlie's insides ached as she heard his voice play in her head. She missed Demi terribly. Being apart felt like the worst form of pain, and she wondered if she was torturing herself more than she was torturing Demi. Charlie knew that feeling sad without Demi wasn't a good enough reason to go back to him. The end of a relationship was supposed to hurt. She knew that much.

I just have to get through this, she thought. *It will get better with time.*

At least it was supposed to. That's what all the self-help bullshit said. She didn't quite understand how life would ever be okay without him. She loved him that much. She wondered if he was doing okay. She wondered where he was and who he was with. These were all questions he would willingly answer, but Charlie was too stubborn to call. She wanted him to think that she didn't care. She wanted him to feel unimportant like she had for the past few weeks.

The nausea that plagued her was crippling, and she wished he was here to baby her. She knew he would give her everything her heart desired. Even before she had gotten pregnant, Demi spoiled her endlessly. Neck rubs and foot massages, randomly. Serving her. Coddling her. Eating her. Affirming her. His obsession with all things Charlie made her feel like a queen. She needed that attention right now. On a day when it took great effort to hold herself up in the shower, she needed it badly. She had no idea it took so much work to bring a child into the world. She was used to beautiful, brown bellies and balloon arches at baby showers. The maternity pictures and over-the-top celebrations covered up the pure hell women went through during those 40 weeks. She would be 12 weeks in a few days, and she couldn't wait to be out of the danger zone. Her OB had told her that her chances for miscarriage dropped drastically at the 12-week mark and her nausea should ease some, so she was eagerly counting the days.

    Charlie was struggling, and she was too damn mad at everybody to ask for help. Demi was on her shit list. Lauren, she just hated, and although she knew it was unwarranted, she just couldn't shake the jealousy she felt whenever Lauren was around. It was almost an admiration. Lauren was just everything that Charlie wished she could be. She was successful, driven, smart, tough, and so damn graceful. It was the respect that Demi had for Lauren that made Charlie admire her most. Lauren had done and said a lot of bullshit over the years regarding Demi and Charlie, but Demi still put her on a pedestal. He still viewed her as someone he looked up to. Charlie would never have that part of him. His respect was impossible to earn. She had no idea that his love was just as hard to receive. He had spoiled her by giving it away to her so freely. At first sight, and at first listen, Demi had emptied his pockets like she had stuck him up. She had robbed him of his heart, and she took that for granted. Demi was a hard, reluctant, untrusting, and unyielding man. He wasn't soft on anyone, but that's all he could be with Charlie. She couldn't see it, though, because she was too busy comparing what he gave her to what he gave to Lauren. Hell, she compared the energy everyone gave to Lauren.

Even my own sister took her side, Charlie thought. The self-pity was high. Charlie had a bone to pick with everybody. She wasn't asking the people she loved to leave Lauren high and dry. She just wanted them not to forget her.

I just want to be there too. It's like my feelings don't even count, she thought. She found herself walking toward DJ's room. It was cryptic to push open the door. It was like a museum to Demi's dead son, and the lump that suddenly formed in her throat seemed to suffocate her. She just felt like crying. The thought of DJ made her emotional in ways she couldn't quite explain. She sat on his bed, and her eyes fell on the book she had never gotten the chance to gift him.

My Big Brother & Me

It was a journal that Charlie had gotten made for DJ to try and get him excited about the possibility of having a sibling. She flipped open the page and stared at the ultrasound picture she had taped on the inside cover.

To DJ, my big brother. I can't wait to meet you. Our daddy tells me about you every night. I'm so glad that God decided to bring us together. You're going to be the best big brother ever. I love you already.

Tears spilled from her eyes. She had never gotten a chance to give it to him. DJ had never even gotten a chance to connect with the idea of their family growing. She had been confident that a new baby would be what was needed to make him start to see her as family. No, she wasn't his parent, but Charlie still felt this loss. Nobody even cared that she was hurting, too.

I can tell him myself, she thought. She had to do something with this guilt. She may not have been welcome to express her sorrow at the funeral, but she could visit him. That wouldn't hurt anyone, would it? She grabbed her keys and coat and then rushed out with a newfound determination. It was freezing outside, but Charlie trudged through the snow and ice anyway. She had been so secluded from the services that she didn't even know where DJ was buried. She called Stassi and waited anxiously for her sister to answer.

"Where have you been? I've been calling you!" Stassi shouted as soon as she picked up the call.

"You know why I'm not fucking with you," Charlie said.

"Charlie, what was I supposed to-"

"Don't make me regret calling you by defending your bullshit," Charlie interrupted.

Stassi sucked her teeth and sighed. "I'm just saying, it's a tough situation. You're my sister, and I love you, but…"

"Just tell me where DJ's grave is, Stassi. If you want to make it up to me, do that. Everybody got to say goodbye except for me."

"Where's Demi? Why can't he take you?" Stassi asked.

"I kicked Demi out," she revealed.

The line went silent.

"Hello?" Charlie shouted.

"Charlie, you're going to break that man," Stassi whispered.

"Since when do you even care?" Charlie asked as she drove. Stassi had been anti-Demi their entire relationship. This new advocacy was strange.

"I don't know, but doesn't a dead kid make everything else seem insignificant? I mean, you're carrying his child, Charlie. You're probably all he has left," Stassi reasoned.

"He didn't act like it," Charlie replied softly.

"I just sent you the address and the directions to DJ's marker. Do you want me to meet you there?" Stassi asked.

"Thanks, Stass. No, I'm good," Charlie replied.

"I understand why you're mad; just remember the circumstances," Stassi added. "Call me later. I love you."

"I love you, too."

It didn't surprise Charlie that DJ's grave was only twenty minutes from their home. She could see Demi insisting that he be buried close. She grabbed the book from her passenger seat and climbed out of the car. The snow was above her ankles as she made her way across the lawn until she found DJ's resting place.

The magnitude of his death overwhelmed her as she stared at his tombstone.

The most loving son, Charlie read the words on his marker silently as her eyes watered.

She leaned down and placed the book in front of his grave, leaning it on his name.

"I'm so sorry, DJ. I wish I had tried harder to connect with you. I wish I got to know you more. I wish you knew that I loved you. I never told you because it didn't feel like that was okay, or that you would be comfortable receiving that from me, but you were a very cool kid." She scoffed and smiled. "You made your daddy so happy and so proud. I loved how light he was whenever you were around. I wish you were here to see your baby sister. I'll make sure this baby knows you. So many people miss you, DJ. I miss you. And I'm sorry. I'm sorry I hurt you this much."

The sound of crunching snow pulled her attention, and Charlie turned to find Lauren pulling next to her car.

She rolled her eyes. "Great," she mumbled as she pulled her coat tighter and watched Lauren approach.

"What are you doing here?" Lauren asked.

"I was just paying my respects," Charlie said. "I'm leaving, don't worry."

Lauren sighed and shook her head. "You can stay; it's fine." Lauren noticed the book and picked it up.

"I bought it before all this happened. It just felt right to still give it to him," Charlie explained.

Lauren nodded and placed the book back.

"He would have really loved being a big brother," Lauren admitted.

"Even if the baby came from me?" Charlie asked. "I was

kind of afraid he'd hate us both."

Lauren laughed. "I would have hated you both. He would have loved you both. He tried to love you," Lauren whispered. "I think he tried hard not to like you because he knew it would hurt me. That was unfair to you. To him, too. Thank you for coming to see him. I worry that now that the funeral is over, I'm going to be the only one to remember him."

"Demi will never forget him, Lo," Charlie whispered passionately. "He could never forget him. That boy was his world."

Lauren nodded because if she spoke, she would cry, and she didn't want to cry again.

"I feel like karma is hitting me right now," Charlie whispered. "I broke up your marriage only for Demi to come right back to you. In the big moments of his life, he's going to run back to you. That's the price I have to pay for dealing with a married-ass man in the first place. You have the power to take him back, and now I'm pregnant and terrified to raise this baby alone."

"It feels great to have Demi's support, Charlie. I won't lie to you about that part, but he doesn't want me, and I don't want him. I do want him in my life, though. I do want to make sure we keep our son's memory relevant. I don't want him to go away like DJ never existed."

"I don't want that either," Charlie whispered.

"So how do we make this work?" Lauren asked.

Charlie scoffed. "I don't think you understand how hard it is to watch you with him. Neither of you understand. It's like you don't see how perfect the picture looks."

"Charlie the picture is bullshit. It looks perfect because we practiced that shit for a lot of years!" Lauren shouted in exasperation. Lauren knew how to pull her shit together. She knew how to make a bitch jealous. She knew how to make the public buy a story, and how to set the table of her life so that she never looked deprived. She put on productions for a living. She and Demi's entire marriage had been a long public performance. They had safeguarded it from the media for years. Of course, they looked good together. It didn't mean they should be together, but she understood how it appeared to the outsiders. "Putting on a front. Never letting the media see us crack. Marriage is a business, and we handled our shit very well. I know how to operate in that space with Demi. I know how to handle our business. But the passion. The shit that takes your breath away. We never had that, and I want that. He has that with you, and you're talking about some shit that's hard to watch. That is what's hard to witness. And Demi ain't coming up off you, so that fear of raising this baby alone? You might as well save that one because he's not that type of man."

"I just don't know about him," Charlie said. "I don't like feeling like I'm measuring up behind you."

"That sounds like a Charlie problem. Not a Demi problem," Lauren said, shrugging.

Charlie felt like she would be sick. "This is all just too much."

The look of sympathy Lauren gave Charlie made Charlie feel pathetic.

"Come on. It's freezing out here. Have you eaten? You literally look green in the face."

"I can't stomach anything," Charlie replied, hopelessly.

"I was like that. I've got a recipe that got me through my whole pregnancy. I'll follow you home and make sure you're settled before I leave."

Charlie hesitated. "Why would you help me?"

Lauren shrugged and shook her head. "I handle his business," Lauren replied. "I don't know, Charlie. Damn, I guess…" she paused, and Charlie saw emotion in Lauren's eyes. "You're carrying my son's sibling and I…"

"Don't want to be left out," Charlie finished for her. The ways women related to each other even when they didn't want to was remarkable. Charlie could have given Lauren a taste of her own medicine, but she knew how bitter it was. She knew how hurtful it would be. "I'd really appreciate the recipe, Lo."

Lauren nodded, and the pair walked back to their cars before heading back to Charlie's house.

***

Nyair knocked on the office door of his mentor. Pastor Cullian was well respected in the community. For as far back as Nyair could remember, Pastor Cullian had been the revered figure in the city. Everyone from the local dope boys to the city council members relied on this man for counsel. He was their elder, and he had taught Nyair a lot about himself, about God, and about the responsibility that his position held in the city. When Nyair had gotten lost in the past, when he had been consumed in an artificial world of money and fame, Pastor Cullian had pulled him out. If it weren't for him, Nyair was sure he would be dead.

"I'm in trouble, sir," he said as soon as the pastor opened the door.

"Nothing a long conversation and the good Lord can't straighten out, son. Come on in," the man said as he shook Nyair's hand. The firm hand and reassuring squeeze to Ny's shoulder made Nyair feel like crying. This man was fatherly. He came with wisdom and a soothing that only God could put inside you. Nyair represented that for a lot of people. It was a great privilege, to stand in their role, but Nyair couldn't help but feel like a fraud.

"What's going on with you, young man?" Pastor Cullian asked. Nyair would always be 'young man' to this elder. He had watched him grow up. He had witnessed his rise and his fall, but most importantly, he had never judged.

"I'm messing up, Pastor. I need to know if I can continue to be a vessel because it's feeling like I'm not worthy," Nyair admitted.

"Let's start with what happened," the old man replied.

"There's a woman," Nyair started.

"There is always a woman," Pastor Cullian said knowingly, chuckling to himself.

"You told me a long time ago that the devil doesn't come to you with his horns out," Nyair said. "I'm slipping. She's literally a temptation that I can't say no to. I've tried. She overpowers everything I know I'm supposed to say and do. I don't want to be the pastor that my congregation can't trust.

I don't want to be the one they whisper about and call a hypocrite. She's a problem for me."

"What is it about her that you can't turn down? And don't tell me it's her looks because you've had your share and your pick of beautiful women. What's bringing her to your doorstep?" the man asked.

"Her grief," Nyair said instantly. "She's needy. She makes me feel..."

"Like you have the power to fix it," the man finished for him. "Fix her. What is she grieving?"

"The loss of her son," Nyair said.

"She's made you her God, son. You can't become a false idol," the man warned. "There is sin in that for the worshiper and the worshipped, and if you're leading in lust, how can you steer her clearly."

"I don't know. What if it has the potential to be more than lust?" Nyair asked.

"An addict can't have a little bit of what they crave.

Nyair heard no lies. A little bit of Lauren was worse than none. He wanted her all the time. Sitting in this very chair his thoughts were consumed with thoughts of their rendezvous. The way she called his name. The smell of her pussy when he put his face in it. The taste of her clit. The way her nipples pebbled at the slightest touch. Even the salt of her tears. Nyair couldn't pray that pussy away. He had tried. He wanted more and more. It was never enough.

"How do you manage your position in the church with your urges as a man without defying God?" Nyair asked.

"You make a saved woman your wife. Your rib stabilizes you, son. Laying with your wife is not a sin. It's a privilege. It's a gift and a duty. Bedding vulnerable women because they are desperate for healing is..."

"It's not like that," Nyair said. "I'm not taking advantage of her."

"Are you sure?" the pastor asked.

Nyair wanted to say that he was, but the more questions Pastor Cullian asked, the more guilty he felt. He didn't know if he was putting Lauren in a position to be a victim. Was he preying on her? It didn't feel that way, but if it looked that way, maybe he was judging it from the wrong lens.

"I'm not sure of anything," Nyair admitted.

"I would advise you to get in your Bible, son, and stay out of you know what, so you can gain some clarity and hear God clearly."

"And what if I pull back, and it hurts her? How is that right?" Nyair asked. "Leaving a grieving mother without help."

"The kind of help you're offering ain't from God, son. Ain't nothing spiritual about that. You're operating out of the flesh."

Nyair left the office with more questions than answers.

Wanting a woman that he couldn't have wasn't a good feeling. He had to ask himself what was driving him. A big part was a sexual desire that Lauren had reignited, but the part that watched her sleep after putting her down in bed told him that it was something deeper. The limitations that came with his lifestyle prevented him from so many things. At most times in his life, it felt like his sacrifice was worth it, but where Lauren was concerned, it left him conflicted. He needed to have a heart-to-heart with her to get her to understand that they had taken things too far, and he would have to figure out how to let her go without letting her drown.

CHAPTER 17

Stassi walked into the firehouse carrying a platter of cold-cut sandwiches, and as soon as the guys inside saw her, they began to whistle and cheer. She blushed as they rushed around her.

"Gray got him a good one!" one of the men yelled as he came flying down the fire pole in the middle of the station. "If he messes up, please give me a call." The man snagged a sandwich from the platter as Grayson walked out of one of the offices.

"I ain't messing up. Don't worry about that," he said.

She smiled as he approached, wearing jeans and a t-shirt with the firehouse logo, and steel-toed work boots. She loved his masculinity and his simplicity.

He removed the platter from her hands and handed it off to one of the men before hoisting her up over his shoulder. She yelped in surprise and laughed as he carried her out of sight as his men cheered boisterously behind his back.

When they were behind the privacy of his office door, he put her down and crossed his arms, staring down at her.

"So, this is my way of apologizing for our date being interrupted," she said.

He nodded. "I didn't require an apology," he replied.

"I mean, you also haven't called me," Stassi said.

"That wasn't punishment. I've been on shift," he replied.

"And you haven't thought about me once?" she asked.

"Food must not have hit if I ain't been a thought at all."

"The food was great. You wet my palette for something else, though," he mentioned slyly.

Stassi was so embarrassed that she couldn't meet his eye contact. She turned her head to the side and folded her lips to stop herself from grinning.

"You are a bit mannish, Mr. Firefighter," she said teasingly.

"I can be," he admitted.

More blushing. He still stood his ground, keeping his distance, arms still folded. His defenses were up. She could tell. He may not have been mad about their date, but he wasn't pleased about it either. His body language spoke volumes. He was going to make her work for this.

"So, you let a girl cook for you, and then you don't call. What am I supposed to think?" she asked.

"When I'm on shift, I check out. That's something you should know if this is going to be a thing. I can't be distracted. I can't think about anything except for what I'm facing in front of me. That's how you keep the fear at bay, the selfishness. You can't think about the people you hope to see again when you're running into a burning building," he said.

"That sounds terrifying. The way you describe it. You

almost have to turn off your emotions to do your job. Sitting at home waiting on a phone call from you from now on is going to be torture," she said.

He unfolded his arms.

That's progress, she thought.

"You're beautiful," he complimented.

She laughed. "You just go off subject. Fuck the flow of conversation."

He chuckled. "You're a distraction. I told you." He peeked out the blinds at his men, who were joking around as they enjoyed their lunch. "Got these fools acting like they never ate a sandwich before."

"I make a pretty good sandwich," she bragged, smiling. "They ain't never ate one like that."

He shook his head. "Apparently," he quipped. "What else you come all the way down here for?"

She stared into his eyes and shook her head. "I just wanted to make sure we were good. If you have any questions for me, I'll answer them. I just…"

"Stassi. It was one date. I ain't really qualified to start questioning you. I get it. There are other suitors in the picture. A little competition never scared me," he said.

She smiled. She didn't realize she was anxious about his reaction until she sighed.

"Good."

"I'd really, really, really like to be shown a little appreciation for the effort I put into dinner," she said. It was her turn to fold her arms. She meant business.

"Is that right?" he asked.

"Damn right," she countered. "And for them sandwiches out there."

He stepped closer to her and put one hand around her waist, pulling her into his body. He was built like a superhero, and he made her feel like a damsel in distress. She loved how he towered over her.

"Now kiss me," she said. "And make it goo…"

His lips covered hers, and Stassi swooned. Yup. This was fairy tale shit. He pulled away way too soon. She wanted more.

"You really should get going. I have a rule. No girls in the firehouse," he said.

"Okay," she whispered. "When is your shift over?"

"In about 9 hours," he said, checking his watch.

"You'll call me?" she asked. "I know I sound desperate, but that kiss wasn't enough. You're putting me out, and I want more, but I don't want you to burn up in a fire because you're thinking of me, so I'ma go, but only if you promise to call."

He chuckled. Her flattery was cute. Her arms were wrapped around his broad waist, and she bent her neck back to look up at him.

"I'ma call you as soon as I'm off," he took his Maltese cross out of his back pocket and handed it to her. "It's like a badge for firefighters."

"You're giving it to me? Don't you need it?" she asked.

He nodded. "I do," he said. "So I'ma have to come get it as soon as I'm off. It's very important."

She smiled and put it in her handbag. She turned to walk

away, and he grabbed her hand, pulling her back to him. This kiss was longer, and deeper, and Stassi was breathless.

"I have a feeling that I'm unprepared for this," she whispered.

"I have a feeling you're right," he said in her ear as he pulled her into his body more. "How I'm supposed to work like this?" he asked. Her stomach pressed into hard dick, and he pulled her closer as she fell back into his kiss. She moaned at just the thought of what he knew how to do with all that dick. This was ho shit. They hadn't even been on two dates. She hadn't even had a good phone conversation with him yet, and she was ready to pop pussy on top of his desk.

"I'm at work, Stassi," he said.

"So, you should let me go, right?" she asked, between lust-filled kisses. It was the way he sucked on her tongue when he kissed her. "God, I want you to suck on my pussy, just like this," she whispered.

"It's so good too. I got a taste of it, and shit been stuck in my mind ever since," he admitted. He pulled back. "You know it's good too, don't you?"

Stassi's panties were ruined. From just words. Words, confidence, and masculinity had her in heat. She was so turned on that she could cum at any little touch.

"That's why you got niggas pulling up to your door. All over this," he said. He slid his hand up her skirt. "Your body's making silk, Stassi," he whispered in her ear as he rubbed her gently with the palm of his hand. "So wet."

No, this nigga ain't one of them talk-a-bitch-through-it niggas, she thought, mind blown.

"Grayson," she whispered, teeth clenched as she leaned back onto the wooden desk.

"Yes, ma'am?" he asked, looking down at the puddles he was splashing in. It was his thumb that was doing the damage. He was riding her clit so hard that Stassi's pussy lips clenched in excitement.

"I can't wait all day," she moaned. "God, I can't wait."

"If I didn't have to make you, I wouldn't, baby," he whispered. "I don't have condoms, and I promise you, these walls ain't meant for screaming."

She groaned as he removed his hand, but before she got up, he lowered his face, sliding those panties aside, and licked her from her taint to her clit, slurping her bud so long and hard that her back arched off the desk. Her head fell back in satisfaction, and her mouth opened. One lick. That was all she got. He removed her panties and put them in his pocket.

"I need those, sir," she protested.

"I'll return them when I'm done," he replied, and Stassi's pussy jumped again. The thought of how he planned to use those panties set her on fire. She didn't know if he planned to smell them or beat off into them, but she was horny as fuck at the notion. She loved a nasty-ass man, and Grayson was proving that beneath the good boy image was a grown-ass man with a vicious sexual appetite. He was like an amusement park ride that she wasn't tall enough to get on. She wanted to strap in anyway and take the ride of her life. Excitement flickered in her eyes, and she wanted to inquire more, wanted to evoke more of him. She wanted to know his kinks, his preferences, what got him off, and what turned him on. She wanted to watch this man do whatever he planned to do with those panties while she played with her pussy. Foreplay before the main event. This wasn't the time nor place, however.

He was assertive in his touch, a bit rough, but still gentle enough to let her know he was only establishing dominance and not inflicting harm. He wrapped four fingers behind her face as he caressed her lips with his thumb. "I'm intrigued by you," he admitted. "More than I care to be."

"Same," she shot back. "You're a complication I never saw coming."

"I'll call you when I'm off to see if you're still up for company," he said.

He placed one last kiss on her lips, and Stassi made her exit. She walked out of the firehouse feeling exposed, like all her newfound friends knew Grayson had just had her in precarious positions.

"Bye, beautiful! Don't forget to come see me after you get tired of that loser! He don't know how to treat a lady!" one of the white boy rookies shouted. "I'll drink your bath water and rub your feet and feed you strawberries in bed! Whatever you want!"

Grayson emerged and put the kid in a playful headlock. "That's enough. Back to work," he said.

She laughed. "Bye, fellas," she said. She shot him one last flirtatious look before letting him get back to his day.

Stassi was smitten, and as she got in her car, Day's name popped up on her phone. She didn't even consider answering it. Somebody else had her attention.

"Oh my God! Lauren, he did not!"

Charlie held her hands over her mouth in shock as Lauren stood over the stove making homemade soup.

"I swear to God he did. Demi would run my baby raggedy. He swore DJ was his personal little servant. DJ, hand me the remote. DJ, go grab this, go grab that. Girl, he asked my four-year-old for some water, and I guess DJ said enough, damn it. That boy scooped Demi a cup right from the toilet bowl. Let him swallow it and everything."

Charlie was in tears she was laughing so hard. "I know he diedddd!" she exclaimed.

Lauren nodded. "Served his ass right," Lauren said. "Bet he didn't ask DJ to get him nothing else ever again."

"His OCD was probably in overdrive!" Charlie snickered.

"Girl, that man was detoxing for a week after that," Lauren laughed. "I swear that feels like yesterday. They grow up so fast."

Charlie leaned against the countertop and tried to fathom how things would be. "I just can't imagine this baby being real. I mean, besides feeling sick, I really don't feel like anybody's mom. Like, what will this baby be like? Look like?"

"I remember asking those questions. I remember trying to envision how Demi and I would mix into one little face. Truth is, I could have never imagined how perfect our chemistry could be. You're going to predict an entire little personality and appearance for this baby, and when it gets here, it'll be more than you could have ever pieced together in your mind. God just works it out that way. Your baby will be a perfect blend."

Lauren prepared a bowl for Charlie. "Try this. If you can't stomach the veggies, you can just drink the broth. It literally got me through all forty weeks of my pregnancy," Lauren said. "You have to take better care of yourself, Charlie. It's not just about you anymore."

Charlie gave a halfhearted smile. "I always thought he'd be here to take care of me."

Lauren lifted a brow. "Listen to me and hear me good. Don't bank on anybody on this earth to take care of you and that baby, except for you. Don't get me wrong, Demi ain't one of these dead-beat-ass niggas out here. He's going to do his part, but your part, the *mommyhood* of it all, is a 24-hour job that doesn't let up. Nobody will know that baby like you. Nobody will love it like you. Nobody will care for it like you. Your priority must be you because if you're not good, that baby isn't good. Demi and everybody else come after you and your child. So, if he's here to take care of you, cool, but if the day ever comes when he isn't, or he can't be around, you stand tall for you and yours. You'll understand that more when you give birth. There is a switch that just flips. It tells you that you have the right to rip a motherfucker apart with your bare hands if they ever try to harm you or your kid. I don't know. Motherhood turns you into a superhero or something. You'll literally go to war with the world over your child."

Charlie took a sip of the soup, and to her surprise, it didn't make her gag.

"Mmm," she moaned, closing her eyes as the soup warmed her entire body.

Lauren smiled. "Good girl," she said. "You eat that, and you'll start to feel better. It'll put some strength back in your legs. I made enough for you to last a few days. I'm going to get out of here."

"Why couldn't we do this before?" Charlie asked.

Lauren paused. "I was at war with you over my family. You were a threat to me, Charlie…To my son's sense of normalcy. You were my enemy."

"And now?" Charlie asked.

Lauren's eyes misted. "I don't have anything left to fight for," Lauren whispered.

Charlie's eyes betrayed her, too. "I don't know what I'm doing, Lo. I don't have a mom. My sister isn't a mom yet. My dad and I are estranged. I don't have anybody. Right now, I don't even have Demi. I know this is weird, but this baby is DJ's blood. I admire you, Lauren. I think you're so strong and smart, and that's probably why I'm terrified that Demi is going to come back to you one day. You make me feel like I'm not nearly enough woman for him. God, and the type of mother you are! I would be okay with you being a part of this baby's village, Lauren. No one can tell this baby about DJ like you. I mean, if you want to. I know it's weird, and I know you kind of hate me, but if you want to be a part of our world, you're welcome here."

Lauren didn't even try to stop her tears. She just stared at

Charlie in amazement.

"You are probably the most endearing person I've ever met, Charlie. From the moment he met you, no one else stood a chance. I've been so hard on you, and you're still here, welcoming me into your child's life to ease the pain of me losing mine."

"Not to ease the pain, Lo. To share it so we all can help you carry it. I just wanted to help you carry it, that's all," Charlie said.

Lauren nodded and wiped her eyes, clearing her throat as embarrassment flooded her.

"Thank you for showing me grace, Charlie. I'm going to head out. Eat that soup and put the rest up for later," Lauren instructed.

Charlie nodded and walked Lauren to the door. It felt like they had made some progress, and Charlie was relieved. Being in battle with another woman was never good for the spirit. As jealous as she had been of Lauren, oddly, she didn't want Lauren out of their lives. Lauren felt like someone Charlie would need or could learn from. That was the beauty of feminine connection; in belonging to a community of women. It came with empowerment when the world made you feel weak. She couldn't put her finger on how or why Lauren held significance in her life, but her intuition was telling her that Lauren had the potential to be more friend than foe.

"He wants me to do what?" Stassi asked in disbelief.

"Mr. Night would like to contract your services for a company brunch. If you check your email, we've sent over a very generous offer. As we know, this is a last-minute engagement. A rush fee has been added to the offer. We just need you to fill out a new W-9 and NDA."

Stassi hadn't even gotten into her house well before she had been hit with this unexpected phone call. He just knew how and when to burst her bubble. Whenever her thoughts drifted to another man, here came Day as if he had a radar on her vagina and could tell when someone else was sniffing dangerously close. She was still frazzled and discombobulated from her rendezvous with Grayson, and here Day's ass was, by way of his damn assistant, trying to throw her a curve ball.

"I don't sign NDAs. Day knows that. I'll look at the email today and let you guys know," she replied. Stassi hung up the phone and shimmied out of her clothes. She felt like a dirty-ass ho. She had let Grayson slut her out in the firehouse, and she was semi-ashamed but wildly intrigued. He was a good boy with a touch of bad, and something about that combination seemed thrilling yet safe. He was different than any man she had ever dated. His level of non-toxic, was perfect. A quick shower reset her day before she threw on a lounge set and gathered herself in front of her laptop.

She opened the computer and found the email from Dynasty. The offer was so lucrative that her heart raced when she saw it.

"This motherfucker here," she scoffed. Day was a man of means. His paper was long, and he was used to the power that came with being the richest man in the room. He yielded that bank account like a sword to win all his battles. She knew he would never offer this money to any other event company. He wouldn't even come close. He was trying to buy her, and his audacity to think she would be that easy was infuriating. She picked up her phone and dialed his number.

"You got that attitude together?" Day asked as soon as he answered.

"I'ma pass on the job," she said, cutting straight to business. The words tasted like shit. Day was playing with M's like children played with toys. He had the capability to change her entire life, and Stassi knew the opportunities he was extending would put her right back in business, but she didn't like the power dynamics he was establishing between them.

"Ayo, hold up, bruh, let me take this," Day said, speaking to someone in the background.

Bet you wasn't expecting that, were you? She thought snidely.

"Anastassia, you trying me," Day warned.

"You've been buying me since day one. You buy everybody around you. It's how you influence the room. Are you offering me this job because I'm good or because you want to win?"

"I been winning, baby. I ain't concerned with shit like that," Day responded. "Lauren isn't an option for obvious reasons. Your work is credible. You're good at what you do, but I can find somebody else if you ain't feeling it," he stated.

"Say less."

"So, this has nothing to do with you trying to make me get over the bullshit you pulled?" she asked.

His pause told her everything she needed to know. "You can't buy forgiveness," Stassi said. "You have to earn it."

"And I intend to, but I also intend on handling this business. I'm able to separate the two," Day said.

"Good, because I'm honestly only interested in business. I'm dating, and I just want to be clear that I don't intend to stop seeing other people. When I was on that, you were off it, so it's just better if we just stick to business."

Stassi wanted him to protest. She wanted him to be jealous and to object, to claim her for himself. She wanted big energy from him. She wanted confirmation that she wasn't crazy for having butterflies in her stomach every time she heard his voice.

"Business it is," he replied. "If that's what you prefer."

Her heart sank. How he could go from full-court pressure, buying cars, and professing his intentions in a room full of people to just business was beyond her. It matched every single rumor she had ever heard about him, though. He lost interest quickly. He swapped models and 'it girls' in and out on his arm monthly. Her frustration with him was immeasurable because when he was in the mood to act right, he pulled her in effortlessly. He gave her glimpses of who he was behind the cameras and behind the fame, but the man the public received was almost intolerable. He was arrogant, dismissive, and inconsiderate.

"Is that what *you* prefer?" he asked.

The audacity of him to give her the option as if she was choosing any of this shit. His actions were dictating the course of their involvement with one another. She was just reacting to his bullshit. The hardest part was knowing that behind the visage was a man that made her feel so damn good.

"You aren't consistent with me, Day," Stassi said. "I prefer that. I prefer a man who is so consistent with the way he moves that I can predict his next step. I want to be able to finish your sentences. I want to be able to look at the clock and know exactly where you are because your routine is the same. Our every interaction changes. One minute you're feeling me, and you want to be with me, the next minute, some weird-ass industry bitch is your focus."

"My focus is on you, Stassi. Even when you think it ain't," he replied. "Even when you deny me access. A nigga moving every single piece around the board just to get you to enter the room so I can see you."

She didn't know if he was sincere, or if he was doing what he did best, having his way with words. It was what he was famous for, after all. Writing music. Using lyrics to tell stories through his art. It sounded good, but was it real?

"You're doing all that," she said with a heavy sigh. "Exerting all that energy, trying to control how I move, when all you got to do is control how you move. I'd come willingly if you acted right, but you don't do right by women, Day, and I ain't trying to have my heart broken. I'd just rather be friends, honestly."

"You want me to be your friend?" He asked the question like it repulsed him. "The shit I think about when I see you…" He paused and scoffed. "I don't think about my friends like that." He sighed in exasperation. "This shit wild, man, but whatever you want, Anastassia. The world is yours. Sign the contract and return it to my office tomorrow. Don't miss this paper because you in your feels. We got work to do."

"Prove something to me, Day. If I'm worth anything at all, prove it."

He was silent, and she wondered what was running through his mind.

"I hear you," was all he returned with before the line went dead. Stassi blew out a sharp breath. She wanted to keep things light with Day because the depths that he could take her would drown her. He was a walking, talking, red flag, and although he checked so many boxes, his lifestyle would ruin her eventually.

CHAPTER 18

Day was used to controlling the room. He only shared power with one individual, and that was Demi. Two kings. One kingdom. They reigned as brothers. They had it all. They had come up dreaming of money and bitches. They had achieved every single goal they had set for themselves. They had wanted the streets, so they took them. They had wanted to go legit, so they did. They hadn't heard 'no' very often, but suddenly, Day was being forced to reconcile with rejection. All the money in the world couldn't buy him favor with Stassi. He knew because he had tried. Day had led with money with Stassi, and now he regretted it because he hadn't taken the time to get to know her true weakness. It wasn't money. She was headstrong, and no other woman had ever given him this hard of a time. He was interested. He was more than interested. Day had a hard time lowering the guard he gave the public, but Stassi had cracked through it. She had seen a different side to him, but she wanted him to be that way all the time and he couldn't. He only reserved that freedom for those he trusted. For her, it felt like he was gaming her. To him, it felt like he was extending trust. He knew he was going to have to cut Kiara Da'vi off if he wanted to prove to Stassi that he was serious.

He needed Da'vi to understand that this was just business. He couldn't give her the clout she was chasing, not anymore. Demi had warned Day over the years of playing the celebrity game with different women, using his presence as currency. "You a street nigga, let's keep it street. Be less accessible for these niggas. Bitches too," Demi had said. He had warned him again and again, but Day had fallen victim to the PR game. Running up sales, building careers, fucking women, courting them, casually leaving them in the wind. He always got what he wanted, and they got what they needed. It was always a fair exchange—until now. Stassi didn't want fame. She wanted to earn her respect, and she wasn't willing to accept his visage. The fact that she was entertaining other niggas gave him a dose of his own medicine. It was a bitter pill to swallow, and he didn't like the shit one bit.

He hadn't had to work for a woman in quite some time. "Prove it." Her words rang in his mind. He knew an ultimatum when he heard one. He was an alpha male, and his ego was telling him to do the opposite. He was insulted that she thought she had the pull to challenge him in the first place. But the part of him that sought her company, the part that desired the unique way she went left when he said right, knew what had to be done. Some women could just sway a man, and she was one of those types for Day.

Day's phone rang, and Demi's photo illuminated the screen just as Kiara Da'vi entered the room. He held up a finger to stall her as he answered the phone simultaneously.

"What up, boy?" Day greeted. He frowned when he heard the noise in the background. Demi was outside. He was never outside.

"Shit, bro. Just out here having a drink. Come fuck with me," Demi said. His somber tone couldn't be missed; neither could the slur. Demi was a general. He had kept his head on a swivel for as long as they had known one another. Being out his body in public wasn't a thing. In fact, being out of body at all wasn't a thing. He knew this one-off was a direct result of DJ.

"I just might do that. Where you at?" Day asked. "Sound like you done had one too many."

"I'm over here on the Northside. You know the old bar off Pierson," Demi stated.

"Yeah, I know the spot. Signature. I know niggas be lurking 'round them parts too. You got security with you, or you dolo?" Day asked.

"I buried my son, my nigga. Didn't need no witnesses tonight, you know?" Demi's voice cracked, but he quickly recovered. Day knew that Demi wanted solitude so that he could cry in peace, and still, Day doubted if Demi had allowed himself to. The breakdown was inevitable. Day knew that when Demi finally lost his shit and allowed himself to process this, it would be ugly for everyone within proximity. Day needed Demi inside where it was safe for everybody.

"You strapped?" Day asked.

"You know it," Demi answered.

"Sit tight. I'll be headed that way. Don't drive, and nigga, don't look at nobody. Ain't no nigga eyeballing you, ain't nobody stepping on your Air Force 1s. Order a water, nigga. Give me 30, and I'ma pull up on you. We'll pour one out for nephew."

"Nigga, what am I 20? I ain't fighting in no bars these days. I'm posted. I'll be here."

CLICK.

Day turned his focus to the lovely girl in front of him.

"Da'vi," he greeted, sitting back in his chair, and swiveling it left, then right, as he steepled his pointer fingers and positioned them over his nose. Any last-minute thoughts of keeping her around were fleeting. He was about to fumble a big bag for Stassi, but it was time. Her entitlement alone meant the cut-off was overdue. She thought that she was owed more than she was, simply because of her brother's initial dealings with Dynasty records. Duke had died years ago, however, and the way Demi and Day had taken a dream and turned it into reality, was far removed from those beginning struggle days. They had taken care of Duke's mama, and Kiara Da'vi had been given an opportunity. Any debt that was owed had been paid. They couldn't change what had happened to Duke in jail, and she could no longer use it to guilt trip or force her prioritization at the company.

"Not Big Demi in the middle of the hood all by himself. He better remember where he at. Nobody cares about them big names in the city. The way y'all walk around with the jewels, pushing big boy wheels in the foreigns, y'all stand out like sore thumbs."

"Yeah, a warning ain't necessary. Niggas know the land and the rules to the land," Day stated arrogantly. They may have been CEOs of a music label, but they were CEOs on the block, too.

"My bad, just saying," she shrugged.

"Look, Da'vi, there's no easy way for me to cut this, but I'm releasing you from the label."

"Wait, what?" He saw her temper go from zero to one hundred. "My brother started this fucking label."

"It's not gon' work out, Da'vi," Day said sternly, cutting her off before she could get on her soap box. "I can't give you what you looking for here. The music is good, but it can't sustain itself. You need a story. I can't be that story no more. I ain't feeling it."

"Since when are you not feeling it? Because I literally have physical video proof that you were feeling it," Kiara snapped. "Been feeling it, nigga. What about the brunch? You promised me, Day!"

"I can talk to your management team, help them develop a plan that will give you longevity in the game. Don't you want that? Like, how long you think you gon' be relevant just from affiliation with made niggas? You're talented, Da'vi…"

"Miss me with the 'you're better than that' speech," Kiara spat.

"That wasn't quite where I was headed, but since you said it, you could be better than a social media gimmick," Day said.

"And you could be better than a washed-up rapper buying pussy, but here we are."

He was certain she had lost her mind. Everybody knew Day wasn't tolerant when it came to disrespect and her anger had her straddling a fine line.

"This is where we part ways, Da'vi. Good luck." His voice was calm, but he was expressionless. The blank stare he hit her with almost made her feel like she didn't even exist, and it was because he had disconnected. Any guilt he had felt had exited stage left. This only pissed her off more.

"I promise you, I'ma have the last laugh. You're ruining my career, and for what? Cuz your dick a little tender over a nobody-ass bitch. Fuck you, Day." She was animated and way too loud for Day's taste. He reached into his desk drawer and pulled out a blunt. He kept one rolled for stresses just like this.

"You can see yourself out. Consider that advance check we cut you severance, my baby."

He was being more than fair. Most companies would have asked for it back.

She stormed out, and Day watched a three-million-dollar investment walk out of his life. It wasn't the smartest play he had ever made, but he was trying to change. He was trying to win over a girl that could possibly be 'the girl,' and he realized that would take some sacrifice. Kiara Da'vi was one of many he was sure to make in his attempt to win favor with Anastassia. Day hit the lights in the office and shrugged into his Amiri jacket before pulling a skull cap over his head. He hit the code to his office safe and then headed out into the night.

When he made it to the parking garage, he immediately saw red. His beautiful foreign car was sitting on two rims, and the paint was scratched from the etch of a key. There wasn't a doubt in his mind that Kiara Da'vi had lost hers. She was in her feelings, so she was making him go in his pockets. He pulled out his phone and hit Demi.

Day
I'ma be a minute. That bitch, Da'vi, don' put a nigga tires on flat. I'ma call the tow and then Uber there. DON'T DRIVE, NIGGA!

Day sent a picture showing the damage, and Demi sent back crying and laughing emojis.

Day chuckled, too. This was young girl shit. "Fucking with her crazy ass. That's what the fuck I get."

Demi
I'm about to make my way to one of my rentals, my nigga. I'll tap in with you tomorrow.

Demi was sick. His body was physically disrupted, and he couldn't decipher if it was grief or anger. He was overloaded with an energy that had him in a foul mood, and as he sat at the bar, he nursed a glass of aged cognac, hoping to take the edge off.

He had never felt this unnerved in his life. He felt exposed and vulnerable, like if anyone even spoke to him, he might break down and cry. The shit hurt. Bad. He had never quite felt anything even remotely close to this before. He wondered what this was. This crippling effect that was taking over his body, and his stomach ached almost like he hadn't eaten in days. Had he? He couldn't even remember. He took a sip of the poison in his hand instead. If he drank enough of it, he knew it would numb him. He didn't have to check the time to know it was late. The dwindling crowd let him know that it was closing time.

"You look like you've had a rough night," the bartender said as she wiped down the bar top. Her voice was sweet, and light, and he glanced up at her pretty face. Her smile was the first smile he'd seen all day. It reminded him that there was happiness somewhere out there in the world.

"You could say that," Demi replied as he spun the tumbler in his hand.

"Well, this one is on me. Last call before the lights go out." The girl was pretty, petite like Charlie, even the same complexion, or maybe it was the liquor telling him that she resembled the woman he had lost. Demi didn't respond, but he allowed her to top him off.

"He's a temperamental one," she teased. "Whatever it is, I promise you, it's not that bad."

"My son died," he said.

The way her smile faded caused his eyes to flood. He cleared his throat and flicked his nose before lifting the glass to his lips. "Agh," he hissed and grimaced as the liquor burned on the way down.

"I'm so sorry," she gasped. "I really wish I could make that go away for you." She touched his hand, and Demi recoiled like she had put fire to his skin, knocking over his drink as it spilled into his lap. He pushed back from the bar in frustration and dusted off his wet clothes, flicking his wet hand as she scrambled for a bar mop.

"I'm so sorry. I umm...I was just trying to be sympathetic..." She rushed around the bar and reached for more napkins before pressing them to his chest, and Demi lost it.

"Just stop!" he shouted, catching her wrist tightly. The more she tried to clean him up, the more places she touched. Demi was overstimulated in the worst way. "I just need all this shit to stop, man."

He released her and gripped the edge of the bar, lowering his head. The room was spinning. He had drunk himself into a vortex of sorrow and rage. He just wanted to go home, but home wasn't waiting. Not with Charlie. Not with Lauren. The woman stood, eyeing him in concern. He grabbed his jacket from the back of the bar stool.

"Wait, you really shouldn't be driving," the girl said. She said it like she cared. "Let me at least sober you up a bit. You don't like being touched. I won't touch you, but at least let me get you some food and some coffee."

"I'm good," he stated. "I can drive."

"Are you sure there isn't someone I can call?" she asked.

"My potnah was supposed to pull up," he responded as he pulled out his phone. He hadn't even realized it had died.

He wanted to call Charlie and put his foot down. He wanted to tell her he was on the way and that they would fight it out until they worked it out, but he was trying to respect her space. The bartender looked at him sympathetically.

It was the look in her eyes that made him feel like less than a man. He had been getting that look since the doctor had delivered the news about DJ. Pity. She pitied him. Everyone did. From friends to strangers, they all saw that he was carrying around baggage, dropping miscellaneous pieces of his heart along this long journey of grief. He kept scrambling, trying to pick himself up off the ground, but it was like the more he tried to recover, the more he failed.

The clock on the wall read 2:10 a.m. He wanted to go to her. His mind wouldn't focus on anything else. He wondered if she was up, agonizing over him the way he was agonizing over her. Charlie played her guitar, smoked weed, and wrote songs when something bothered her. Sometimes, they would stay up all night sitting in the middle of their living room floor, burning one while she did her thing. He would be a fly on the wall on those nights. Watching her in her element was a privilege. Getting a front-row seat to her process was his comfort zone. Her fingers plucking strings, his fingers plucking her. Demi ate pussy to acoustics every night. It was a fucking vibe. Their entire life. Their whole bond was unlike anything he had ever felt before. He didn't want to lose her. He didn't even know how he had fumbled her. He took the coffee down in a few swallows, eager to sober up so he could go to her. If she wanted him to beg, so be it. He would.

He stood and placed a few hundred dollars on the bar top before he turned and walked out of the building.

He knew he was fucked up, but it wouldn't be the first time he had to make it home on one too many. He hit the alarm and the remote start on his car as he walked across the dark parking lot. It wasn't until he got right up on his door that he saw the reflection of the man behind him in the window. It was too late to react.

POP! POP! Two gunshots were all it took to end his misery. He felt nothing and everything all at once as his body tried to open his car door. He collapsed on the inside of the seats as he heard a familiar voice.

"Did you kill him? Is he dead?"

Bitch-ass nigga, Demi thought. It was Justin's voice. Justin had sent somebody to kill him, and Demi didn't know if it was justice or karma that had come back for him as he bled out all over his seats.

He couldn't move his head, but he reached up with a bloody hand, desperately feeling around his steering wheel for the call button.

There was only one number programmed into his car's system. When he pressed it, it dialed Charlie's number. Blood poured from his mouth, and he could feel himself suffocating slowly as it filled his lungs. The phone went straight to voicemail.

"Bii—rddd!" he gritted. It took all his might to get her name out. "He..." He grimaced because he knew he wouldn't be able to get much more out, and he had to choose these words carefully. He started to say help me, but he knew that once she got this message, it would be too late. So, instead, he told her what he wanted her to know most. "I love…" He was sipping air in, but not enough, and his vision blurred. "You."

I love you, Bird. I'm sorry, he finished the thought in his head before everything went still.

The Next Morning

Knock! Knock! Knock!

Charlie sighed as she put down the paintbrush in her hands. She had been trying to busy herself to distract from her loneliness. Painting her daughter's nursery had sounded like a good idea before she started. It was proving to be a task. She was grateful for the unexpected interruption. She placed the brush down and made her way to the front door, pulling it open without checking the security monitor.

"What do you want?" Charlie asked as soon as she saw Stassi standing on her doorstep.

"I want to see how you're doing. You haven't returned any of my calls," Stassi said. "I'm worried about you!"

"Now you're worried," Charlie replied sarcastically. "The selective concern is crazy."

"Charlie, I'm sorry, damn." Stassi didn't have a problem giving in first. She understood why Charlie was upset. "Bitch, are you gon' make me stand out here in the cold? I know I got some ass kissing to do, but can I be warm while I do it?"

Charlie hated that she could never remain firm with Stassi. She sucked her teeth and turned around. "Bring your disloyal ass inside," she spat before storming off to the living room.

"You're starting to poke out a little," Stassi said, noticing Charlie's tiny baby bump.

"It's crazy, right?" Charlie asked. "The things I'm feeling. The way my body is changing from the inside out is so weird. I've never experienced anything like this before. It's harder than I thought it would be."

"I'm sorry it's been hard for you. I know it's unfair. This is supposed to be a happy time, and so much sadness has interrupted that. I didn't mean to make you feel left out, but it honestly isn't anything to envy being a part of. That little boy dying the way he did. It's the saddest thing I've ever witnessed. I haven't slept right since all this started. Watching Demi and Lauren wasn't easy. I almost understand why Demi wanted to leave you out of it, sis," Stassi admitted. "How are you two?"

"I don't want to talk about Demi," Charlie said. She hadn't accepted one phone call from him. He texted her daily. She never responded. She was trying incredibly hard to stick to her guns, but she missed him terribly. Talking about it wouldn't make anything better, so she would rather not. She had to figure out things on her own. He was willing to give her anything she wanted. She knew he was at her mercy. The problem was she didn't know how to undo the damage that had been done. She had no answers on how to fix their problems. They both felt like they were in the right, so even though Demi was willing to wave the white flag, she wasn't sure if going back would solve their issues. She still wouldn't feel like she had a place in his life because he didn't understand the problem to begin with. She was sure he thought she was being emotional, hormonal, and unreasonable, and hell, maybe she was. She just didn't know anymore.

"Okay," Stassi said. "Well, do you want to talk about your career? Because you've been holed up here, doing absolutely nothing but self-loathing, and it's not healthy."

"What career?" Charlie scoffed. "What am I supposed to do? Market an album with a big-ass belly?"

"Yes," Stassi said. "You're supposed to share your whole journey with the people who love your music. You're heartbroken, so sing about it. That nigga pissing you off, so get in the studio and write a song about that shit. Give us what Mary gave us with *Share My World*. Give us what Keyshia gave us with *Love*. If it hurts, sing, Charlie. If you love him, sing that too. But this shit that you're doing…Rotting here. It ain't the move. Do anything but that."

"I can barely pull myself out of bed, my morning sickness is so bad," Charlie protested.

"So, shit, write about that!" Stassi joked. "I want you to snap out of this shit. Get back to being you. Write. Get on stage. I want you to turn that baby into everybody's baby. Make your pregnancy into everybody's pregnancy. If you sit down for these nine months, your dream is going to fade away. Day has some events he wants me to plan for the company, and I think you should perform, Charlie. I think you should sing your heart out. If it's broken, let it bleed."

"Nobody wants to see a pregnant girl on stage," Charlie shot back. She didn't want to give up her dream, but she knew it was time to be realistic, too. She and Demi wouldn't likely end up together, and this baby would be the death of all her plans. It was terrifying, but somehow, it still felt like the most important job she had ever had. She didn't know what was ahead of her, but the responsibility she felt growing inside her felt like something she couldn't just abandon. This baby was proof that the love of her life existed once. He had been in front of her eyes before DJ died. She had watched him fade away like a mirage as soon as his son left this earth. Now, she was in the desert searching for her next reprieve alone. She was waiting for rescue, but it felt like Demi would never find her again. She felt it. He had dropped her off in that desert the day he asked her to leave the hospital. He had promised to return for her, but every day since, she had been dying slowly, thirsting for his presence. Even now, at this moment, the pit in her stomach was growing because he felt impossible to reach. She felt him, wherever he was, drifting further and further from her.

"I don't think I can share what I'm feeling and who I am right now on stage, Stass," Charlie said. "I don't even know who I am. I'm insecure. I'm terrified. I'm up, then I'm down. I'm unreasonable. I'm moody. Bitchy. Horny. Selfish. Angry. Jealous."

"Bitch, you sound like every single woman I know. You are us. Sing for us." It felt like Stassi was trying to talk her off a ledge; hell, or was she trying to talk her onto one?

"I'll make you a deal. Just go live. Go live like you used to do when you had 500 followers, get your guitar, and just sing. If folks don't care, I won't say shit else about it. You know the bloggers are all waiting for you or Demi or Lo to speak about DJ's death anyway. They got the funeral images all on Shade Room. The comments full of speculation. Just go live and sing your truth. If nobody cares, then I'll back off. I'll bet a whole bunch of folks care, though, Charlie. A bunch of people want you to sing their story. The pregnancy doesn't make the story less important."

Charlie was hesitant. She had never been afraid to open her mouth to sing until now.

"What are you afraid of?" Stassi asked.

"To be stupid in front of everybody," Charlie whispered. It was the judgment she couldn't handle. It was the feeling like she had won this grand love when Demi had come back to her, only for her to end up here. It was karma coming for her lick back. The public shame would be the nail in her coffin.

Stassi stood, and Charlie could see the look of "bitch please" all over her face.

"Where's your guitar?" Stassi asked.

"It's in the room, Stass, but…"

Stassi was already halfway down the hallway. "But nothing!" She returned with the guitar and gave it to Charlie.

"Bitch, stupid in public and stupid in private is still stupid," Stassi said.

Charlie's mouth fell open in shock at the insult. "You just might be the worst motherfucking support system in the whole world," Charlie said.

"I'm just saying. Shit, we all been there. These niggas have us out of body, doing crazy-ass shit, feeling crazy-ass shit, capping for they asses, sucking them, fucking on 'em real good, feeling ourselves, like we ir-re-fucking-placeable, only for us to find out eventually that we all the same. All our asses out here looking stupid for these niggas. We all have our day. We all birds of a motherfucking feather. So, sing, bitch. Cuz you ain't the first, and you won't be the last. Sing our pain."

Stassi went live before Charlie had time to protest.

"Sing what?" Charlie asked.

"Whatever you want," Stassi stated.

Charlie popped open her case and pulled the guitar out. She grabbed a pick and then cradled it in her grasp. The guitar was beautiful. She named her Destiny because Demi had gifted it to her, and she felt he was hers, her destiny. Her *eventually* anyway. Why fight because they were going to end up together eventually anyway, was her explanation. This time didn't feel like that, but the beautiful instrument in her hand reminded her of him—of them. She closed her eyes and strummed a few strings.

Fingers wrapped around a delicate champagne glass, Lauren sat, sipping, as her free hand scrolled through social media. She was halfway through a bottle of Bollinger vintage. It was numbing, just like she liked it. It was medicinal to all things that ailed her.

She didn't even know how Charlie had come onto her timeline. She didn't follow her, but before her very eyes was her adversary. Or was she? She had thought about that long and hard over the past few weeks. Her disdain for the girl was justified, but it was so hard to keep up. They were victims of circumstance, a circumstance that Demi had created.

Lauren didn't even want to listen. Charlie wasn't someone she hated anymore, but the initial shock of her triggered pain in Lauren every single time they crossed paths. It was like she was forced to forgive Charlie over and over again at every encounter. Charlie looked like every heartbreak she had ever felt was competing for her tears, and Lauren placed four fingers over her mouth as Charlie hummed a tune that was so familiar. No words, just a melody floating through a tight-lipped grimace as Charlie played that damn guitar. She wasn't even saying the words to the song, and the emotion of it oozed through Charlie's body and through this screen into Lauren. Her eyes misted as she watched the numbers of the live run-up. Charlie finally added words.

"I'm thinking of youuuuu. In my sleepless solitude tonighttt…"

Lauren felt a streak of devastation collide with her soul. She hadn't known exactly when Demi had met Charlie, but this song, this rendition of it, it put a motherfucking time stamp on the entire affair. Lauren remembered when Demi had suddenly begun playing the song in his car out of the blue years ago. She had gotten in his car one day to run to the pharmacy, and to her surprise, Mariah Carey had come crooning through the speakers. She had questioned it then. She had known him so well that she knew it wouldn't be something he would normally listen to. He had lied back then, telling her he was thinking of sampling the song for an artist, but now she knew. It was a song he had heard Charlie sing. A tear fell from Lauren's eyes. Her heart pounded. She wanted to log off, but she couldn't. Trauma and heartbreak were cruel that way. Just when you thought you were growing, the smallest detail would reveal a new part of you that hadn't healed yet. It hurt to hear Charlie singing this song, yet still, it was beautiful. The pure emotion from this damn girl. *How is she this vulnerable in a world this cold?* Lauren thought. She envied that. The weakness. The softness. She had never been that girl. She was strong, and swift, and striking, and successful, but she realized as she watched the girl whom Demi had fallen for, that all he wanted was a woman who was soft. A woman who could make a man weak. Demi knew how to be strong. He didn't need Lauren to reinforce his strength. He needed one like Charlie who made him feel something different. Lauren realized now that she never had a chance in her marriage. If Charlie had the ability to make humans feel this way with sound, she couldn't imagine how deeply Demi had fallen into a trance with her in his arms. The song was beautiful, and the way she played the song, giving it her own sound, made it completely unique to Charlie. Lauren knew where this heartbreak was coming from. She heard the throaty emotion that was breaking Charlie. She knew the rasp came from what she was feeling in real-time. Charlie was beautiful. Her talent was breathtaking, and as Lauren tilted the glass to her lips, she finally felt acceptance. Lauren didn't want anything less than the feeling Charlie was singing about.

Lauren sent a star emoji into the cyber verse and then clicked out of the live, but not before noting that there were five hundred thousand people watching. Charlie was a fucking star. She was Demi's North Star, and she envied them. He was lost right now, but she knew he would find his way back to Charlie because she shone bright enough for him to navigate through this pain. Lauren's doorbell rang, and she lugged her sadness to the door. They answered it. She and her grief. Bound to one another. She feared it would be this way forever. The pair inhabited these walls, like lovers. She was sure they would be inseparable 'til death do them part. Damn, how had her life become this dismal? As soon as she looked up into the eyes of this intruder, this unannounced visitor, she felt like help had arrived. The look of concern in his eyes was hard to decipher. Was he worried about her or himself? He was lost. She was sure of it. He wasn't supposed to seek her, yet here he was. Here they were. He made her feel like Charlie's song. Instantly. He was soothing after a burn. He was the peroxide after a cut. The bandage after a break.

She didn't say anything. Neither did he. She wanted him to speak first so that she didn't say the wrong thing.

"You're in my head, Lo," he said. She crossed the threshold out into the cold, out into the wild with him. She reached up and pulled him near, palming the back of his neck as she pulled him down into her space. Forehead to forehead. "You have no idea how bad I got it for you."

"So have it bad then," she whispered. She caressed his entire aura. The back of his neck, the side of his face, the lobes of his ears, as she stared at him with need. "I don't have a lot right now, Nyair. I see everything you're thinking; so, if you came over here to tell me I'm about to lose this, too, just don't."

"I got to, Lo," he said.

"You don't," she protested.

"What would you have me do, Lo? I chose a life. I made a vow," Nyair said. "What do you want from me? I have an addiction, Lauren. To sex." She gasped. It should have scared her, but it turned her on instead. "I want it when I want it, and I can't control it. I'm hard just thinking about the way you get wet for me." He gritted his teeth, and Lauren was breathless because she felt it, she felt him, hardening by the second as he placed his hands around her waist and pulled her closer. If he was addicted, she was too. Even the sound of this confession made her crave him. Her pussy was alive with need, nectaring in this very moment as his dick pressed into her. "Sex leads to drugs and alcohol. It leads to lying and late nights, ecstasy, and endless orgasms. I lived a lifestyle that was dangerous, Lo. People get hurt when I let this shit get out of control. A girl I was responsible for lost her life behind this shit."

It was like a record had scratched as Lauren's eyes widened and her breathing hitched.

"Come in, Ny."

Nyair had expected her to pull back at the revelation of his sins. Instead, she pulled him nearer. She led the way inside, took his coat, and then paved the way to her couch.

"Tell me. Tell me everything you think is going to scare me away," she said. "Nothing scares me anymore. Nothing. Not the girlfriend who died in the car accident when you were younger. Not the sex addiction or the drugs and alcohol that led you to God. Not the failed NFL career. Nothing. If my situation doesn't scare you off, yours can't make me blink."

His surprise was understandable. He didn't share his past with many.

"I looked you up. Even the sealed records. I know already, Ny. You don't have to pretend to be this perfectly saved man. You don't have to redeem your past here. You can have desires here. You can just be here because some days that's all I'll be able to do. Just be. It's so much easier to just be when I'm with you," Lauren said. "Is it just me? Cuz I'm pretty sure I'm losing my mind. I just watched a video of Charlie singing a love song to my ex and I wished them well, so I'm pretty sure I've lost my mind. Tell me I'm crazy, Nyair. Tell me I'm going through depression and that I'm not really in love with you, but that this is some kind of trauma bond."

"I can't tell you that," Nyair said. Lauren stopped breathing. He took her hand. "I walked away from the church today, Lo."

And just like that, Lauren was terrified. That was a big step, too big of a step. She hadn't asked for that. She would never require that of him.

"Why would you do that?" she asked. "Why would you do that?" She screamed it this time.

"Because I don't have any indication when I'ma get my fill of you," he admitted. "And I don't think it's the trauma. I think it's servitude. I think it's companionship. I think it's trust. And I can't get the taste of you off my tongue. I think about it all the time. My mouth waters if I think about it too hard, Lauren. Like now, I just want to hear you begging in my ear."

"Begging for what?" she asked. It was rhetorical. She just wanted to hear him say it, because God knows, she wanted to beg for that dick. She knew he was ready. It was calling to her. Her womanly influence enticing him without doing anything at all.

"For me."

"You don't even know how bad I want you," Lauren scoffed. "But I don't want you to give up your life for me. So much of what I love about you is wrapped up in your faith. You see me as more than a mother who lost a son because you trust God to see me through this. How am I supposed to feel good about you just giving up your whole life? For what? So that we can keep fucking on the low? So you can make me cum when I'm sad? What makes this okay? How can I have you without you losing everything?"

"You'd have to be…"   He paused.

"Have to be what?" She was insistent. If he knew what she needed to become to make this easier for him, he needed to tell her. Because the way he made things easier for her was worth whatever adjustments came with the territory.

"The shit I want to do with you is supposed to take place between a man and his wife, Lo."

The dread that crossed her face couldn't be hidden. To go there again. To trust the very institution that had failed her before. Was he asking what she thought he was asking?

"I don't…I don't know what to…are you asking…why does it have to be so…" She had a hundred questions, but none were brave enough to force themselves out of her mouth.

"All of that," Nyair said for her. "I asked myself all of that before I drove over here and here's what I think. I think you should believe me when I tell you that I'm stuck. My every thought for the past few months has led back to you. Before DJ passed away. If I'm honest, before you were even divorced, I thought of you more often than I should have. You're beautiful. You carry your shit so beautifully. Your career, your motherhood, your marriage— when you were in one. You carry all these things like a queen. You command people, and I'm stuck when you enter my space. I'm so focused on you. I want to be so precise with you, and I know the timing is bad and you're grieving, so I'm not asking you for a microwave commitment. But for me to do this, I do need to make a commitment, Lo. I do need to tell you that I love you…"

"Nyair…"

"I know it doesn't make sense that we've come to this, but this is where I am with it," Nyair said.

"How do I do this? How do I even deserve this after what I let happen to my son?" she asked.

Her question penetrated his core. It was a taste of the torment she walked around with, and it stung badly enough to wet his eyes.

"How do you not deserve a man that's gon' love you back to life after you've been to the edge of death over your son? You want to follow him there. I want to keep you here, baby. I want to marry you one day, when you're ready, after a lot of therapy, a lot of prayer, and a lot of healing. I want you to be my wife, Lauren."

"So that you can feel better about having sex with me? Is this some sick way to make it right with God?" she asked. "Does marriage solve anything? If you're addicted, you're addicted regardless. Right?"

"It's my way to do right by you. I don't want to be the man you're using to distract you from all this. I don't want you to let me use your body for pleasure without having intentions of sticking around for the hard parts. I want you to put it on me when you can't carry it, Lo. I want you to hand it here. I want to lick every wound," he said, placing a finger to her chin and tilting her gaze to his. "I can have your body whenever I want. You'll give it to me cuz I know what to do with it. I don't need to finesse you for that. I want to marry you because somewhere in between the mess we been making of one another, love made itself at home. I don't want you to be alone, Lo. I want you for myself. And you're right, addiction is addiction, and if you tell me it's too much, I'm here to slow it down, but I'm too deep in to stop."

"I'm so overwhelmed right now," she admitted, sniffling as he pulled her into an embrace.

"Me too," he countered. "I didn't see you coming. But choose this anyway. Ain't that what you said to me?"

Lauren shook her head. "I said love me anyway."

"I'm trying to, but you got to be willing to receive it," Nyair said. "We can keep going how we going and end up hurting each other at the end of it, or we can try to do this right. All you have to do is say yes."

"I don't think you know what you're getting yourself into here. I don't feel like I'm supposed to feel good things right now. I'm not supposed to smile. I'm not supposed to have joy. It's not right. I'm not supposed to have you. Not right now. Why did you have to come to me right now? When I'm not ready!"

He reached for her hand, and as their fingers intertwined, she held on for dear life. He lifted their fists to his lips and kissed her knuckles.

"Three letters, one word. That's all I want to hear." He went into his inner jacket pocket and retrieved a velvet red box. The words Cartier were emblemed on top. "I ain't forget the most important part either. I've thought about this." He smiled coyishly at her, licking full, perfectly mauve-tinted lips as he flipped open the lid. "Y-E-S?" He spelled out the answer for her but left the option to choose lingering in the air.

Lauren's eyes burned so badly that she couldn't even see the four karats in front of her. Why God would take her through a fire that blazed so wildly to get to this point, she would never understand. She had so much baggage. She had experienced so much loss. The intense and sudden change, the missing her only child, it would all make her so difficult to love.

"Getting over this will be a burden, Ny. You have your pick. Why would you choose a love this hard?"

"You're not going to get over this, baby. You'll feel the absence of your son for the rest of your life. I don't want to get you over losing DJ. I want to love you through it. You're not a burden, Lo. You're a responsibility. You require attention and obligation. You need time and commitment. You need physical restoration. I'm doing that. I been doing that, and I can feel how desperate your body's been for a nigga to just touch you the right way, to please you, with intention. You been missing that, and I'm enjoying giving you that, but you need mental restoration too, Lo. Spiritual restoration. Emotional restoration. Have faith in me, Lo. Have Faith in God that He'll give you what you deserve."

This man. This man. This man.

"I'm a mess," she whispered.

"You're a message," he corrected. "For somebody, somewhere. Some mother. Some woman. When I'm done loving you right, you'll be somebody's message."

"Yes," Lauren said, shrugging and sighing because…fuck it. She had nothing left to lose, and she couldn't deny that through all this pain, the one emotion she felt clearly was her affection for him. She could eat, breathe, and sleep this man if he let her. She loved him. Their taboo, poorly timed, and inconvenient bond was everything.

"Yeah?" he confirmed, unable to hide his excitement and relief.

She nodded as he slipped the beautiful pear-shaped ring on her finger. "Please, take care of me, Nyair."

"I intend to, baby. A nigga gon' do that real well."

"Stop cussing, Pastor. Your congregation already gon' think I'm a bad influence."

He snickered. "Yeah, we got some things to do."

"Your little church groupies are going to hate me," Lauren sniffled as he cleared the tears from her pretty face.

"Yeah," he said. "We can handle that business, though. There's going to be some naysayers. I'm up for fighting for this. If you with it, I'm with it."

Lauren nodded, and he leaned in to kiss her lips. "It's us versus whoever, but we going to do this right so that our *us* includes God. Ain't nobody beating us like that. There's one condition, though."

"What's that?" she asked.

"I need to restore my discipline. We need to press pause on the physical until we've invested in the spiritual connection. We started wrong. We started with lust. Let's fill up on love until it's official."

It sounded like a challenge. She was so physically turned on by Nyair. It was on sight every time, when he entered her space. Even now, she wanted to be conquered by him. This wouldn't be easy—for either of them—but she knew it was best for them. He sensed her hesitation.

"I know it ain't the easiest..."

"I'll follow where you lead me," she replied simply. It was a soft girl response. She wanted to go into this marriage submitting so she would trust his guidance.

It was the simplest answer, and the blush it pulled out of him told her it was the perfect answer.

"I never expected to have this with another man again. Actually, I don't think I've ever had it. Thank you for being here," she continued.

"Thank you for allowing me to be here," Nyair responded. "Us versus everything and everybody. Me, you, and the Big Homie. Three stranded chord."

She had heard that biblical reference before. A marriage wasn't made of two, but three, and it was that steel chord of God that kept it from unraveling. She and Demi never had that foundation. They never knew they needed it to keep their union strong.

For the first time since losing her son, Lauren felt hopeful. Maybe, just maybe, her life wasn't over.

CHAPTER 19

Stassi smiled as she watched the comments go crazy as Charlie performed. "You're at a million viewers," she said excitedly. "Girl, you was about to let the devil steal your joy. This is your gift. Y'all tell Charlie this is hers already. All she got to do is sing, and all the success is going to come to her," Stassi said, flipping the camera toward her.

"I know, I know, I just have so much to think about now," Charlie said.

"That's another conversation for when we off live," Stassi said. "Right now, I want y'all to tell Charlie what y'all want her to sing about on the upcoming deluxe version of her album." Stassi scrolled through the comments, laughing. "Oh, your fans are wild."

"What they saying, girl?" Charlie asked, curiously.

"Fuck niggas and city girl shit," Stassi answered.

"That ain't where I'm at with it, but we can probably throw together a track or two for the girls that's outside," Charlie said, laughing. Stassi's forehead creased suddenly as the comments slowly crept in.

"What's wrong?" Charlie asked as she noticed Stassi's disposition change.

Novelista - I heard Demi Sky got shot in Flint.

Realmimigirl - Charlie, that married man you sleeping with got his karma. Heard he got wet up.

OhhheyyVee - Y'all heard it here first. RIP, Demi Sky.

Stassi's expression changed as she scrolled through the comments frantically, suddenly panicked.
"Who said that? Where are y'all getting this from?" Stassi asked.
Charlie heard the concern in Stassi's voice, and she set her guitar to the side. "Stassi, what the fuck is happening right now? Who said what?"
Stassi clicked out of the live and handed the phone to Charlie. "Call Demi! Right now. They're saying he was shot, Charlie."
Charlie's world stopped spinning.
"What do you mean?" She snatched her phone from Stassi's hand and immediately scrolled for evidence. "Who said that? Where, Stass?" She was out of her mind. Her heart galloped with the steam of thoroughbreds. "These bitches are always trolling. I'll just call him. That's why I didn't want to do this shit. I hate online shit. He's fine. Demi's fine." Stassi didn't know what to say, and Charlie prayed silently as she dialed him up.
The sound of his voicemail connecting annihilated her.

"My sweet Bird. Sing a song for me. Everybody else, it's textable."

Normally, she would leave him a note or two before hanging up. This time, she pressed end and dialed him right back as if the second call would render a different result.

"He isn't answering. Call Day, Stassi! See if he's heard from him!" Charlie commanded.

Stassi did as she was told, but the unending ring in her ear made her feel nothing but dread.

"He isn't answering either. We aren't on the best of terms, though. He might not answer for me," Stassi said.

Charlie dialed Day's number next.

"This cannot be happening," Charlie cried out. Stassi scrolled through social media, and sure enough, she found what she was looking for.

"Charlie, he's on Shade Room. It's saying he died." Stassi couldn't hide her shock. She knew how Demi got down. Had he taken his frustration out in the streets and gotten caught up? He may be a gentle giant with Charlie, but he was menacing to everyone else. She knew his background. Had she sent her man out into the world in a mind state that had cost him his life?

Charlie stood there, in shock as her stomach plummeted. "Stassi, tell me you're lying!"

Stassi read comment after comment, but it was all speculation, and it got worse and worse as she kept scrolling. Repeating the gossip would only make things worse.

"We've just got to get down there, Charlie. These people don't know what they're talking about," Stassi reassured.

"Some people are saying he's dead. Some people saying he killed somebody. Some are saying he's arrested. It's all gossip. None of this might be true. If he's in jail, he'll need his lawyer. You know who that is, right?"

"Ummm…yeah, some guy…umm, Einstein, I think. I don't know. He gave me his card and told me to put it up one day. I can't remember," Charlie said. She rushed into her bedroom, and Stassi followed as Charlie went into her closet. She frantically pulled handbags from the shelves, dumping all types of shit out of them as she rummaged through the junk. Remnants of nights out covered her closet floor as she searched high and low for the attorney's business card. "It's in one of these bags. It has to be. Where is it?!"

"Okay, calm down. Lauren has to know his lawyer, right? She's his…"

Charlie's eyes welled with tears, and she stopped all her efforts. "His wife. You can say it. She's his wife, and she'll know how to help him." Charlie fisted a handful of locs as she shook her head in disbelief. She sat down in the middle of her chaotic closet and reluctantly dialed Lauren's number.

"Hello?" Lauren answered in confusion.

"I'm sorry to call you like this…"

"Are you crying, Charlie?" Lauren asked. "What's wrong? What's happened?"

"I don't know," Charlie replied. "The blogs are saying something happened to Demi. I don't know if he's in jail or if he's hurt. Everybody is saying something different. I need his lawyer's number. I don't know where he is. I heard rumors that he's been shot. I don't know what to believe."

There was no pause, no hesitation, no need to gameplan. They were opposites. Charlie was the soft to Lauren's hard, the weakness to Lauren's strength, and it wasn't that Demi needed one more than the other. He needed them both for different things. Circumstances like these shone a light on Charlie's naïveté. She was young. She had no connections. No power on her own. Lauren, on the other hand, was armed with not only knowledge but resources to make shit shake. It was insane the way one man could convince two women they weren't enough, all the while they envied the qualities each other possessed. Lauren admired Charlie's softness, while Charlie envied Lauren's strength. Each attributing their lack of 'something' to the reason why Demi may choose differently. The power of men was too hefty when it turned women into unnecessary enemies. Today, they were on the same page.

"First, I need you to calm down. Are you there by yourself?" Lauren asked.

"My sister is here," Charlie said.

"Okay. Get yourself together. We don't know anything yet. Let me make some calls and find out what the hell is going on, and I'll call you back. Get dressed. I'll let you know where to meet me."

"Demi might be hurt," Lauren said aloud as soon as she hung up the phone. She lifted her eyes to meet Nyair's.

"I don't expect you not to care, Lo. He's your family. Y'all just lost something monumental. Where is he? I can take you where you need to go if you need some support, or I can fall back if you need to go alone to figure things out," Nyair responded.

If a king needed a visual, she was staring at it.

"I'm not sure where he is, but I'd love some help figuring it out." Her sigh of relief held so much. There would have to be a merging of her past with her present, and Nyair was proving to not be intimidated by that fact.

"Say less," he said. "Where did this happen?"

"I think at a bar on the Northside of Flint, according to these comments," she said as she scrolled through social media. "I'm not sure, though."

"Let's get to the bottom of it," Nyair said.

He pulled out his phone, and with the press of one button, he was on the line with the chief of police in Flint. The one thing about Nyair was he was very well-connected in his city. There wasn't a city official that he hadn't collaborated with. Within minutes, he had a rundown of the situation.

Lauren sat anxiously as she watched him conduct the call. Her stomach was in knots. She was trying to follow Nyair's conversation and piece together what had happened, but she could only hear one end of it. When he finally ended the call, she could tell from the look on his face that it was bad.

"Just tell me," Lauren said.

"He's been shot. He's in surgery. The police have no idea who did this, but it's not looking good, Lo."

Lauren's brain exploded.

"Oh my God," she whispered. "How is this happening? Where was he shot? How bad is it?" she asked.

Lauren's brain was firing off a thousand questions, and only a few were sneaking from her mouth. She couldn't process this, but she had to. "Where is he?"

"He's at Genesys Hospital. We should get there now," Nyair said.

"Yeah, yeah, let me just grab my purse and my keys," she said as she moved around the room, retrieving the items. "Where is my phone?" she asked. "I just had it."

Nyair stopped her. "Hey, hey. Your phone is in your hand," he said, shaking her gently. "Take a beat. You're in shock. You're panicking. It's going to be okay."

"If he dies…"

"Let's just get there," Nyair said, kissing her forehead.

"I have to call Charlie back. She's pregnant. How do I tell her this? We aren't even friends. I shouldn't be the one to tell her something like this."

"I know it's a thing there between y'all. I saw it at the funeral, and I get it. You don't always get to choose who God places in your life, though, Lo. Who else does this girl have?"

Lauren nodded and sent Charlie a text message, asking her to meet her at the hospital, then Nyair took her hand and led her into another battle—one she wasn't prepared to fight.

Charlie only had bad experiences walking into the hospital. The last time she had been there with Lo, she had learned DJ had passed away. The time before that, she had learned that Demi was married. The way her body responded this time was palpable. The anxiety of what she was about to walk into made her tremble in fear. Her hands shook so badly that she had to ball her fists to control it.

"This way," Stassi said as they rushed down the hallway.

When Charlie saw Lauren, pacing at the end of the corridor, she stopped walking. Lauren glanced up at her, and Charlie slowly pushed forward.

"Is he okay?" Charlie asked.

"He's been shot, Charlie. In the back. He's coded twice. They're doing everything they can," Lauren said, voice cracking under the weight of their reality.

Charlie's legs lost strength, and she put her hand against the wall to stop herself from falling.

"Ohhh," she moaned. Her grief was audible, and she bent over in agony as she heard Lauren tell the rest of the story to Stassi.

Looked like robbery.
Blood loss.
Shot twice.
If he makes it.

That's all Charlie could absorb. She wasn't sure if the sickness she felt was her baby or her devastation, but she rushed to the nearest trash can.

A nurse rounded the station desk and ushered Charlie to a chair.

"She's pregnant," Stassi informed.

"I'll get you some ginger ale and crackers. Wait here."

"He can't die on me," Charlie cried. "I should have never asked him to leave. This is all my fault. He was supposed to be with me."

"Let's just wait and see what the doctors say," Nyair said gently, placing his hand on the small of Lauren's back and turning her toward him.

"Where's Day?" Stassi asked. No one had even thought to question it. Everyone was so focused on the tragedy that they didn't notice that Demi's right-hand man was missing.

Lauren pulled away from Nyair.

"Call him, Stassi," she said. Her tone made Charlie look up in concern.

"He's probably at the studio," Stassi said. "It's going to voicemail. He cuts his phone off when he's producing. I'll go get him and bring him here."

Lauren shook her head. It was too odd to be a coincidence.

"Something's wrong," Lauren said. "No way something this big goes down, and Day isn't here."

"She's right," Charlie whispered.

"Don't jump to conclusions. Y'all stay here, and I'll be back," Stassi said.

"You don't have to stick around," Lauren said to Nyair. "I can call you when I leave here. I'll come straight to you."

"I'm going to go downtown to see if I can find out who they think did this," Ny said. "If anything changes, or if you need me for anything, don't hesitate, okay?" Nyair instructed.

Lauren nodded, and he kissed her lips, shocking Charlie before he nodded her way, acknowledging her before he departed.

Lauren took a seat in the chair beside Charlie.

"I can't lose him," Charlie whispered.

"Neither can I," Lauren added. Lauren held out her hand, and Charlie looked at it skeptically before sighing and grabbing onto her. Charlie leaned into Lauren, resting her head on Lauren's shoulder as they sat side by side, united under the worst circumstances. Hours passed, and Stassi had searched everywhere. Day wasn't at his studio, the offices, or at his home. Charlie sat, bouncing her leg anxiously as Lauren scrolled mindlessly through her phone, trying to pass the time as they awaited Demi's surgeons.

"Oh my God," Lauren whispered as she showed her phone to Charlie.

#TSRUPDATEZ
Industry Mogul, Dayton Night, Accused of Sexual Assault. Kiara Da'vi sues for $20M.

"This can't be happening," Lauren whispered. It was too convenient to be a coincidence, and her mind raced as she wondered if both events were tied to each other. Somebody was coming for their entire circle, and Lauren feared that Demi and Day may not come out of this unscathed.

To Be Continued...

Made in United States
Troutdale, OR
06/30/2025